CARTOON NETWORK

STEVEN UNIVERSE

FIELD RESEARCHING

kaboom!

WWW.BOOM-STUDIOS.COM

STEVEN UNIVERSE ONGOING Volume Three, September 2018. Published by KaBOOM!, a division of Boom Entertainment, Inc. STEVEN UNIVERSE, CARTOON NETWORK, the logos, and all related characters and elements are trademarks of and © Cartoon Network. (S18) Originally published in single magazine form as STEVEN UNIVERSE ONGOING No. 9-12 © Cartoon Network. (S17) All rights reserved. KaBOOM!™ and the KaBOOM! logo are trademarks of Boom Entertainment, Inc., registered in various countries and categories. All characters, events, and institutions depicted herein are fictional. Any similarity between any of the names, characters, persons, events, and/or institutions in this publication to actual names, characters, and persons, whether living or dead, events, and/or institutions is unintended and purely coincidental. KaBOOM! does not read or accept unsolicited submissions of ideas, stories, or artwork.

BOOM! Studios, 5670 Wilshire Boulevard, Suite 400, Los Angeles, CA 90036-5679. Printed in China. First Printing.

ISBN: 978-1-68415-244-5, eISBN: 978-1-64144-106-3

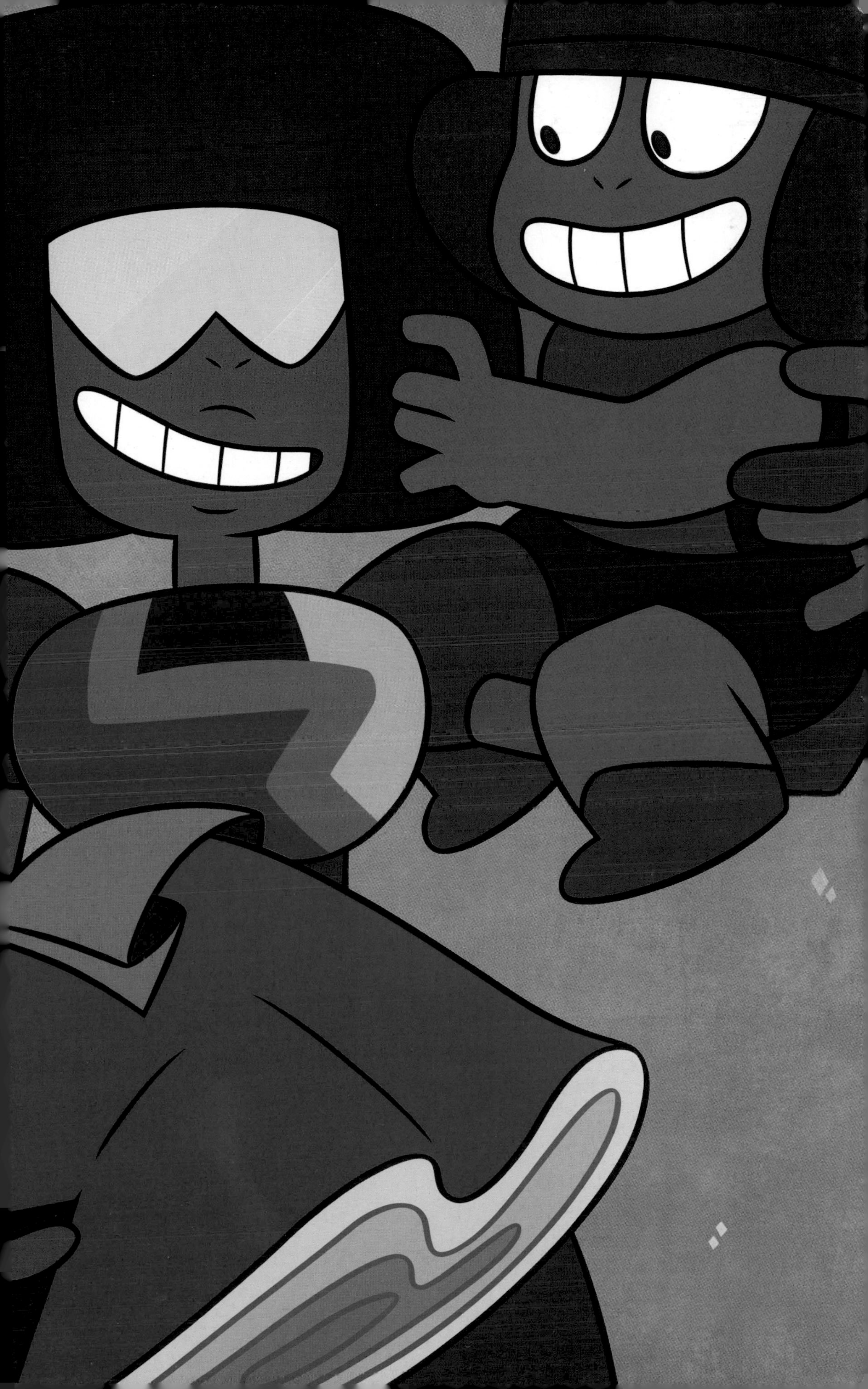

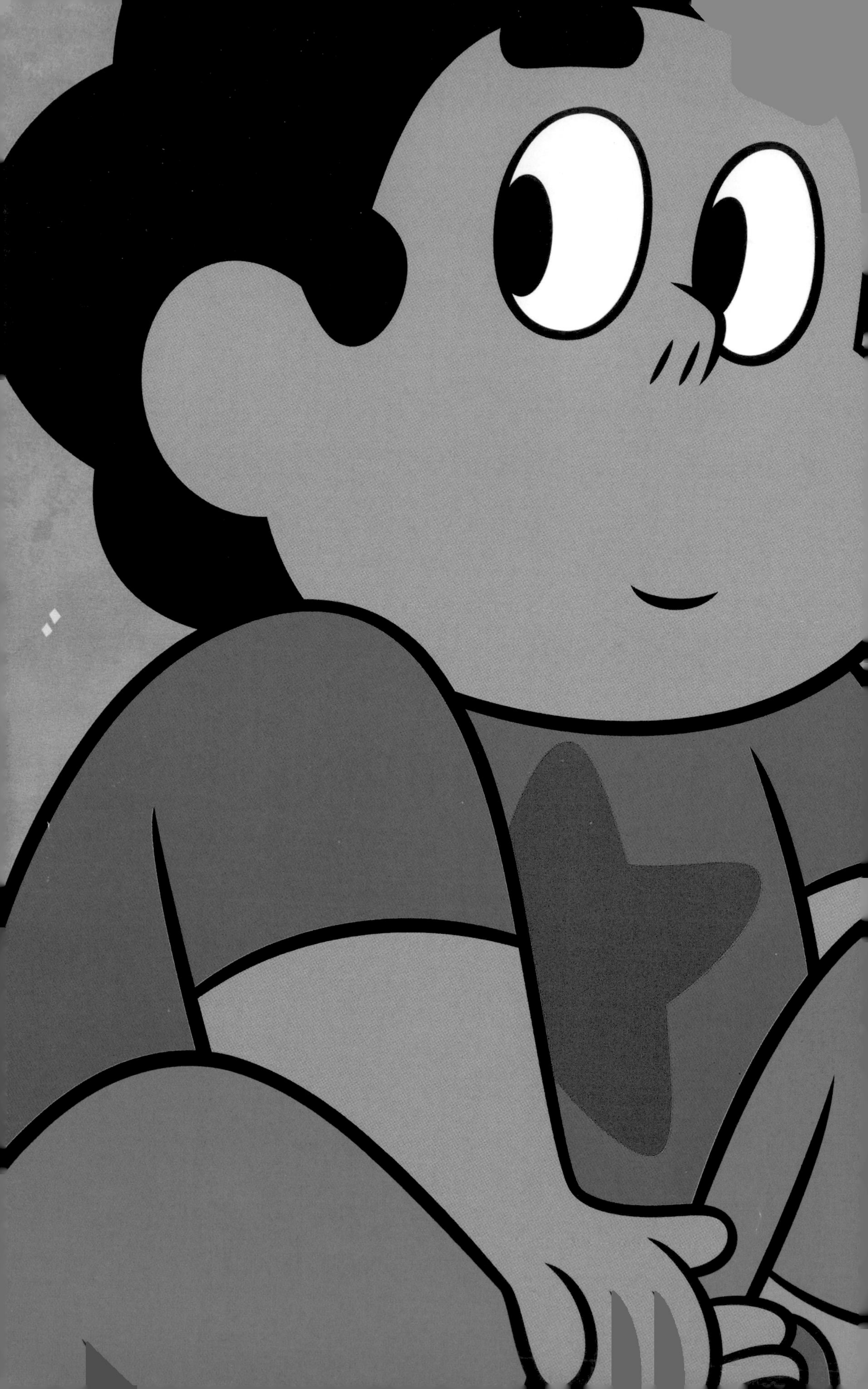

CARTOON NETWORK

STEVEN UNIVERSE™
FIELD RESEARCHING

created by
REBECCA SUGAR

written by
GRACE KRAFT

illustrated by
RII ABREGO

colors by
WHITNEY COGAR

letters by
MIKE FIORENTINO

cover by
MISSY PEÑA

series designer
GRACE PARK

collection designer
JILLIAN CRAB

assistant editor
MICHAEL MOCCIO

editor
WHITNEY LEOPARD

**Special thanks to
Marisa Marionakis, Janet No, Curtis Lelash, Conrad Montgomery, Jackie Buscarino, Alan Pasman and the wonderful folks at Cartoon Network.**

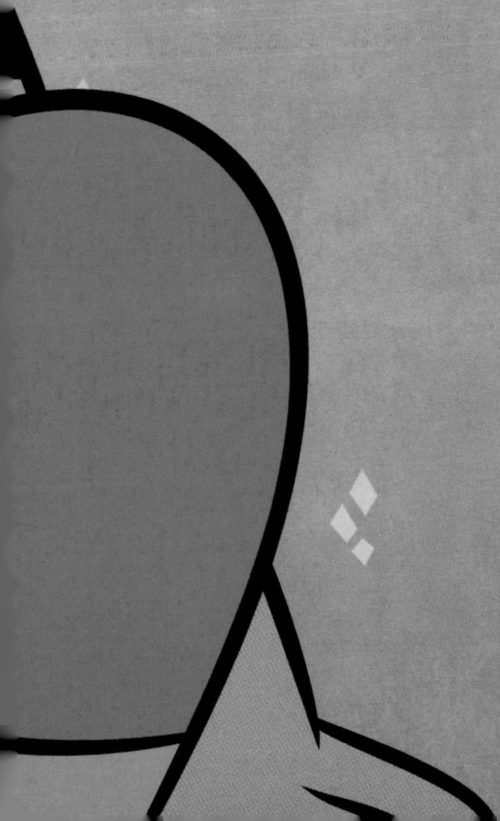

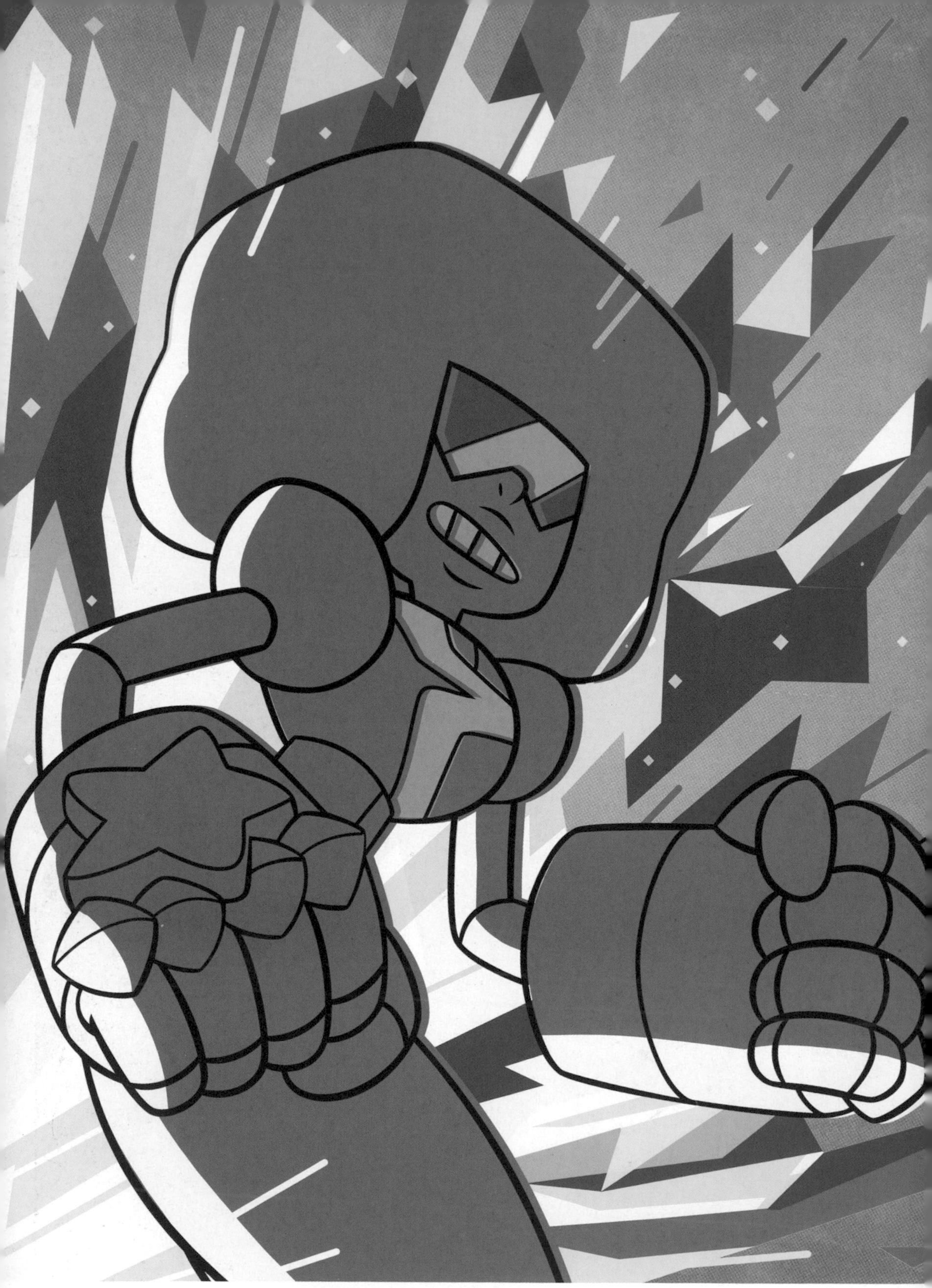

CHAPTER NINE

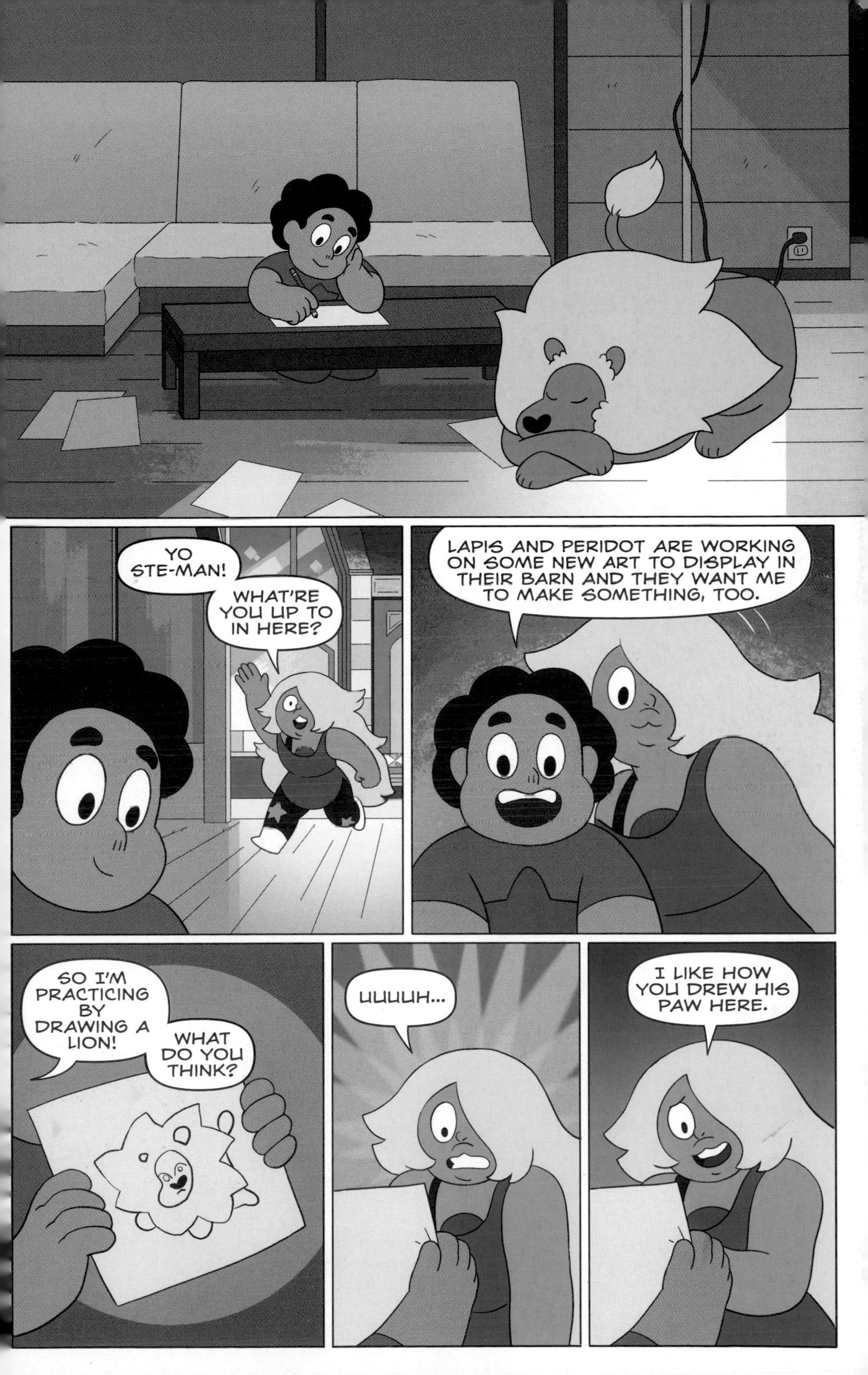

YO STE-MAN!
WHAT'RE YOU UP TO IN HERE?
LAPIS AND PERIDOT ARE WORKING ON SOME NEW ART TO DISPLAY IN THEIR BARN AND THEY WANT ME TO MAKE SOMETHING, TOO.
SO I'M PRACTICING BY DRAWING A LION!
WHAT DO YOU THINK?
UUUUH...
I LIKE HOW YOU DREW HIS PAW HERE.

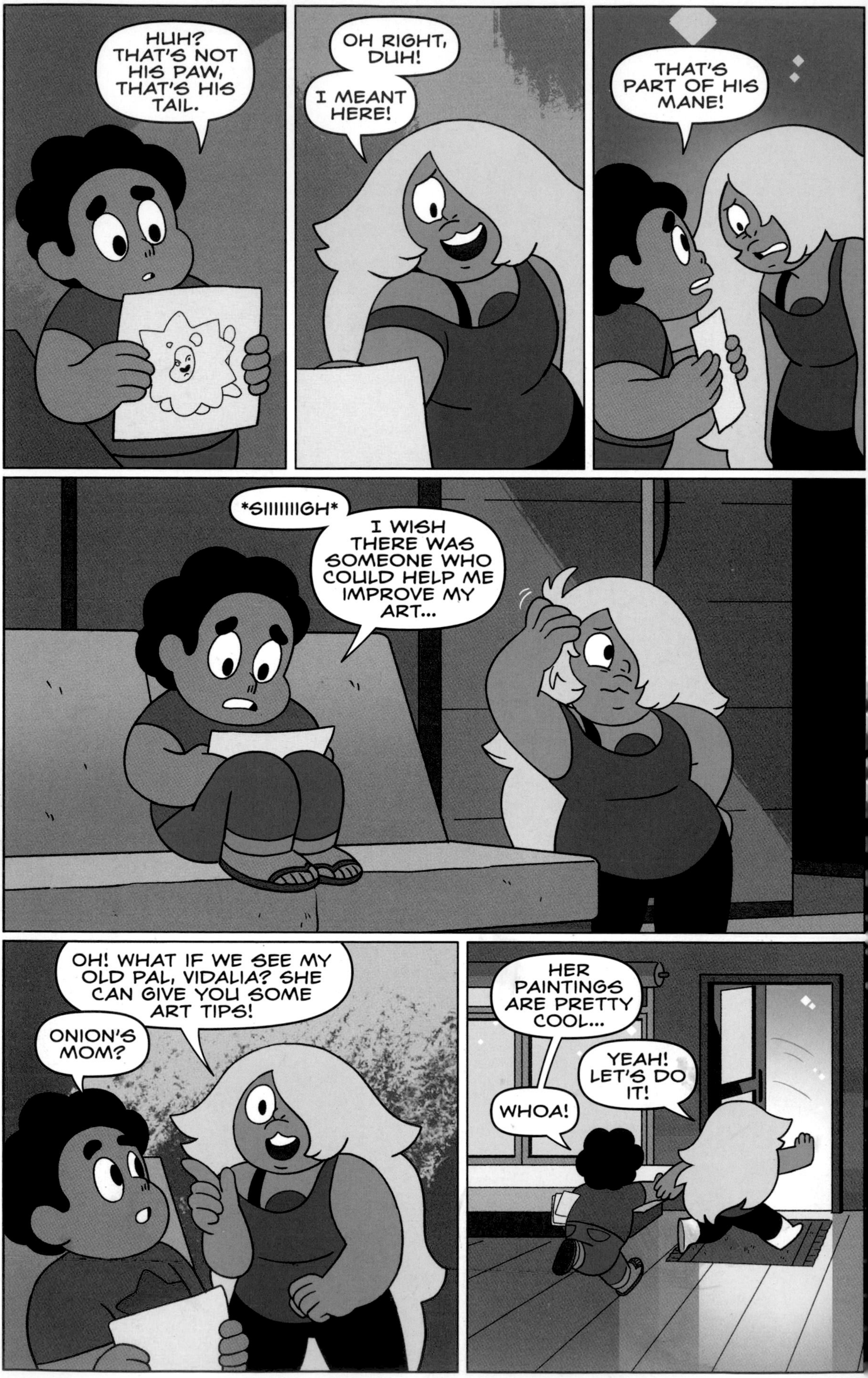
HUH? THAT'S NOT HIS PAW, THAT'S HIS TAIL.
OH RIGHT, DUH!
I MEANT HERE!
THAT'S PART OF HIS MANE!
SIIIIIIGH
I WISH THERE WAS SOMEONE WHO COULD HELP ME IMPROVE MY ART...
OH! WHAT IF WE SEE MY OLD PAL, VIDALIA? SHE CAN GIVE YOU SOME ART TIPS!
ONION'S MOM?
HER PAINTINGS ARE PRETTY COOL...
WHOA!
YEAH! LET'S DO IT!

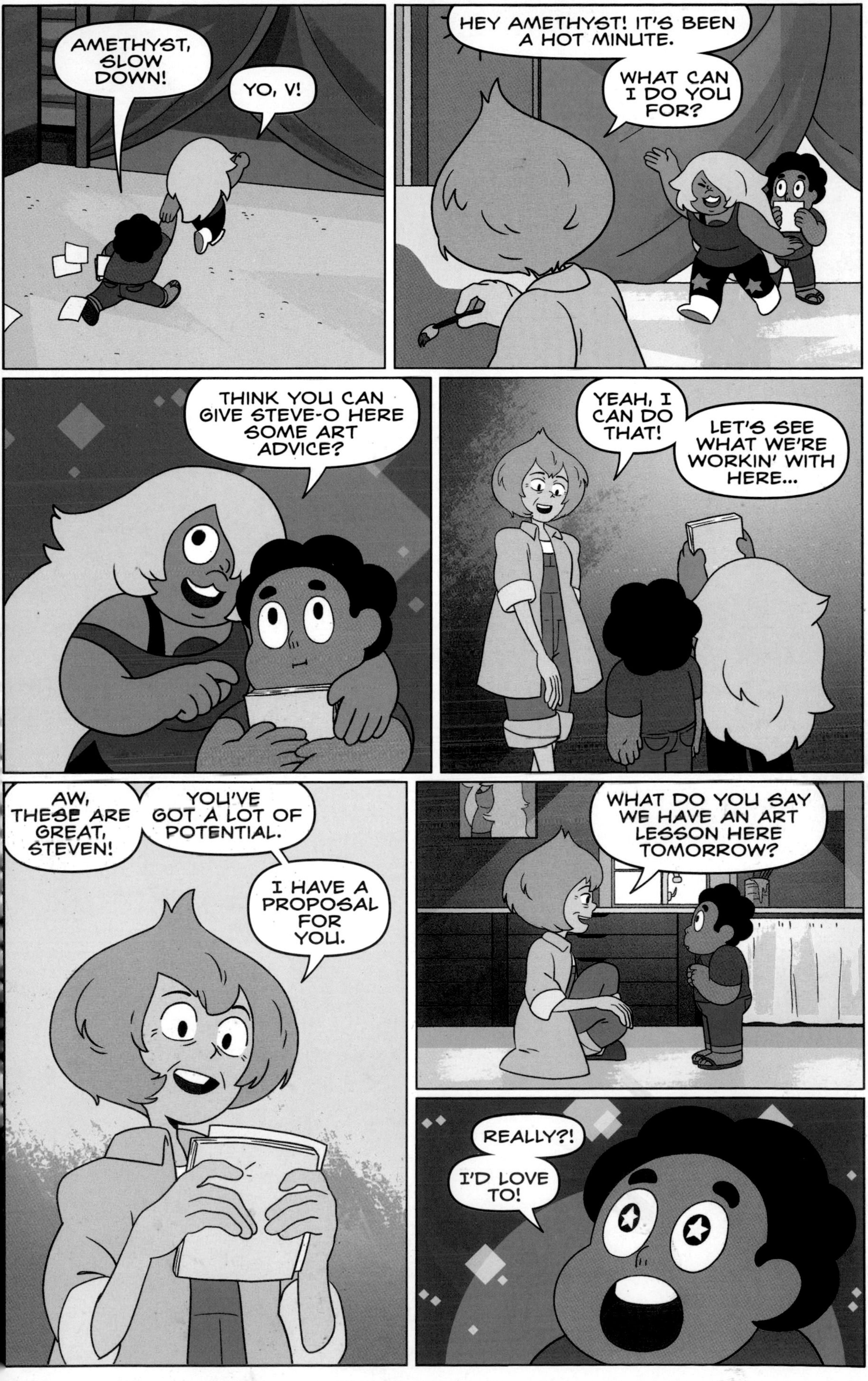

AMETHYST, SLOW DOWN!
YO, V!
HEY AMETHYST! IT'S BEEN A HOT MINUTE.
WHAT CAN I DO YOU FOR?
THINK YOU CAN GIVE STEVE-O HERE SOME ART ADVICE?
YEAH, I CAN DO THAT!
LET'S SEE WHAT WE'RE WORKIN' WITH HERE...
AW, THESE ARE GREAT, STEVEN!
YOU'VE GOT A LOT OF POTENTIAL.
I HAVE A PROPOSAL FOR YOU.
WHAT DO YOU SAY WE HAVE AN ART LESSON HERE TOMORROW?
REALLY?!
I'D LOVE TO!

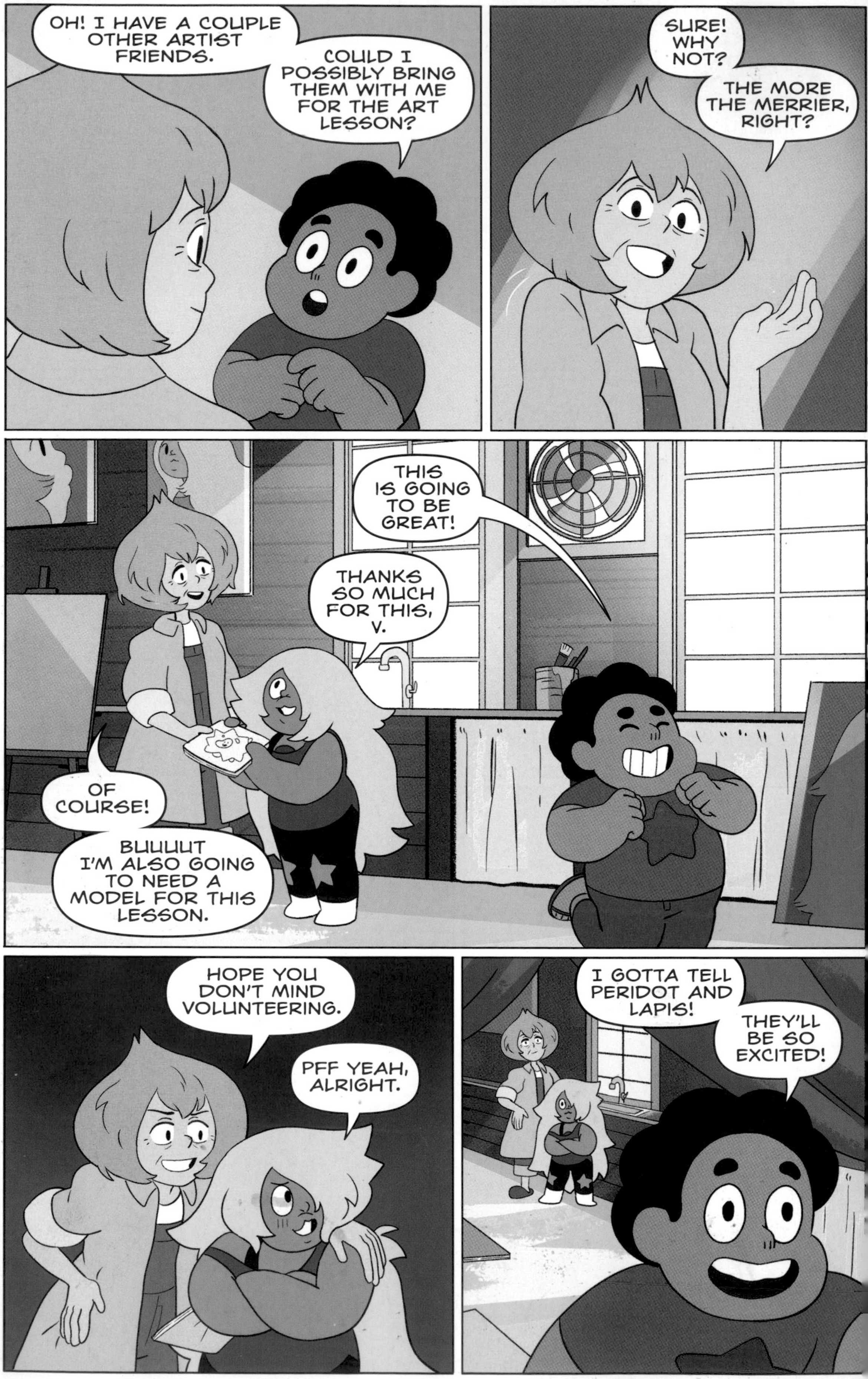
OH! I HAVE A COUPLE OTHER ARTIST FRIENDS.
COULD I POSSIBLY BRING THEM WITH ME FOR THE ART LESSON?
SURE! WHY NOT?
THE MORE THE MERRIER, RIGHT?
THIS IS GOING TO BE GREAT!
THANKS SO MUCH FOR THIS, V.
OF COURSE!
BUUUUT I'M ALSO GOING TO NEED A MODEL FOR THIS LESSON.
HOPE YOU DON'T MIND VOLUNTEERING.
PFF YEAH, ALRIGHT.
I GOTTA TELL PERIDOT AND LAPIS!
THEY'LL BE SO EXCITED!

YOU VOLUNTEERED US FOR WHAT NOW?

AN ART LESSON WITH VIDALIA!

SHE'S AN OLD FRIEND OF AMETHYST'S, AND SHE'S REALLY GOOD AT PAINTING!

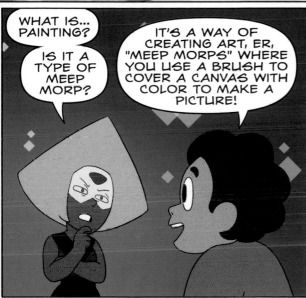

WHAT IS... PAINTING?

IS IT A TYPE OF MEEP MORP?

IT'S A WAY OF CREATING ART, ER, "MEEP MORPS" WHERE YOU USE A BRUSH TO COVER A CANVAS WITH COLOR TO MAKE A PICTURE!

SOUNDS AWFULLY... PRIMITIVE. AND UNIMAGINATIVE.

HMMM...BUT IF THIS "VIDALIA" IS A FRIEND OF AMETHYST'S, SHE MUST BE SOME-ONE AT LEAST AS IMPRESSIVE AS MYSELF.

BUT I DOUBT A HUMAN WOULD HAVE MUCH TO TEACH US ABOUT MEEP MORPS THAT WE DON'T ALREADY KNOW.

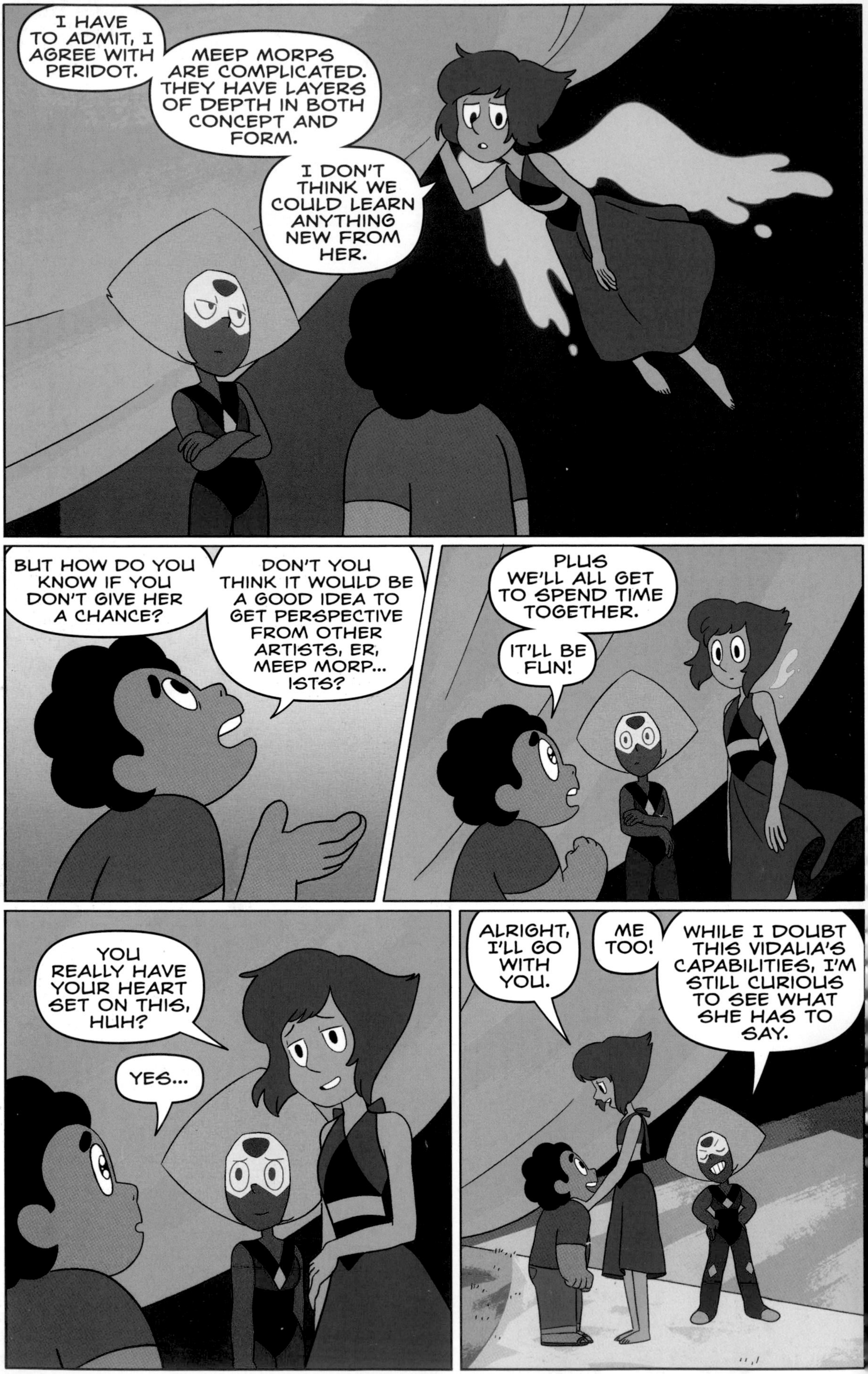

I HAVE TO ADMIT, I AGREE WITH PERIDOT.
MEEP MORPS ARE COMPLICATED. THEY HAVE LAYERS OF DEPTH IN BOTH CONCEPT AND FORM.
I DON'T THINK WE COULD LEARN ANYTHING NEW FROM HER.
BUT HOW DO YOU KNOW IF YOU DON'T GIVE HER A CHANCE?
DON'T YOU THINK IT WOULD BE A GOOD IDEA TO GET PERSPECTIVE FROM OTHER ARTISTS, ER, MEEP MORP... ISTS?
PLUS WE'LL ALL GET TO SPEND TIME TOGETHER.
IT'LL BE FUN!
YOU REALLY HAVE YOUR HEART SET ON THIS, HUH?
YES...
ALRIGHT, I'LL GO WITH YOU.
ME TOO!
WHILE I DOUBT THIS VIDALIA'S CAPABILITIES, I'M STILL CURIOUS TO SEE WHAT SHE HAS TO SAY.

ALRIGHT STEVEN AND, UH, STEVEN'S FRIENDS!

ARE YOU ALL READY TO LEARN THINGS ABOUT ART?

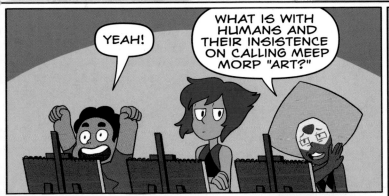

YEAH!

WHAT IS WITH HUMANS AND THEIR INSISTENCE ON CALLING MEEP MORP "ART?"

NOW, I DON'T WANT ALL OF YOU TO JUST TRY AND COPY WHAT YOU SEE.

SO FOR OUR FIRST LESSON, WE'LL START WITH A BASIC ART BUILDING BLOCK, FIGURE DRAWING!

WITH OUR FANTASTIC MODEL, AMETHYST!

YO!

I WANT YOU TO SEE AND FEEL THE FORCES WITHIN THE POSE.

FEEL THE WEIGHT AND RHYTHM OF THE FIGURE.

TRANSFER YOUR EXPERIENCE WITH THE MODEL'S POSE ONTO THE PAPER.

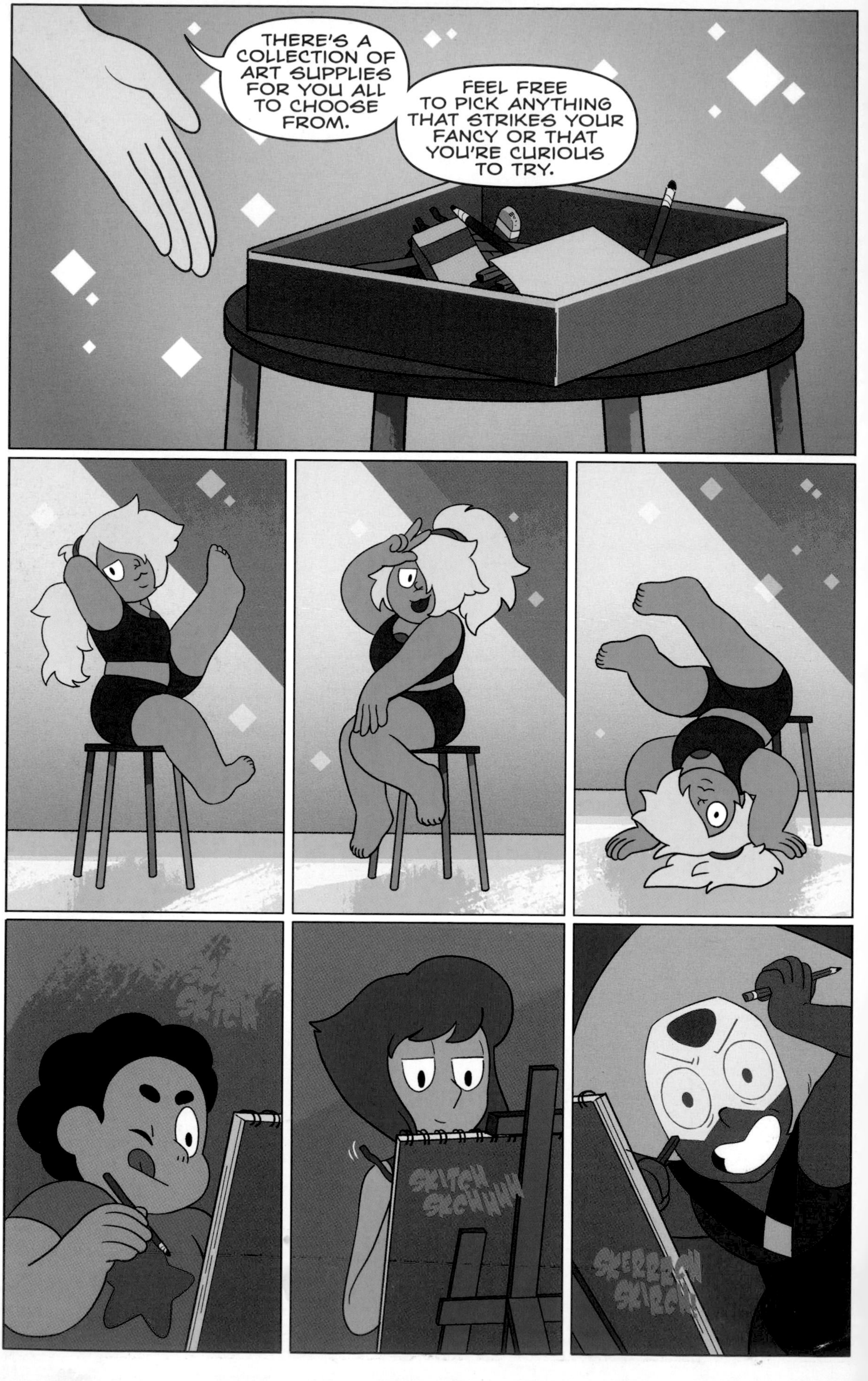
THERE'S A COLLECTION OF ART SUPPLIES FOR YOU ALL TO CHOOSE FROM.
FEEL FREE TO PICK ANYTHING THAT STRIKES YOUR FANCY OR THAT YOU'RE CURIOUS TO TRY.
SKITCH SKCHHHH

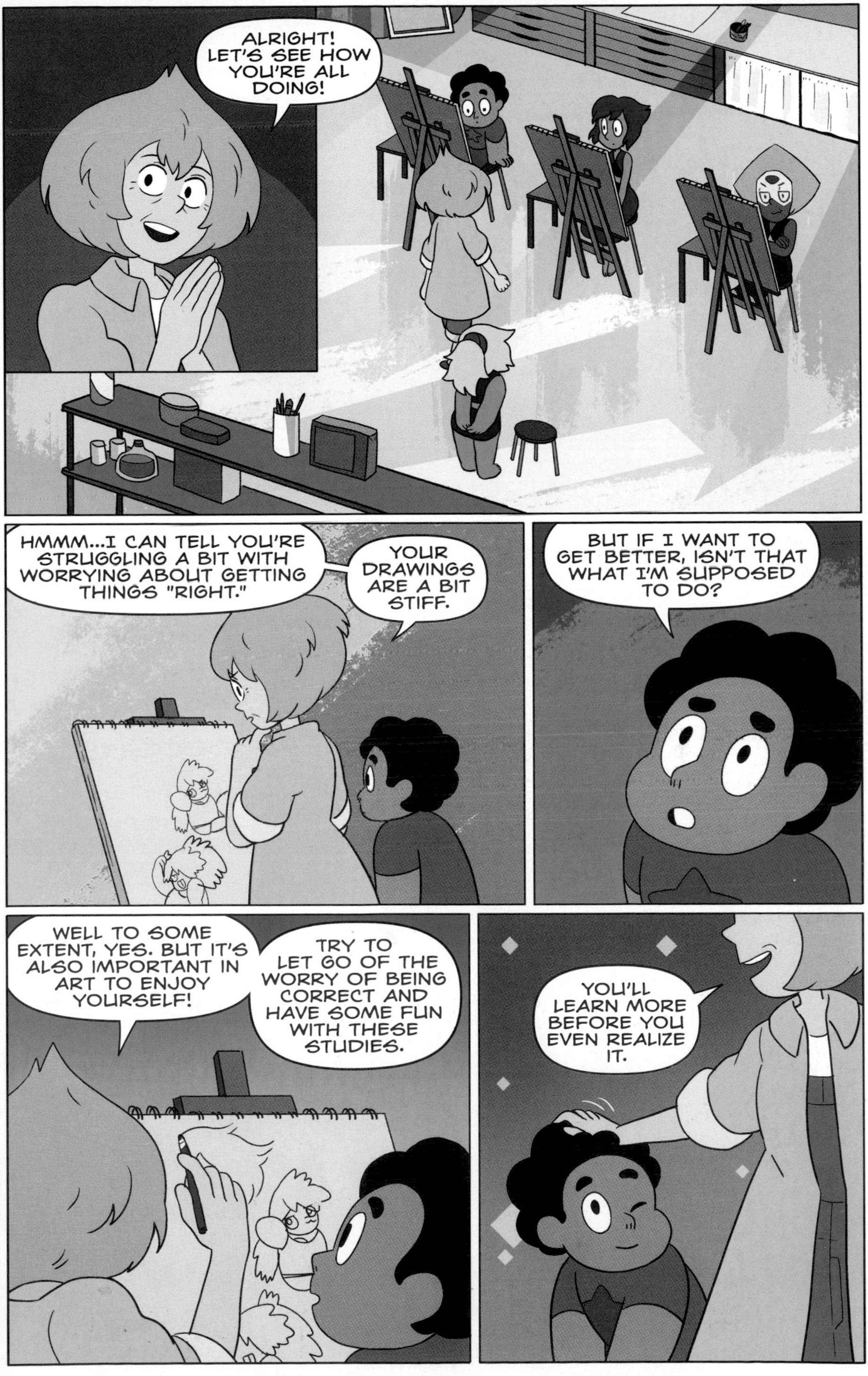
ALRIGHT! LET'S SEE HOW YOU'RE ALL DOING!
HMMM...I CAN TELL YOU'RE STRUGGLING A BIT WITH WORRYING ABOUT GETTING THINGS "RIGHT."
YOUR DRAWINGS ARE A BIT STIFF.
BUT IF I WANT TO GET BETTER, ISN'T THAT WHAT I'M SUPPOSED TO DO?
WELL TO SOME EXTENT, YES. BUT IT'S ALSO IMPORTANT IN ART TO ENJOY YOURSELF!
TRY TO LET GO OF THE WORRY OF BEING CORRECT AND HAVE SOME FUN WITH THESE STUDIES.
YOU'LL LEARN MORE BEFORE YOU EVEN REALIZE IT.

HMM, LAPIS WAS IT?
YOUR DRAWINGS ARE VERY... LOOSE AND FLOWY.
BUT ALSO COME OFF A BIT HESITANT AND DIRECTIONLESS.
MAYBE YOU CAN TRY TO BE MORE CONFIDENT IN THE MARKS YOU ARE PUTTING ON THE PAPER?
BE DECISIVE AND EXPRESS YOUR OWN OPINION!
I DON'T KNOW IF I WANT TO...FORCE THAT MUCH CONTROL?
WELL, I'M NOT SAYING YOU NEED TO FORCE ANYTHING.
BUT ART IS ALL ABOUT COMMUNICATING YOUR OWN EXPERIENCE.
AND THESE STUDIES ARE YOUR REACTION TO WHAT YOU'RE SEEING IN FRONT OF YOU.
THE DRAWINGS YOU HAVE HERE ARE GREAT, I SEE A LOT OF YOUR IDEAS AND INTERPRETATION.
BUT I THINK YOU'RE DRAWING MORE OF WHAT YOU WANT TO SEE AND THAT'S GETTING IN THE WAY OF SEEING WHAT'S ALREADY THERE AND BUILDING ON IT.
THAT SOUNDS... KIND OF CONTRADICTORY.
HAHA, DON'T I KNOW IT! THAT'S ART FOR YOU.
BUT, THIS IS JUST JUST MY PERSONAL FEEDBACK.
IT'S UP TO YOU WHAT VALUE YOU FIND IN IT.

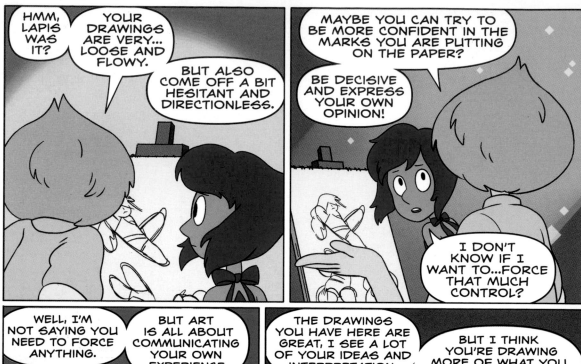

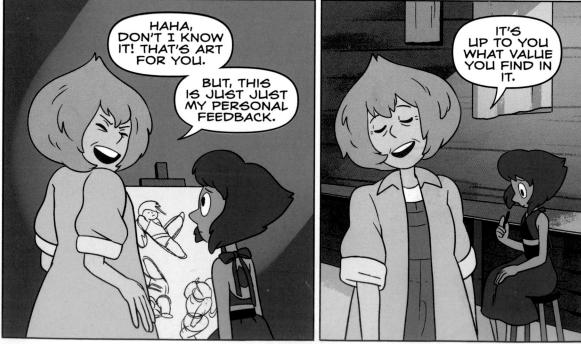

OH! PERIDOT, RIGHT?

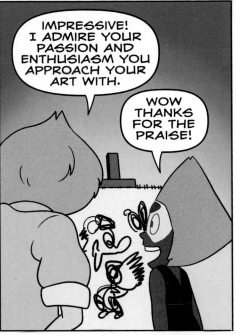

IMPRESSIVE! I ADMIRE YOUR PASSION AND ENTHUSIASM YOU APPROACH YOUR ART WITH.

WOW THANKS FOR THE PRAISE!

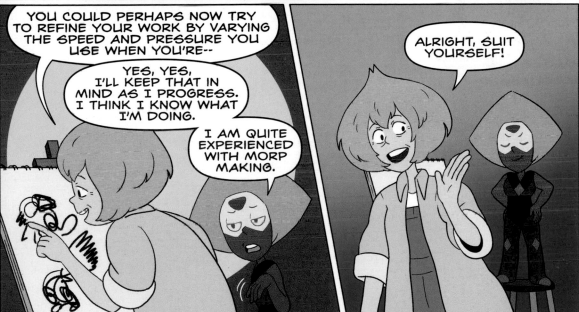

YOU COULD PERHAPS NOW TRY TO REFINE YOUR WORK BY VARYING THE SPEED AND PRESSURE YOU USE WHEN YOU'RE--

YES, YES, I'LL KEEP THAT IN MIND AS I PROGRESS. I THINK I KNOW WHAT I'M DOING.

I AM QUITE EXPERIENCED WITH MORP MAKING.

ALRIGHT, SUIT YOURSELF!

DID YOU HEAR THAT LAPIS? SHE SAID SHE LIKES MY ENTHUSIASM!

SHE CLEARLY RECOGNIZES THAT I'M ALREADY AN EXPERT AT MORPS!

OH, THAT'S... GREAT.

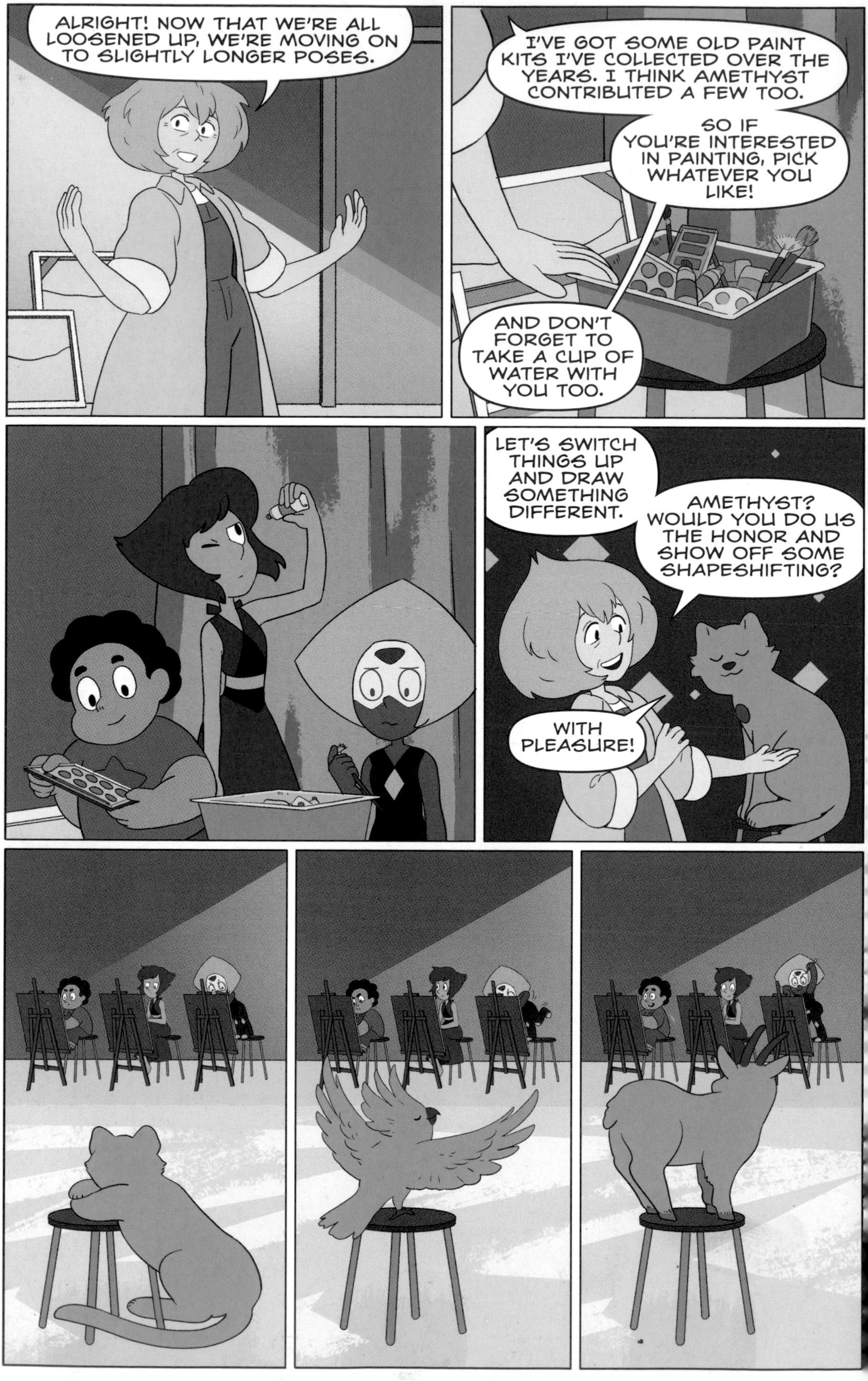
ALRIGHT! NOW THAT WE'RE ALL LOOSENED UP, WE'RE MOVING ON TO SLIGHTLY LONGER POSES.
I'VE GOT SOME OLD PAINT KITS I'VE COLLECTED OVER THE YEARS. I THINK AMETHYST CONTRIBUTED A FEW TOO.
SO IF YOU'RE INTERESTED IN PAINTING, PICK WHATEVER YOU LIKE!
AND DON'T FORGET TO TAKE A CUP OF WATER WITH YOU TOO.
LET'S SWITCH THINGS UP AND DRAW SOMETHING DIFFERENT.
AMETHYST? WOULD YOU DO US THE HONOR AND SHOW OFF SOME SHAPESHIFTING?
WITH PLEASURE!

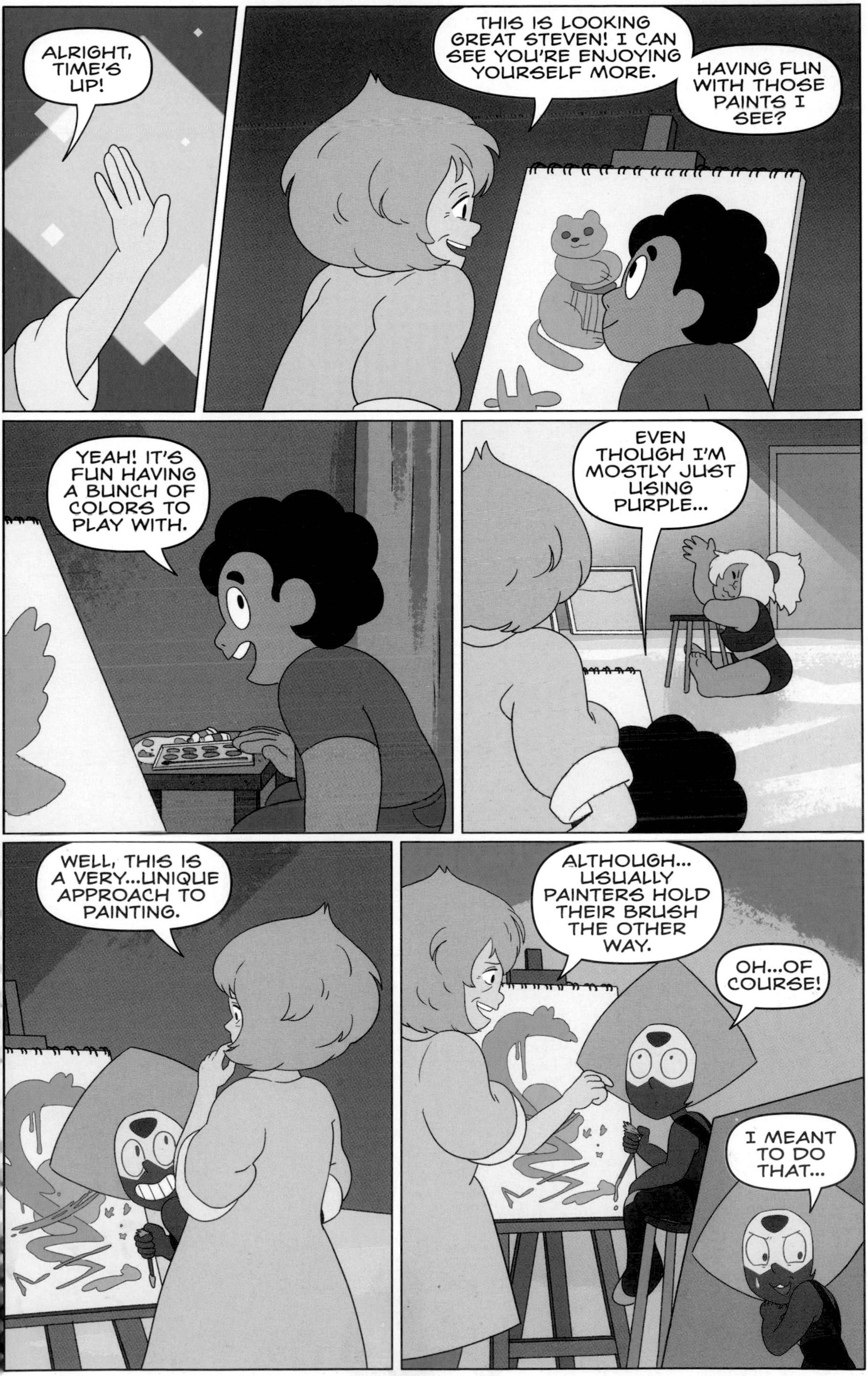
ALRIGHT, TIME'S UP!
THIS IS LOOKING GREAT STEVEN! I CAN SEE YOU'RE ENJOYING YOURSELF MORE.
HAVING FUN WITH THOSE PAINTS I SEE?
YEAH! IT'S FUN HAVING A BUNCH OF COLORS TO PLAY WITH.
EVEN THOUGH I'M MOSTLY JUST USING PURPLE...
WELL, THIS IS A VERY...UNIQUE APPROACH TO PAINTING.
ALTHOUGH... USUALLY PAINTERS HOLD THEIR BRUSH THE OTHER WAY.
OH...OF COURSE!
I MEANT TO DO THAT...

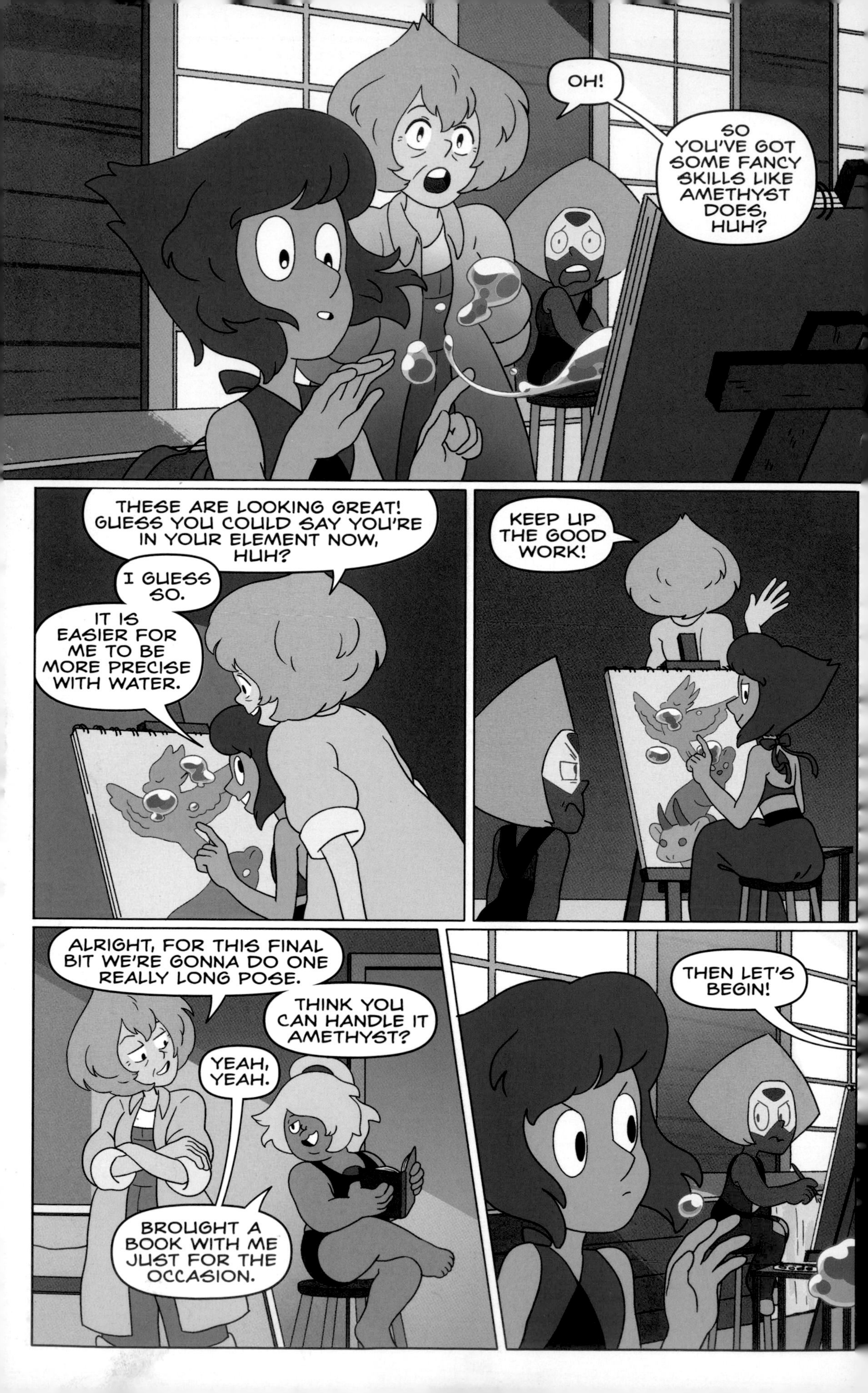
OH!
SO YOU'VE GOT SOME FANCY SKILLS LIKE AMETHYST DOES, HUH?
THESE ARE LOOKING GREAT! GUESS YOU COULD SAY YOU'RE IN YOUR ELEMENT NOW, HUH?
I GUESS SO.
IT IS EASIER FOR ME TO BE MORE PRECISE WITH WATER.
KEEP UP THE GOOD WORK!
ALRIGHT, FOR THIS FINAL BIT WE'RE GONNA DO ONE REALLY LONG POSE.
THINK YOU CAN HANDLE IT AMETHYST?
YEAH, YEAH.
BROUGHT A BOOK WITH ME JUST FOR THE OCCASION.
THEN LET'S BEGIN!

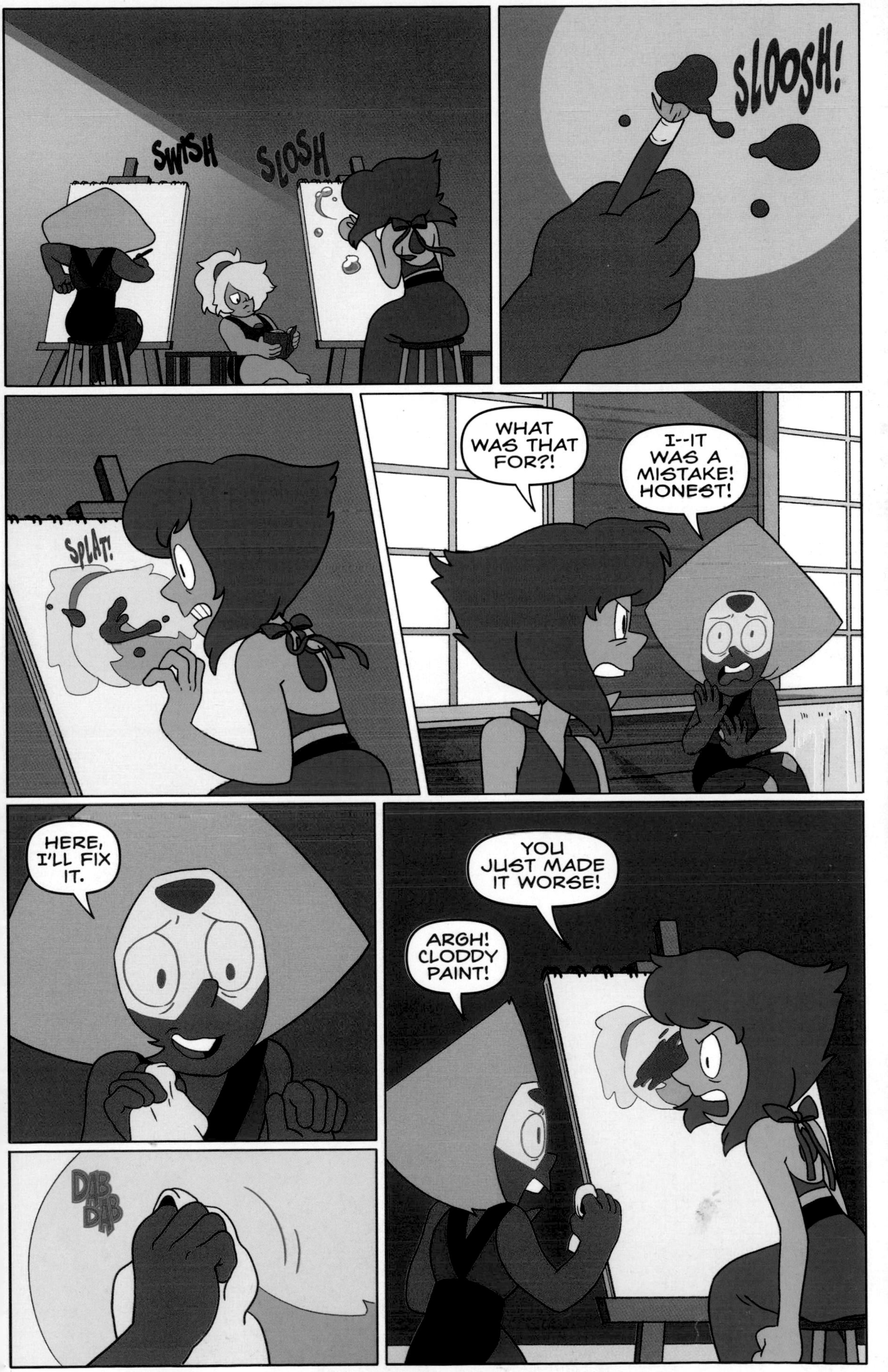
SWISH
SLOSH
SLOOSH!
SPLAT!
WHAT WAS THAT FOR?!
I--IT WAS A MISTAKE! HONEST!
HERE, I'LL FIX IT.
DAB DAB
YOU JUST MADE IT WORSE!
ARGH! CLODDY PAINT!

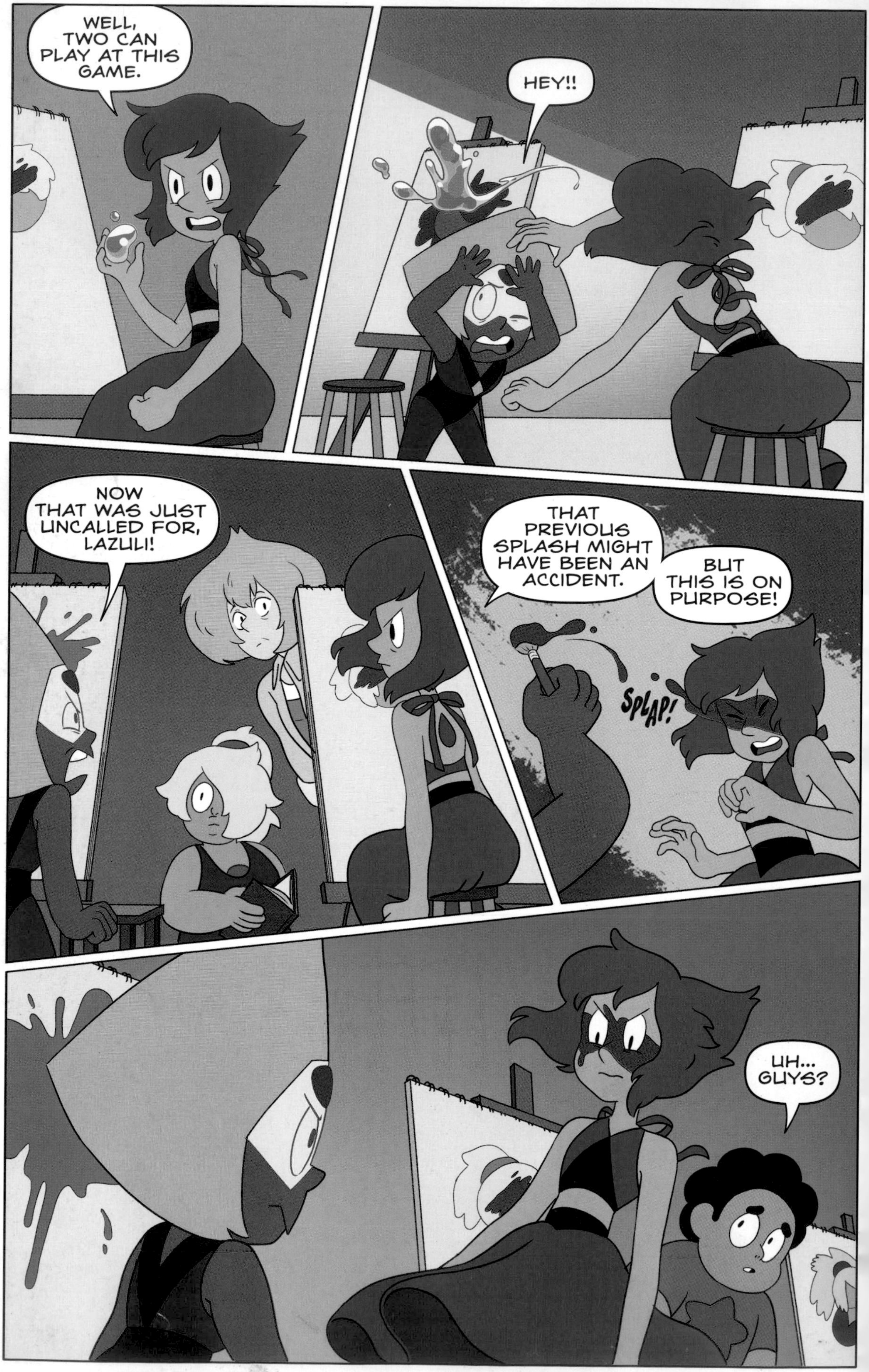
WELL, TWO CAN PLAY AT THIS GAME.
HEY!!
NOW THAT WAS JUST UNCALLED FOR, LAZULI!
THAT PREVIOUS SPLASH MIGHT HAVE BEEN AN ACCIDENT.
BUT THIS IS ON PURPOSE!
SPLAP!
UH... GUYS?

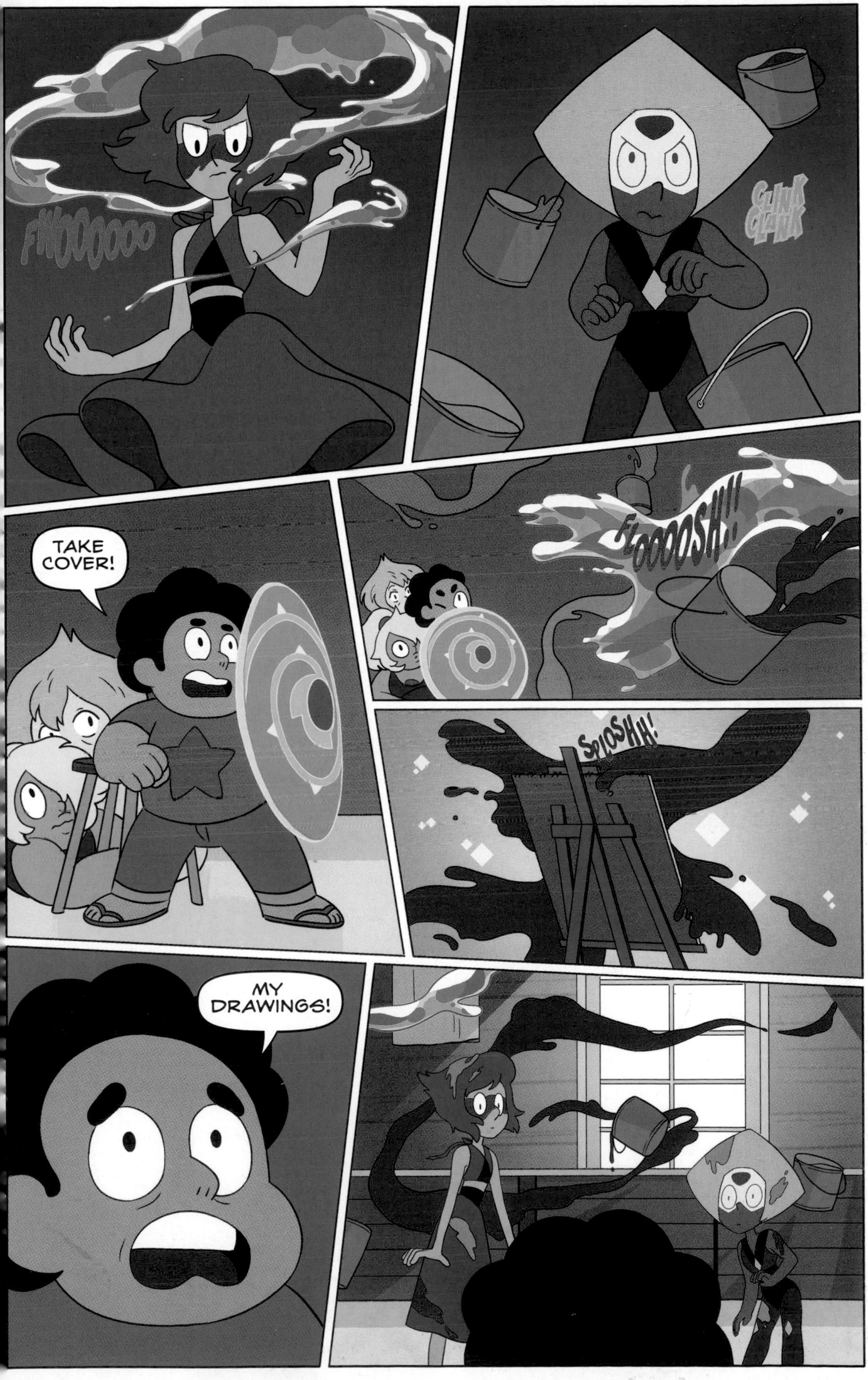
FWOOOOOO
CLINK CLANK
TAKE COVER!
FLOOOOSH!!
SPLOSHH!
MY DRAWINGS!

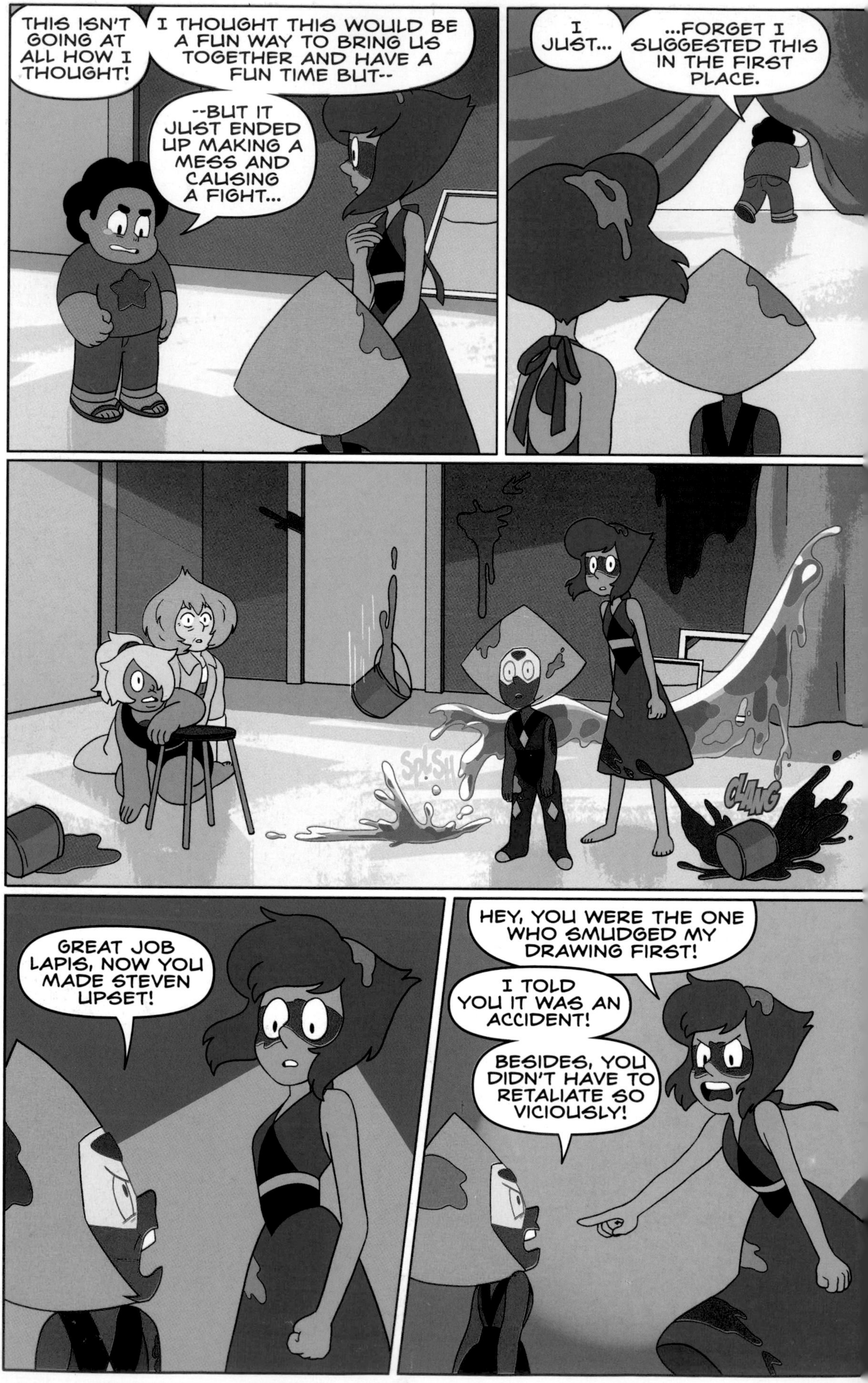
THIS ISN'T GOING AT ALL HOW I THOUGHT!
I THOUGHT THIS WOULD BE A FUN WAY TO BRING US TOGETHER AND HAVE A FUN TIME BUT--
--BUT IT JUST ENDED UP MAKING A MESS AND CAUSING A FIGHT...
I JUST...
...FORGET I SUGGESTED THIS IN THE FIRST PLACE.
SPLASH
CLANG
GREAT JOB LAPIS, NOW YOU MADE STEVEN UPSET!
HEY, YOU WERE THE ONE WHO SMUDGED MY DRAWING FIRST!
I TOLD YOU IT WAS AN ACCIDENT!
BESIDES, YOU DIDN'T HAVE TO RETALIATE SO VICIOUSLY!

I...YOU'RE NOT WRONG, I GUESS.

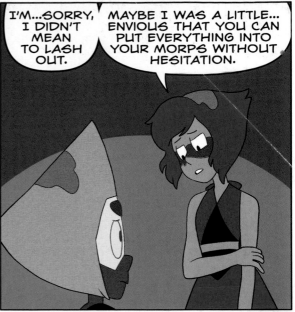

I'M...SORRY, I DIDN'T MEAN TO LASH OUT.

MAYBE I WAS A LITTLE... ENVIOUS THAT YOU CAN PUT EVERYTHING INTO YOUR MORPS WITHOUT HESITATION.

YES, WELL...MAYBE I ALSO LET MY JEALOUSLY GET THE BEST OF ME.

YOUR TECHNIQUE WITH THE PAINTS WAS VERY IMPRESSIVE.

BUT YOU GUYS DON'T HAVE TO BE ALL JEALOUS OF EACH OTHER AND FEEL LIKE YOU'VE GOT TO COMPETE.

YEAH! YOU CAN LEARN AND IMPROVE ON THOSE VERY POINTS YOU ADMIRE ABOUT THE OTHER.

THAT SOUNDS PRETTY AGREEABLE TO ME.

YEAH, SOUNDS A LOT EASIER TOO.

AND AS OUR FIRST COLLABORATIVE PIECE AFTER MAKING THIS PACT, I PROPOSE WE...FIGURE OUT A WAY TO FIX THIS MESS.

I THINK I MIGHT HAVE AN IDEA.

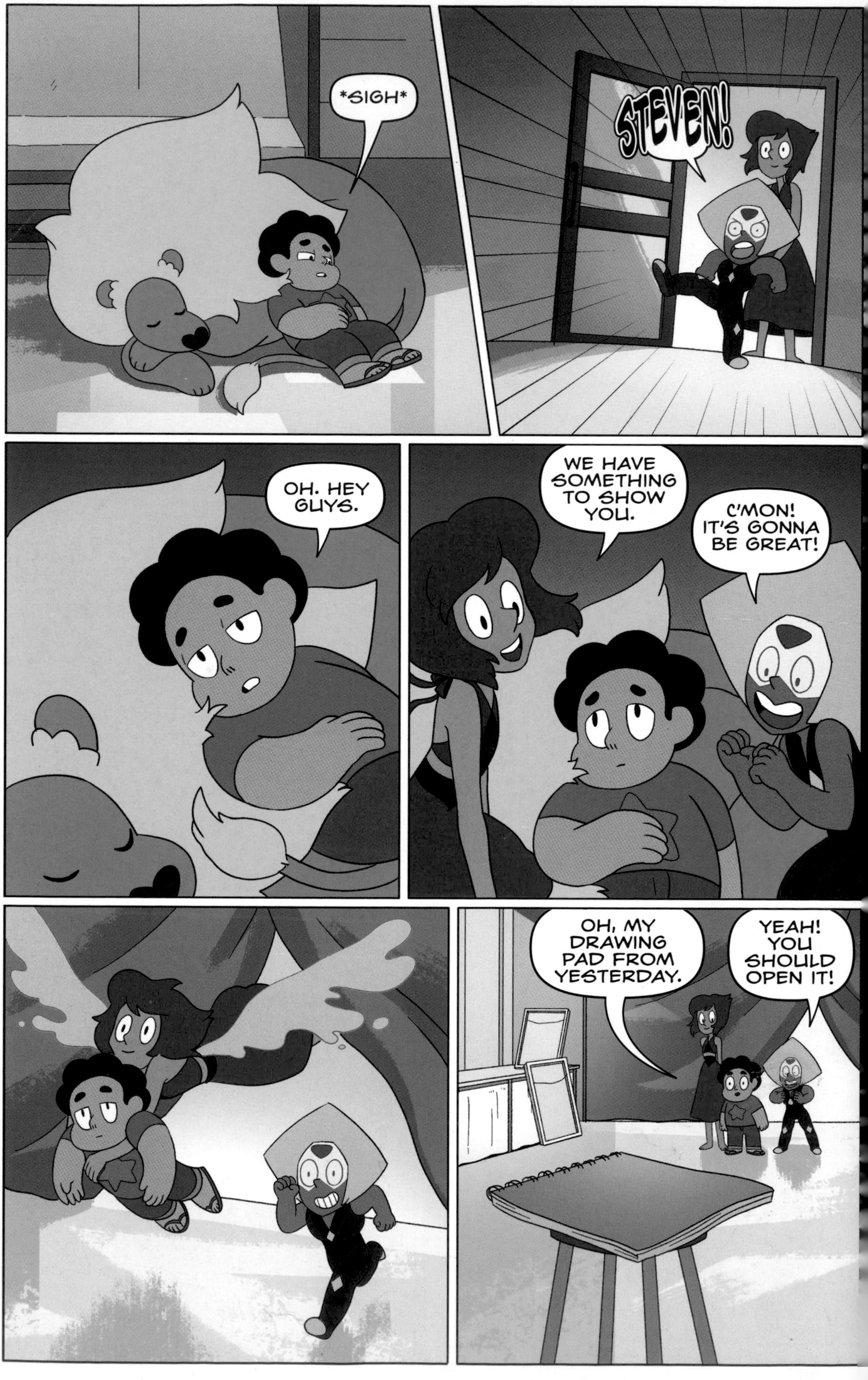
SIGH
STEVEN!
OH. HEY GUYS.
WE HAVE SOMETHING TO SHOW YOU.
C'MON! IT'S GONNA BE GREAT!
OH, MY DRAWING PAD FROM YESTERDAY.
YEAH! YOU SHOULD OPEN IT!

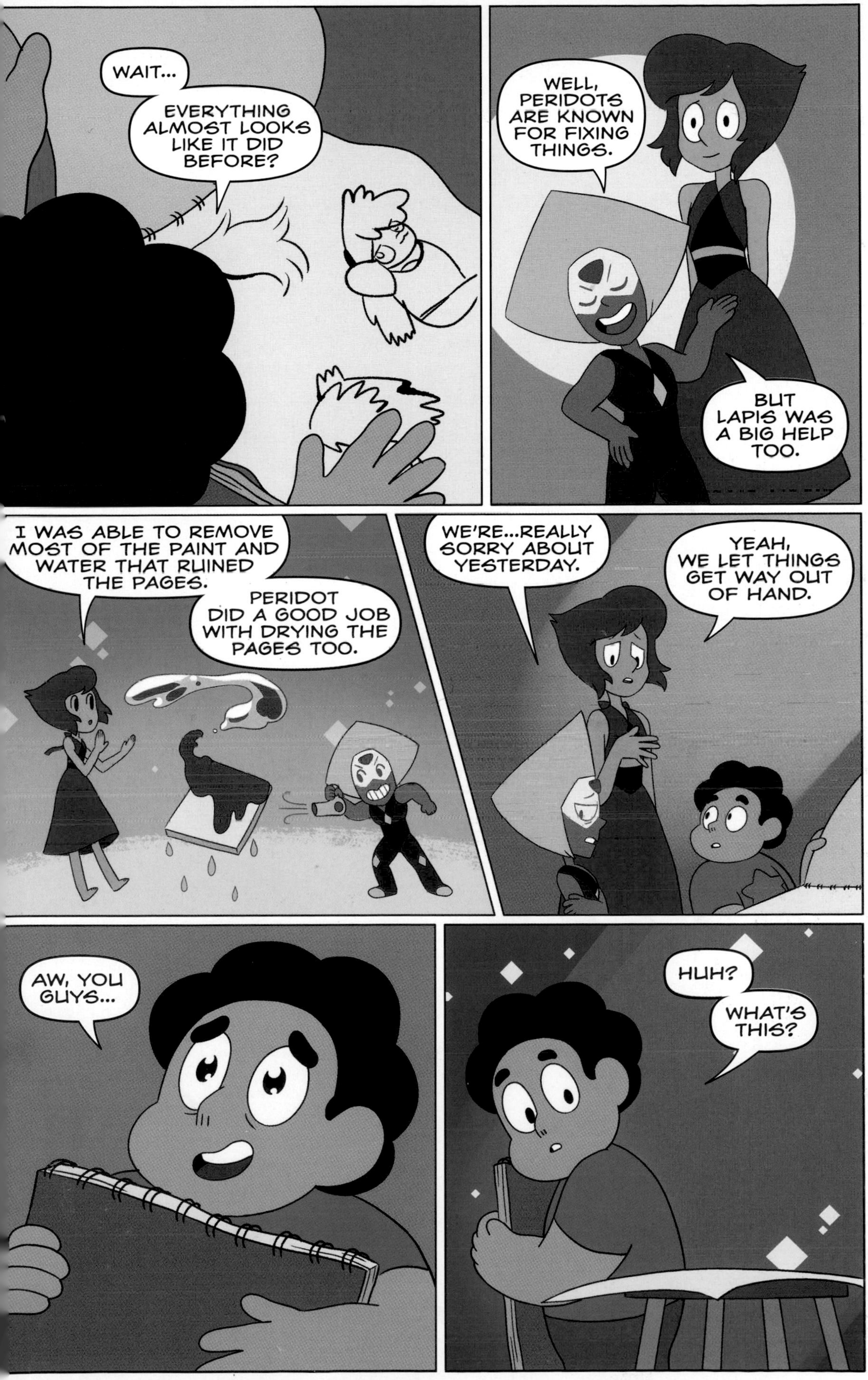

WAIT...
EVERYTHING ALMOST LOOKS LIKE IT DID BEFORE?
WELL, PERIDOTS ARE KNOWN FOR FIXING THINGS.
BUT LAPIS WAS A BIG HELP TOO.
I WAS ABLE TO REMOVE MOST OF THE PAINT AND WATER THAT RUINED THE PAGES.
PERIDOT DID A GOOD JOB WITH DRYING THE PAGES TOO.
WE'RE...REALLY SORRY ABOUT YESTERDAY.
YEAH, WE LET THINGS GET WAY OUT OF HAND.
AW, YOU GUYS...
HUH?
WHAT'S THIS?

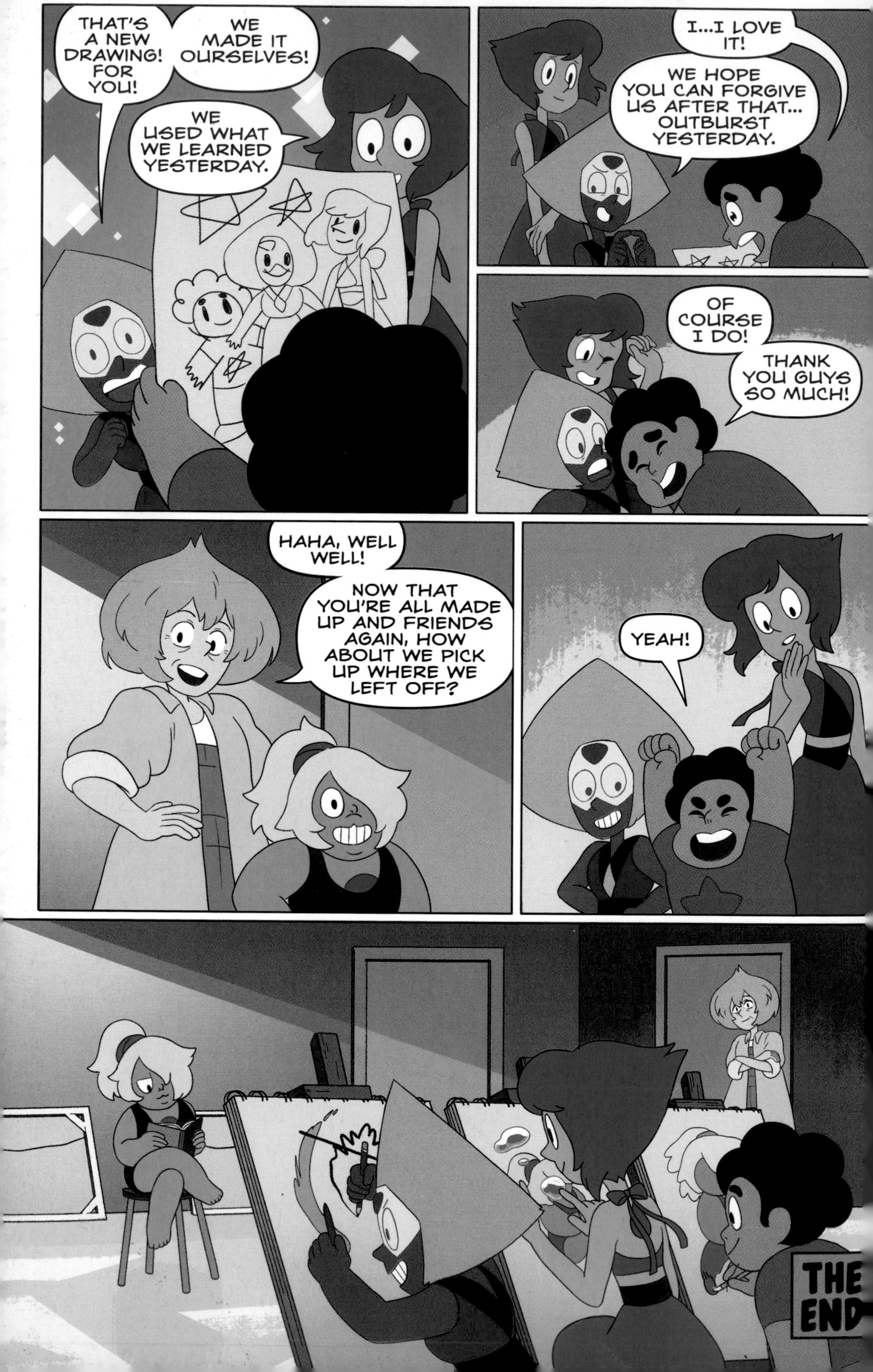
THAT'S A NEW DRAWING! FOR YOU!
WE MADE IT OURSELVES!
WE USED WHAT WE LEARNED YESTERDAY.
I...I LOVE IT!
WE HOPE YOU CAN FORGIVE US AFTER THAT... OUTBURST YESTERDAY.
OF COURSE I DO!
THANK YOU GUYS SO MUCH!
HAHA, WELL WELL!
NOW THAT YOU'RE ALL MADE UP AND FRIENDS AGAIN, HOW ABOUT WE PICK UP WHERE WE LEFT OFF?
YEAH!
THE END

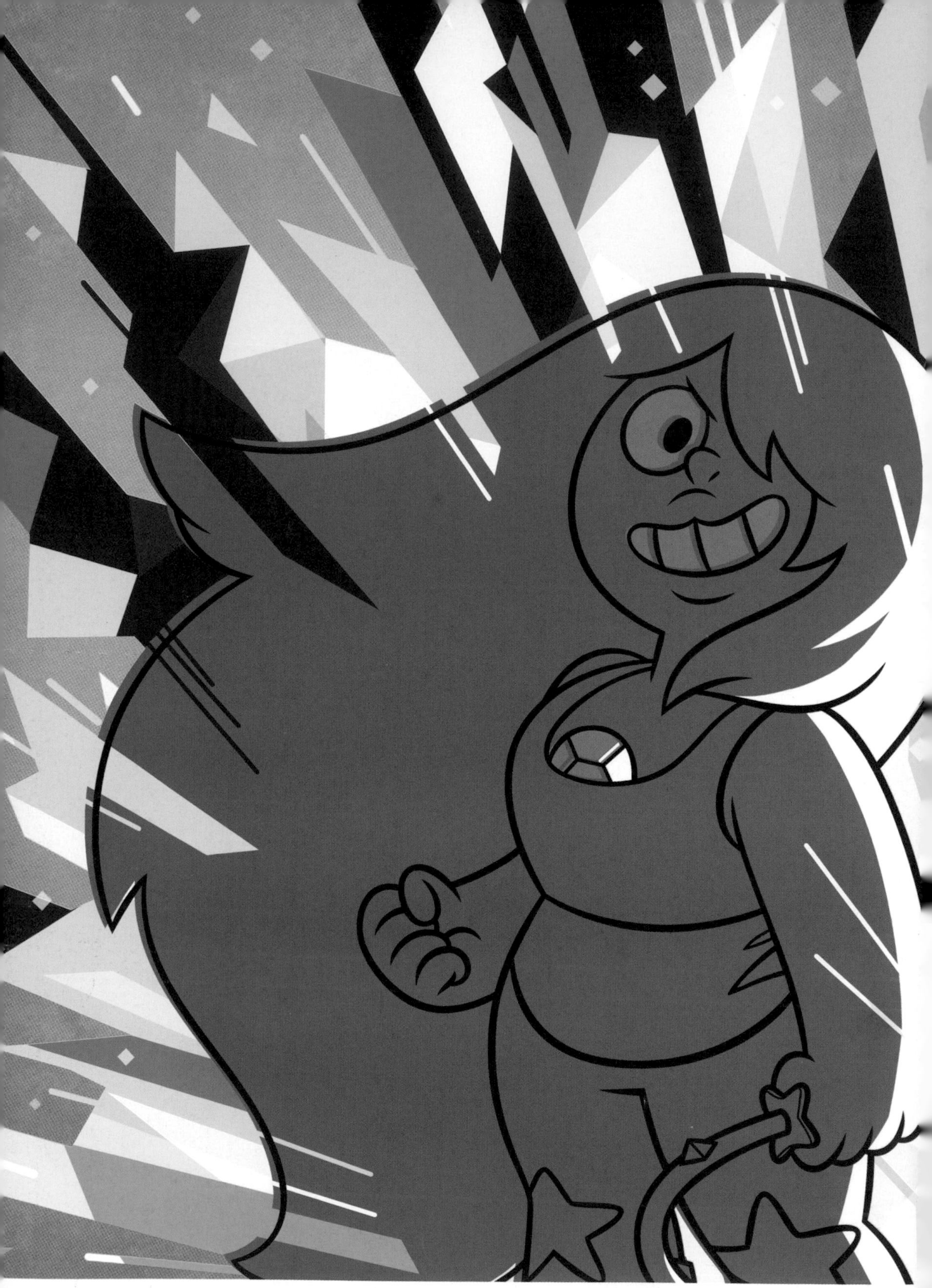

CHAPTER TEN

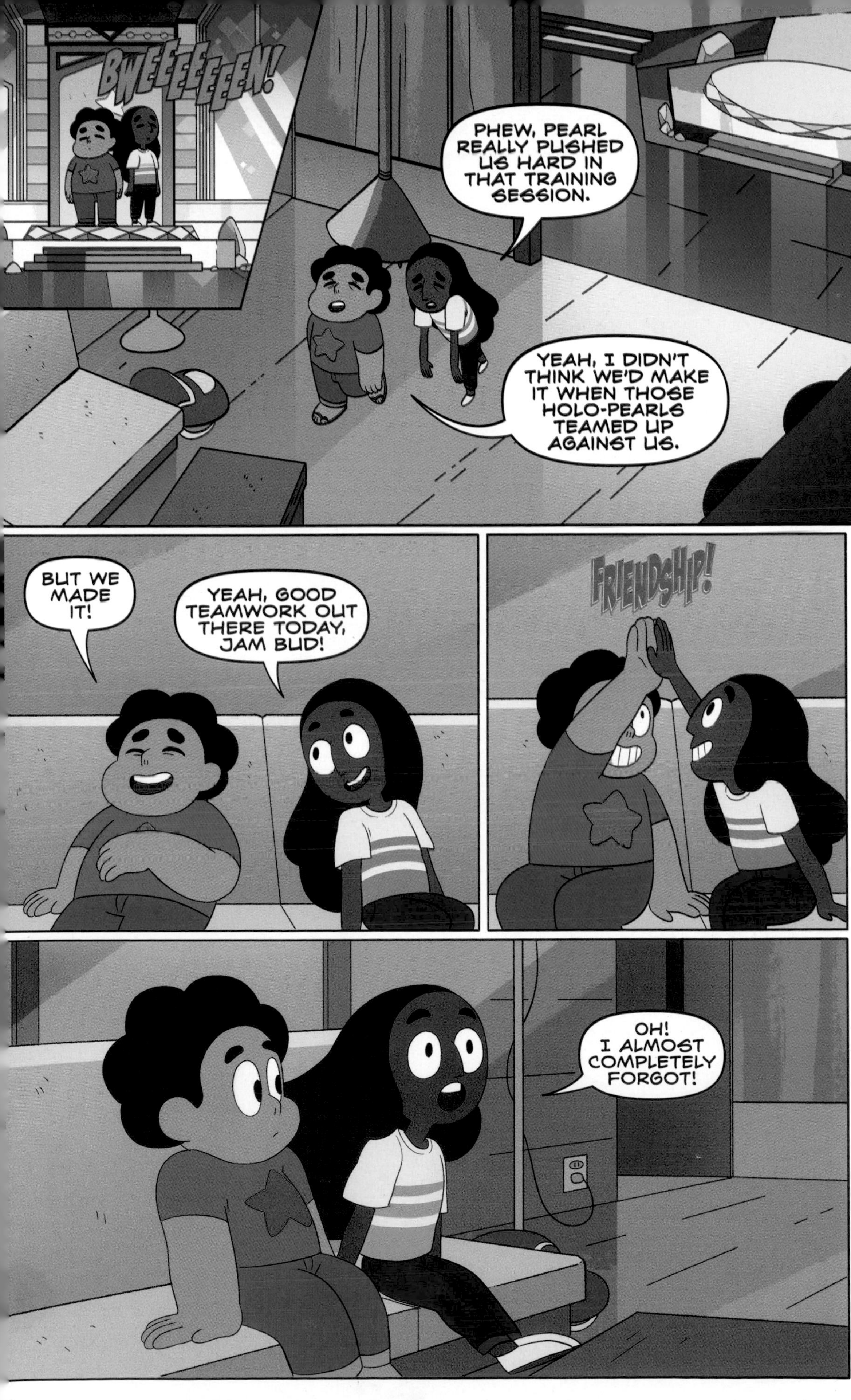
BWEEEEEEEN!
PHEW, PEARL REALLY PUSHED US HARD IN THAT TRAINING SESSION.
YEAH, I DIDN'T THINK WE'D MAKE IT WHEN THOSE HOLO-PEARLS TEAMED UP AGAINST US.
BUT WE MADE IT!
YEAH, GOOD TEAMWORK OUT THERE TODAY, JAM BUD!
FRIENDSHIP!
OH! I ALMOST COMPLETELY FORGOT!

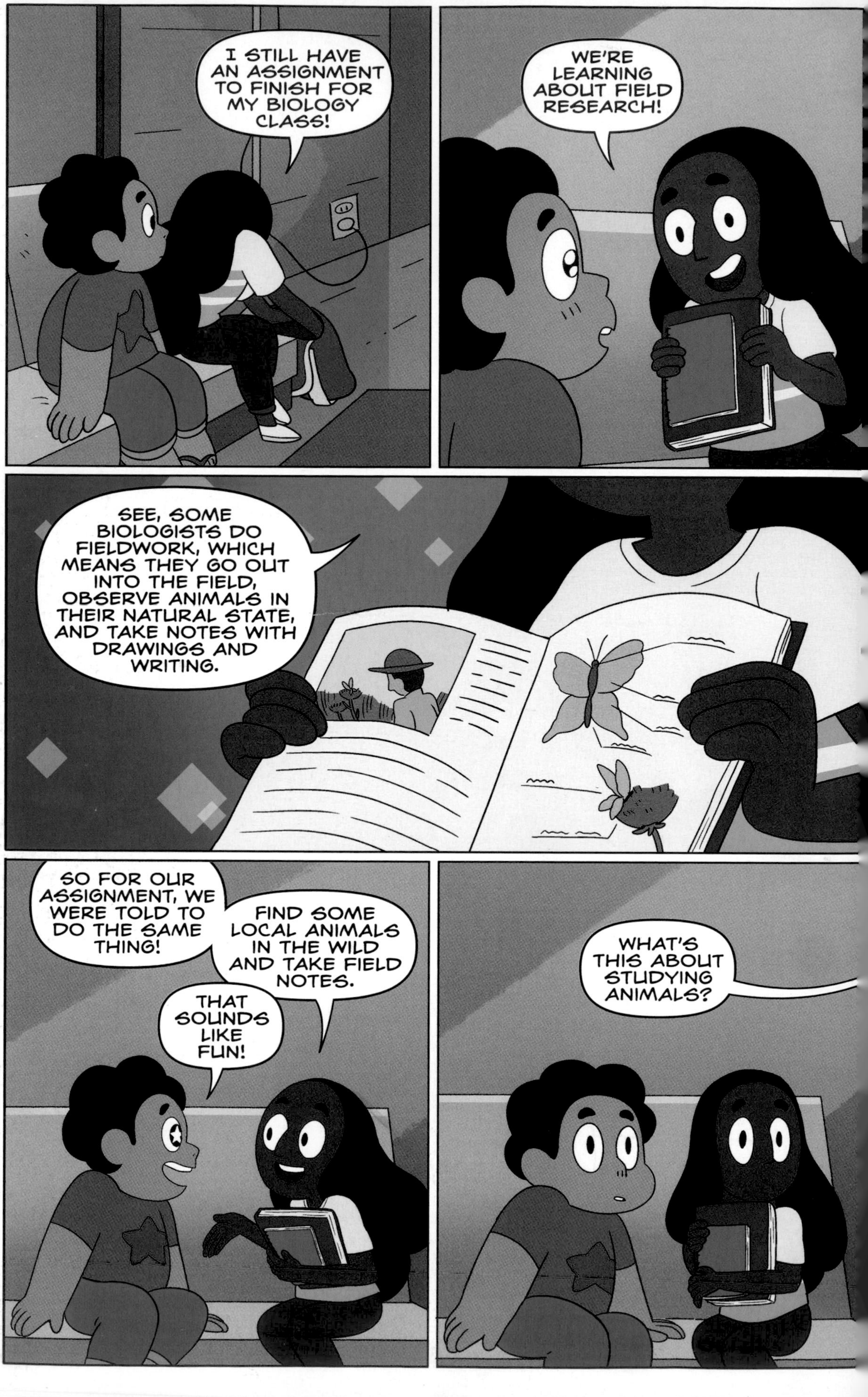
I STILL HAVE AN ASSIGNMENT TO FINISH FOR MY BIOLOGY CLASS!
WE'RE LEARNING ABOUT FIELD RESEARCH!
SEE, SOME BIOLOGISTS DO FIELDWORK, WHICH MEANS THEY GO OUT INTO THE FIELD, OBSERVE ANIMALS IN THEIR NATURAL STATE, AND TAKE NOTES WITH DRAWINGS AND WRITING.
SO FOR OUR ASSIGNMENT, WE WERE TOLD TO DO THE SAME THING!
FIND SOME LOCAL ANIMALS IN THE WILD AND TAKE FIELD NOTES.
THAT SOUNDS LIKE FUN!
WHAT'S THIS ABOUT STUDYING ANIMALS?

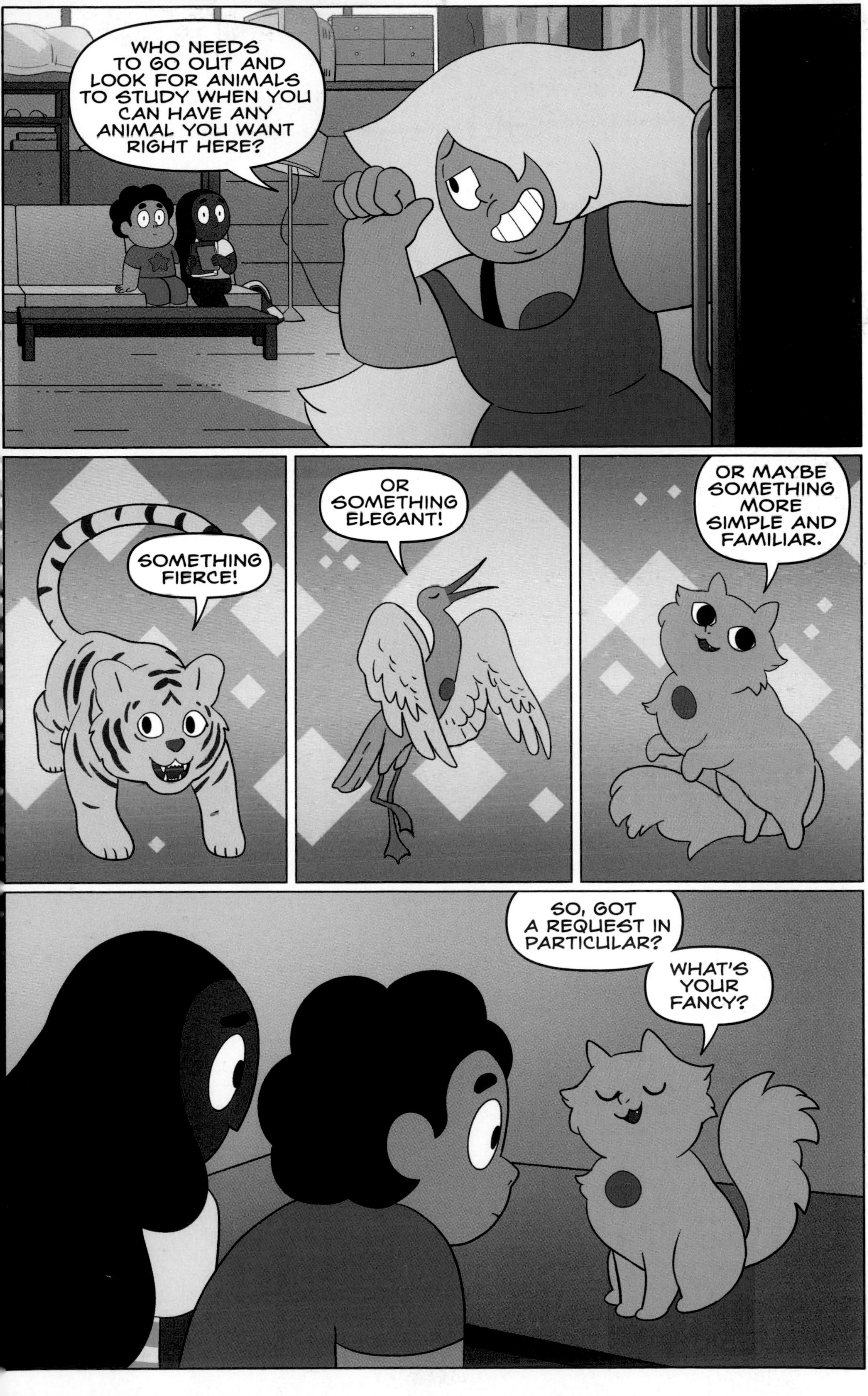
WHO NEEDS TO GO OUT AND LOOK FOR ANIMALS TO STUDY WHEN YOU CAN HAVE ANY ANIMAL YOU WANT RIGHT HERE?
SOMETHING FIERCE!
OR SOMETHING ELEGANT!
OR MAYBE SOMETHING MORE SIMPLE AND FAMILIAR.
SO, GOT A REQUEST IN PARTICULAR?
WHAT'S YOUR FANCY?

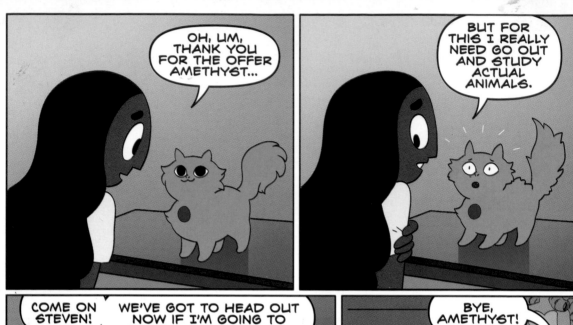

OH, UM, THANK YOU FOR THE OFFER AMETHYST...

BUT FOR THIS I REALLY NEED GO OUT AND STUDY ACTUAL ANIMALS.

COME ON STEVEN!

WE'VE GOT TO HEAD OUT NOW IF I'M GOING TO GET THIS DONE BY THE END OF TODAY.

I'M RIGHT BEHIND YOU!

BYE, AMETHYST!

WE'LL BE BACK LATER!

ACTUAL ANIMALS, HUH?

GUESS I JUST NEED TO SHOW THEM HOW CONVINCING I CAN BE!

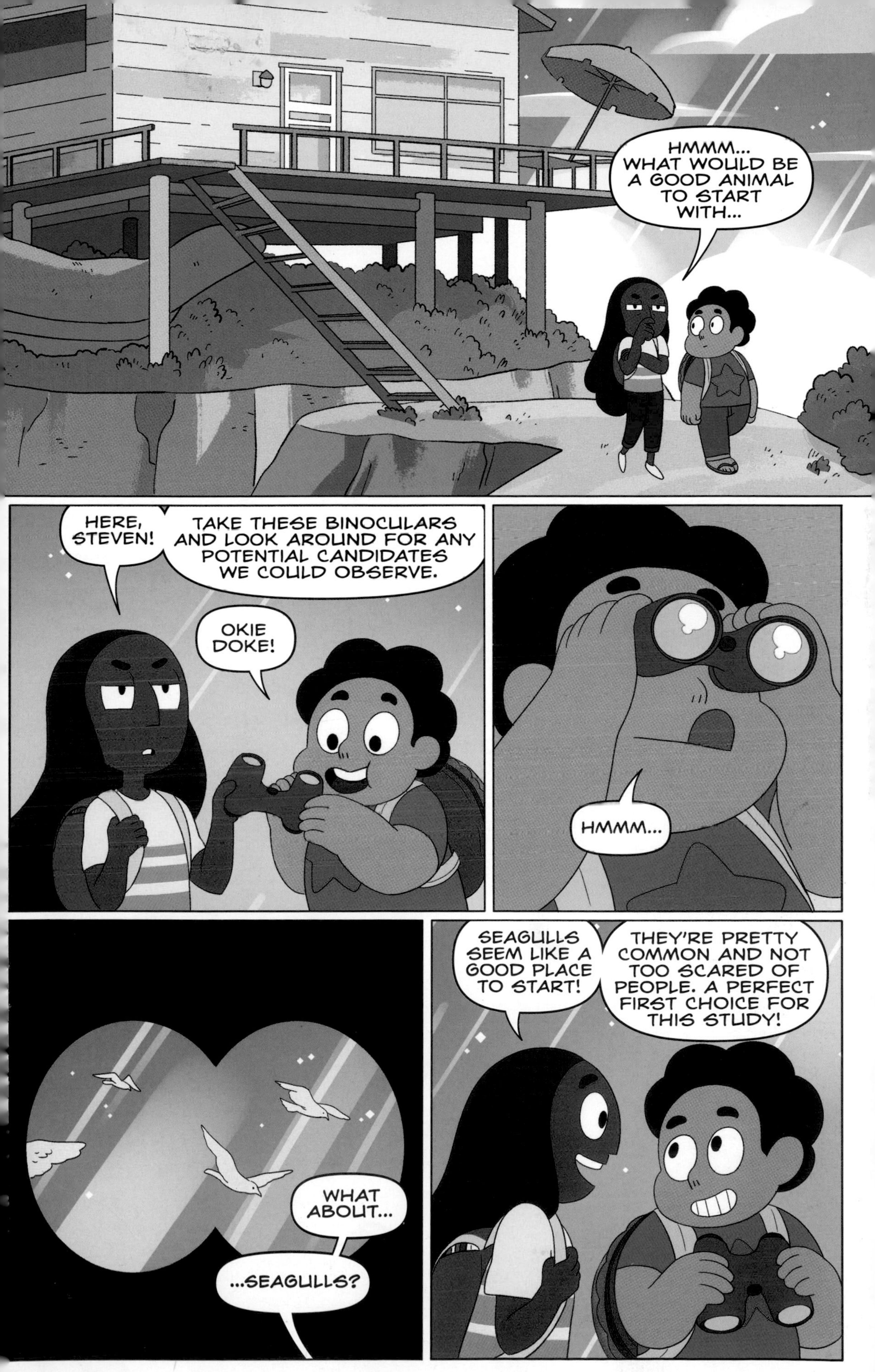
HMMM... WHAT WOULD BE A GOOD ANIMAL TO START WITH...
HERE, STEVEN!
TAKE THESE BINOCULARS AND LOOK AROUND FOR ANY POTENTIAL CANDIDATES WE COULD OBSERVE.
OKIE DOKE!
HMMM...
WHAT ABOUT...
...SEAGULLS?
SEAGULLS SEEM LIKE A GOOD PLACE TO START!
THEY'RE PRETTY COMMON AND NOT TOO SCARED OF PEOPLE. A PERFECT FIRST CHOICE FOR THIS STUDY!

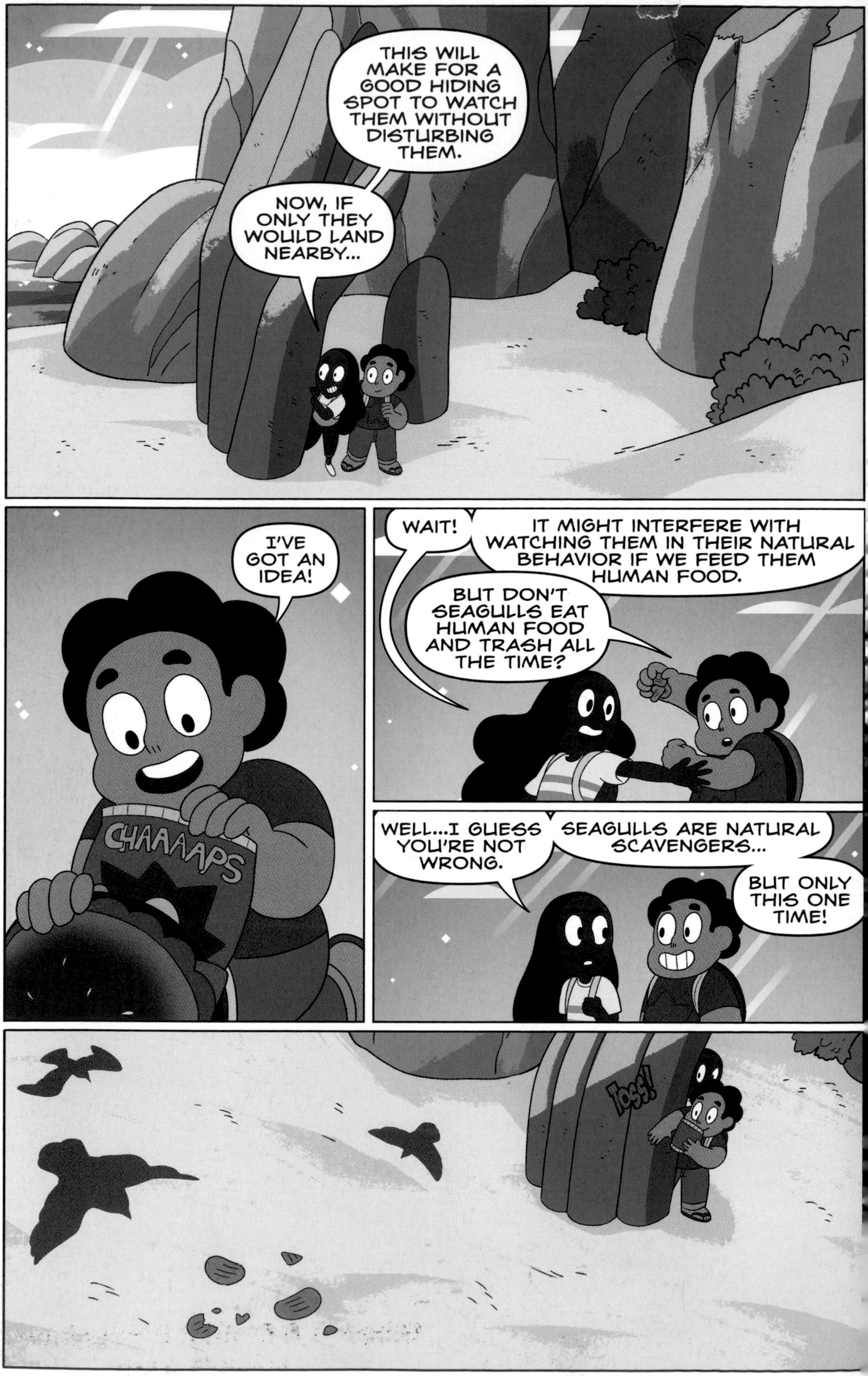
THIS WILL MAKE FOR A GOOD HIDING SPOT TO WATCH THEM WITHOUT DISTURBING THEM.
NOW, IF ONLY THEY WOULD LAND NEARBY...
I'VE GOT AN IDEA!
CHAAAAPS
WAIT!
IT MIGHT INTERFERE WITH WATCHING THEM IN THEIR NATURAL BEHAVIOR IF WE FEED THEM HUMAN FOOD.
BUT DON'T SEAGULLS EAT HUMAN FOOD AND TRASH ALL THE TIME?
WELL...I GUESS YOU'RE NOT WRONG.
SEAGULLS ARE NATURAL SCAVENGERS...
BUT ONLY THIS ONE TIME!
TOSS!

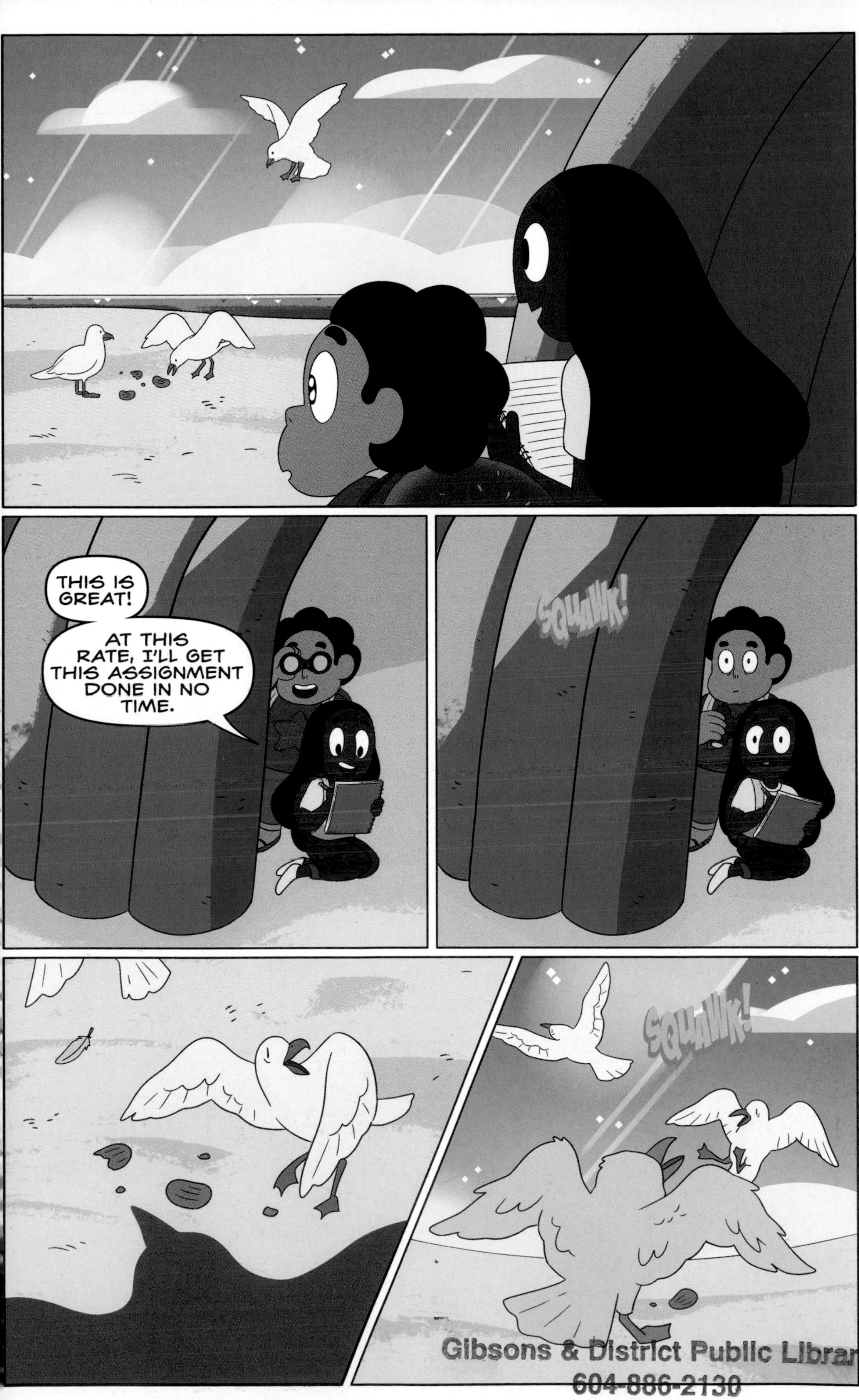
THIS IS GREAT!
AT THIS RATE, I'LL GET THIS ASSIGNMENT DONE IN NO TIME.
SQUAWK!
SQUAWK!

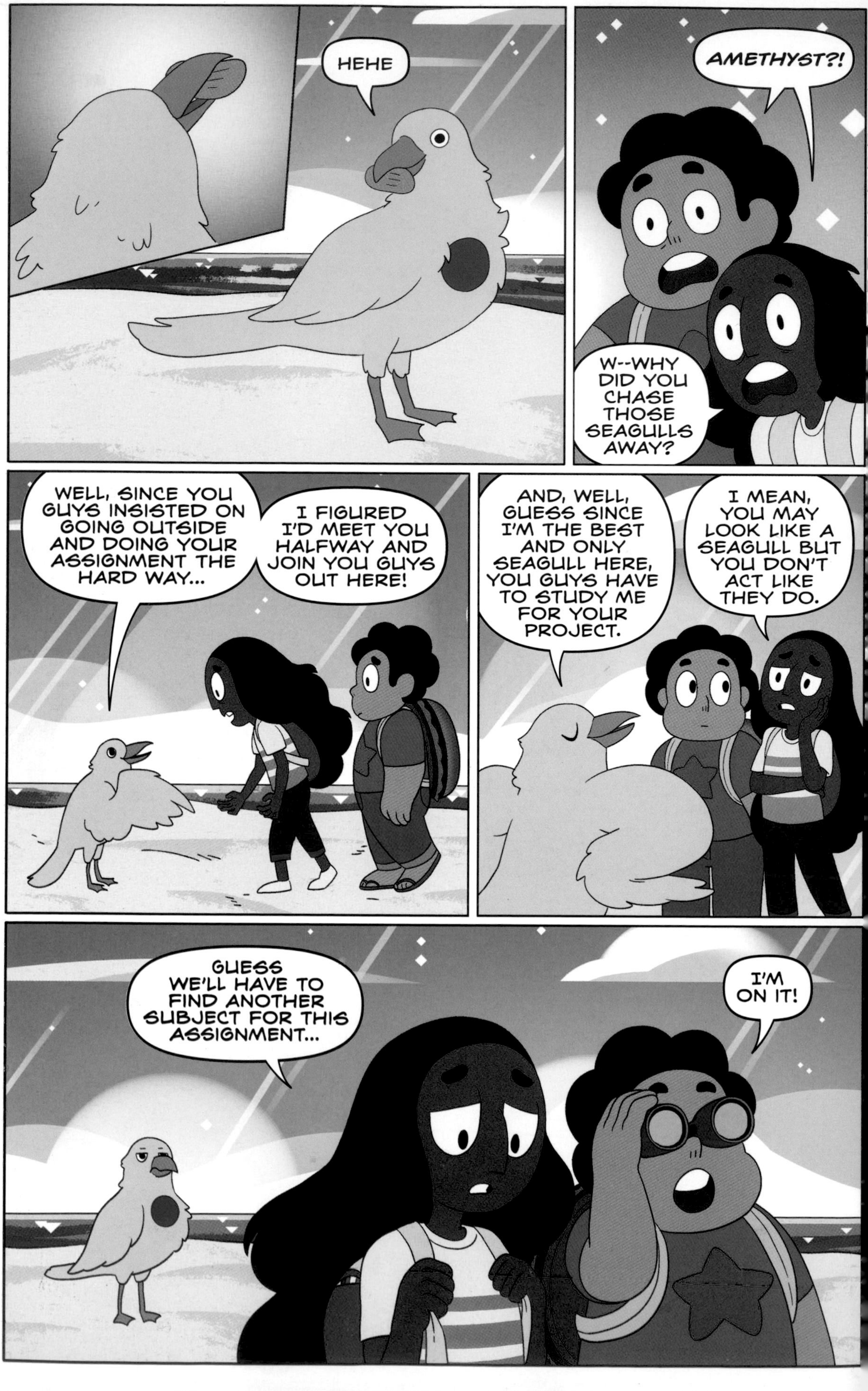
HEHE
AMETHYST?!
W--WHY DID YOU CHASE THOSE SEAGULLS AWAY?
WELL, SINCE YOU GUYS INSISTED ON GOING OUTSIDE AND DOING YOUR ASSIGNMENT THE HARD WAY...
I FIGURED I'D MEET YOU HALFWAY AND JOIN YOU GUYS OUT HERE!
AND, WELL, GUESS SINCE I'M THE BEST AND ONLY SEAGULL HERE, YOU GUYS HAVE TO STUDY ME FOR YOUR PROJECT.
I MEAN, YOU MAY LOOK LIKE A SEAGULL BUT YOU DON'T ACT LIKE THEY DO.
GUESS WE'LL HAVE TO FIND ANOTHER SUBJECT FOR THIS ASSIGNMENT...
I'M ON IT!

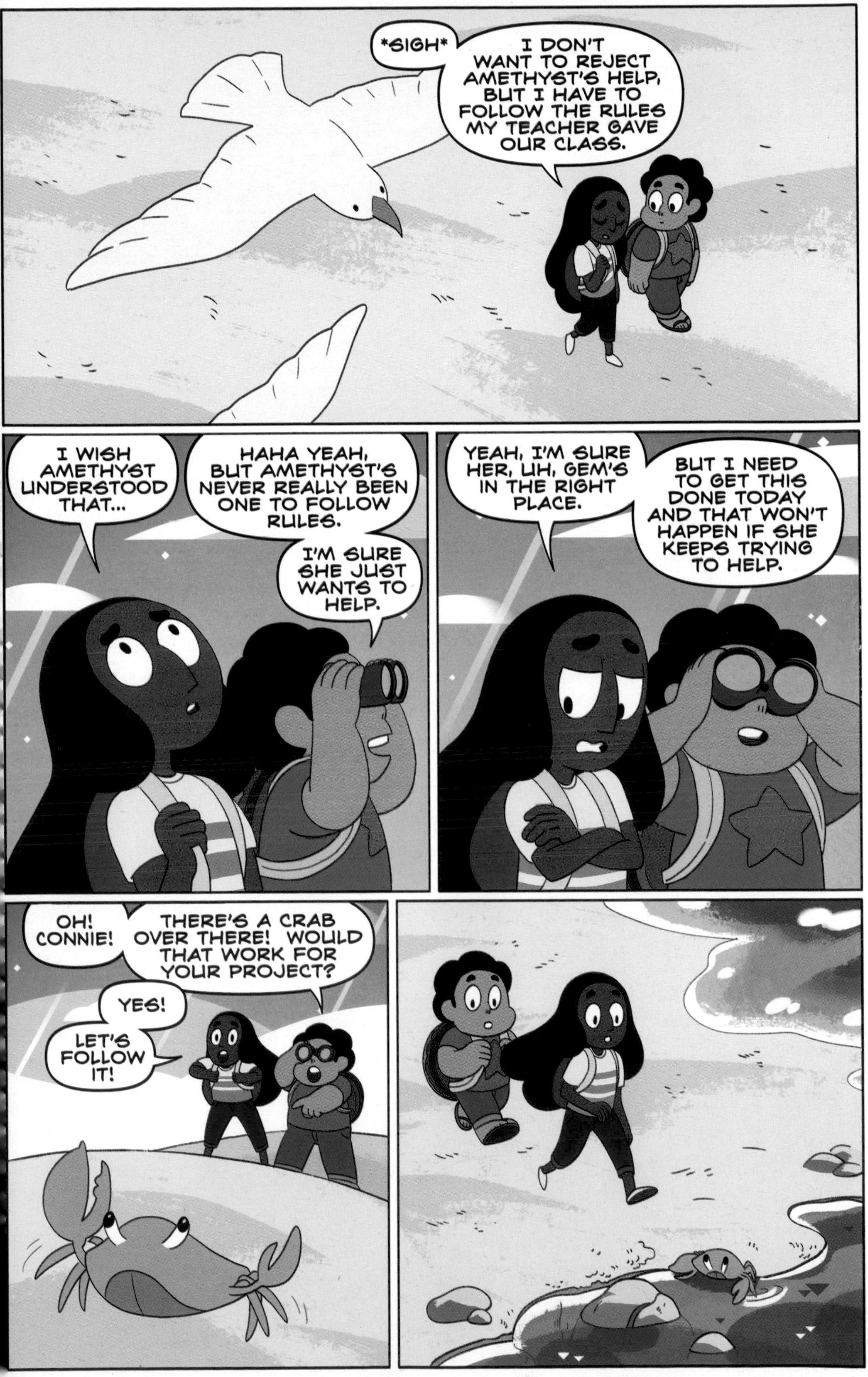
SIGH
I DON'T WANT TO REJECT AMETHYST'S HELP, BUT I HAVE TO FOLLOW THE RULES MY TEACHER GAVE OUR CLASS.
I WISH AMETHYST UNDERSTOOD THAT...
HAHA YEAH, BUT AMETHYST'S NEVER REALLY BEEN ONE TO FOLLOW RULES.
I'M SURE SHE JUST WANTS TO HELP.
YEAH, I'M SURE HER, UH, GEM'S IN THE RIGHT PLACE.
BUT I NEED TO GET THIS DONE TODAY AND THAT WON'T HAPPEN IF SHE KEEPS TRYING TO HELP.
OH! CONNIE!
THERE'S A CRAB OVER THERE! WOULD THAT WORK FOR YOUR PROJECT?
YES!
LET'S FOLLOW IT!

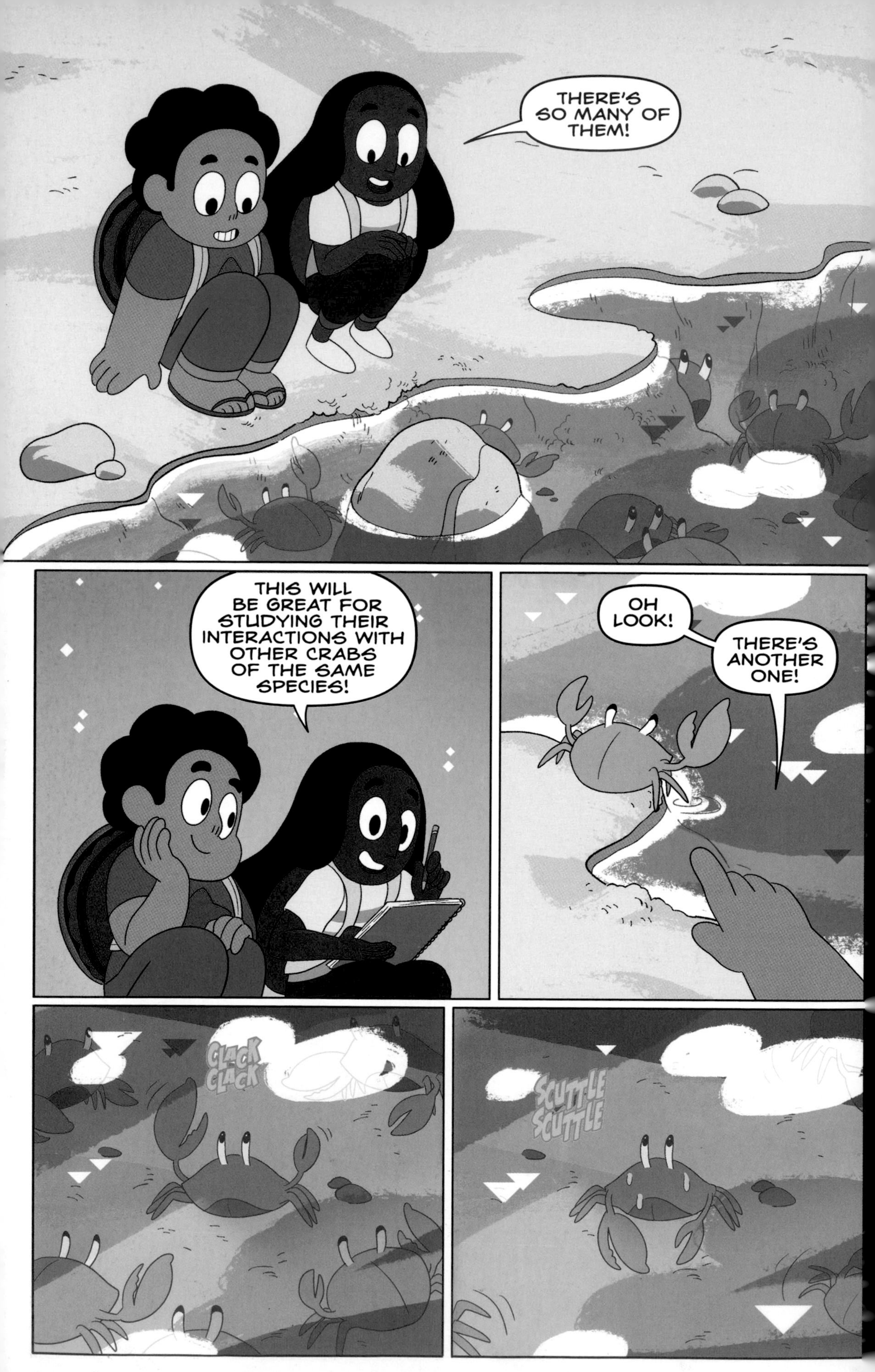
THERE'S SO MANY OF THEM!
THIS WILL BE GREAT FOR STUDYING THEIR INTERACTIONS WITH OTHER CRABS OF THE SAME SPECIES!
OH LOOK!
THERE'S ANOTHER ONE!
CLACK CLACK
SCUTTLE SCUTTLE

GRAB

FLIP

YEP! IT'S AMETHYST.

ALRIGHT ALRIGHT! YOU CAUGHT ME.

WHAT'S THE BIG DEAL? I THOUGHT I WAS A PRETTY CONVINCING CRAB.

YES, BUT YOU STILL AREN'T A CRAB.

YOU DON'T KNOW HOW THEY NORMALLY BEHAVE AND WHY.

AND THAT'S WHAT THIS ASSIGNMENT IS ABOUT: STUDYING ANIMALS IN THE WILD TO LEARN MORE ABOUT THEM.

THOSE WERE THE RULES, AT LEAST.

WELL RULES STINK!

UGH! I GET IT, ALRIGHT?

YOU DON'T WANT MY HELP, AND MY SHAPE-SHIFTING ISN'T GOOD ENOUGH FOR YOU!

AMETHYST, WAIT!

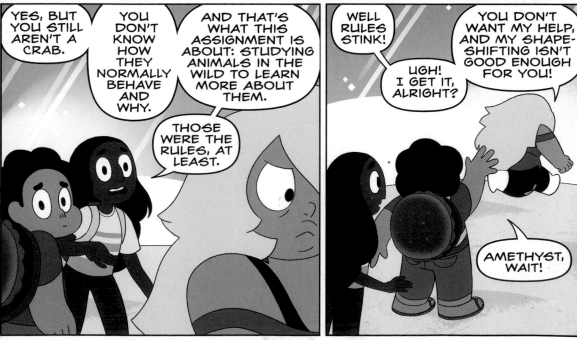

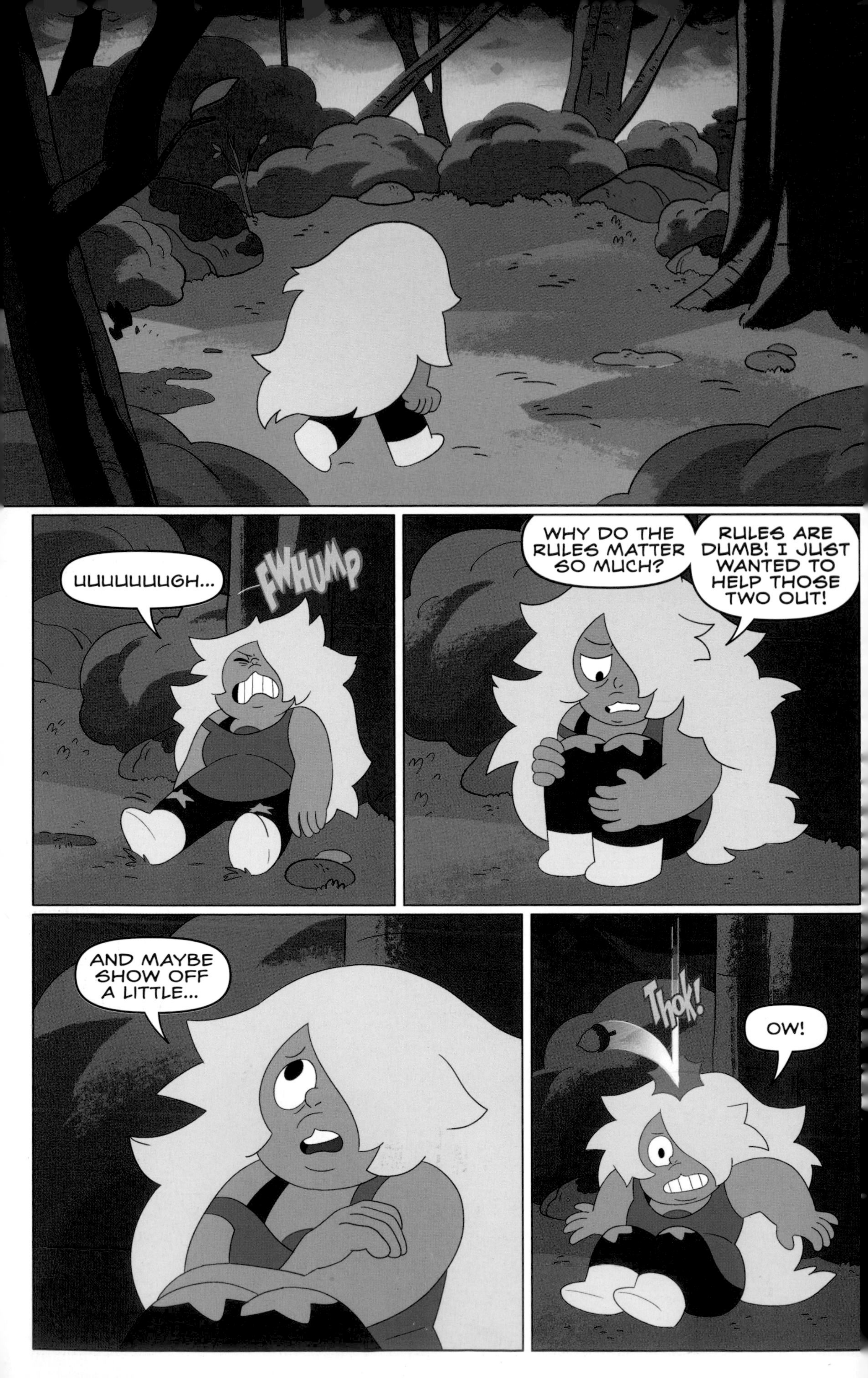
UUUUUUUGH...
FWHUMP
WHY DO THE RULES MATTER SO MUCH?
RULES ARE DUMB! I JUST WANTED TO HELP THOSE TWO OUT!
AND MAYBE SHOW OFF A LITTLE...
THOK!
OW!

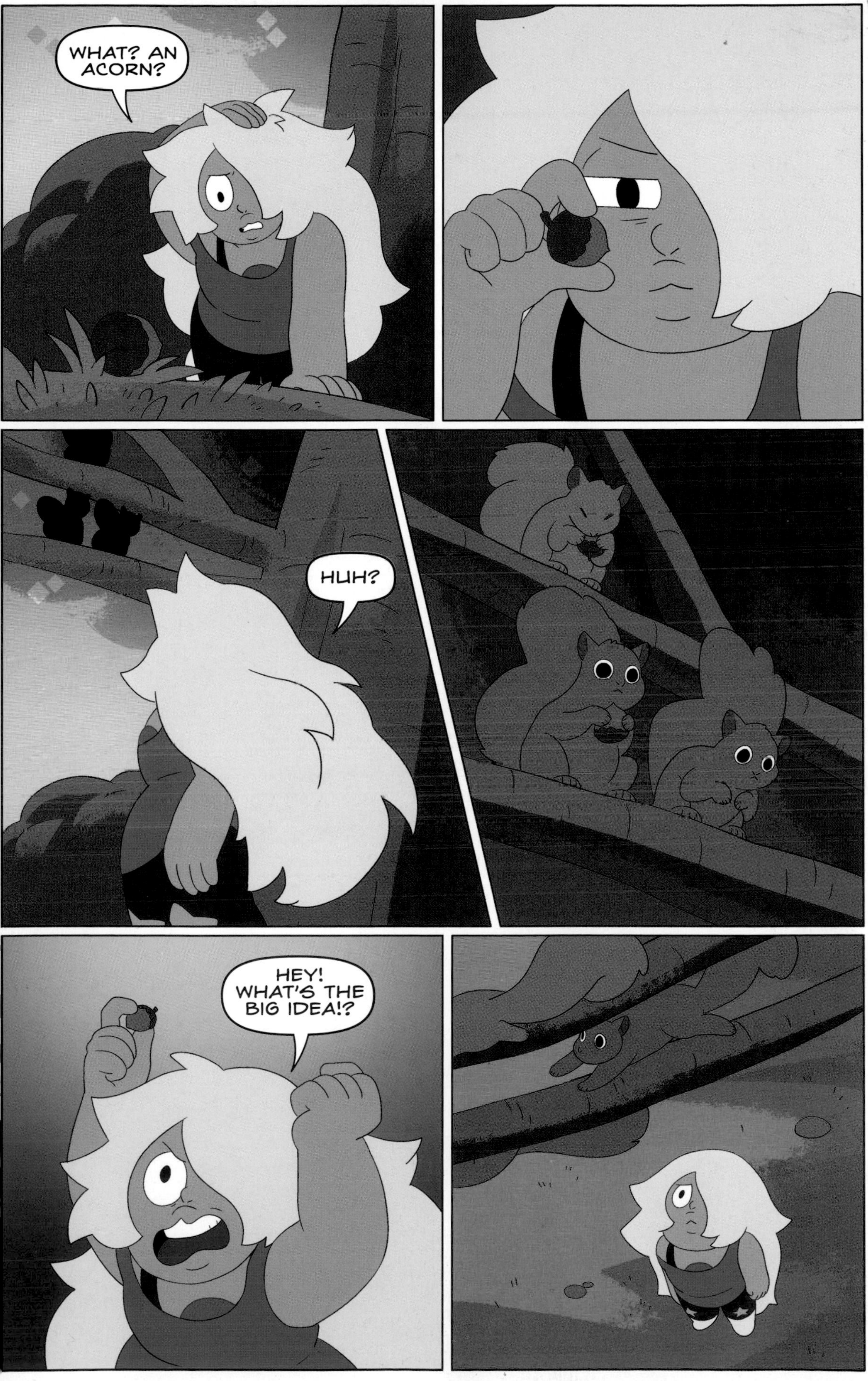
WHAT? AN ACORN?
HUH?
HEY! WHAT'S THE BIG IDEA!?

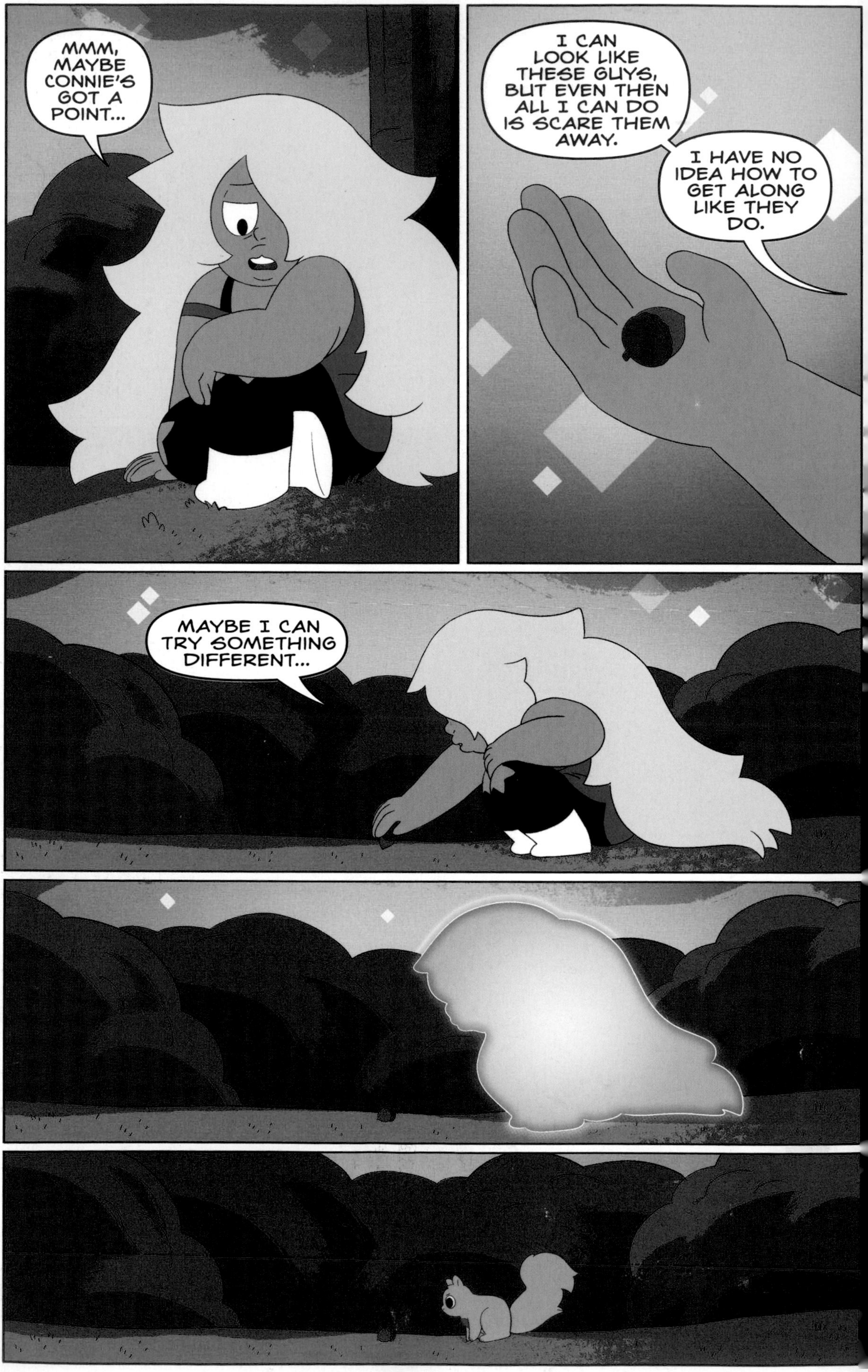
MMM, MAYBE CONNIE'S GOT A POINT...
I CAN LOOK LIKE THESE GUYS, BUT EVEN THEN ALL I CAN DO IS SCARE THEM AWAY.
I HAVE NO IDEA HOW TO GET ALONG LIKE THEY DO.
MAYBE I CAN TRY SOMETHING DIFFERENT...

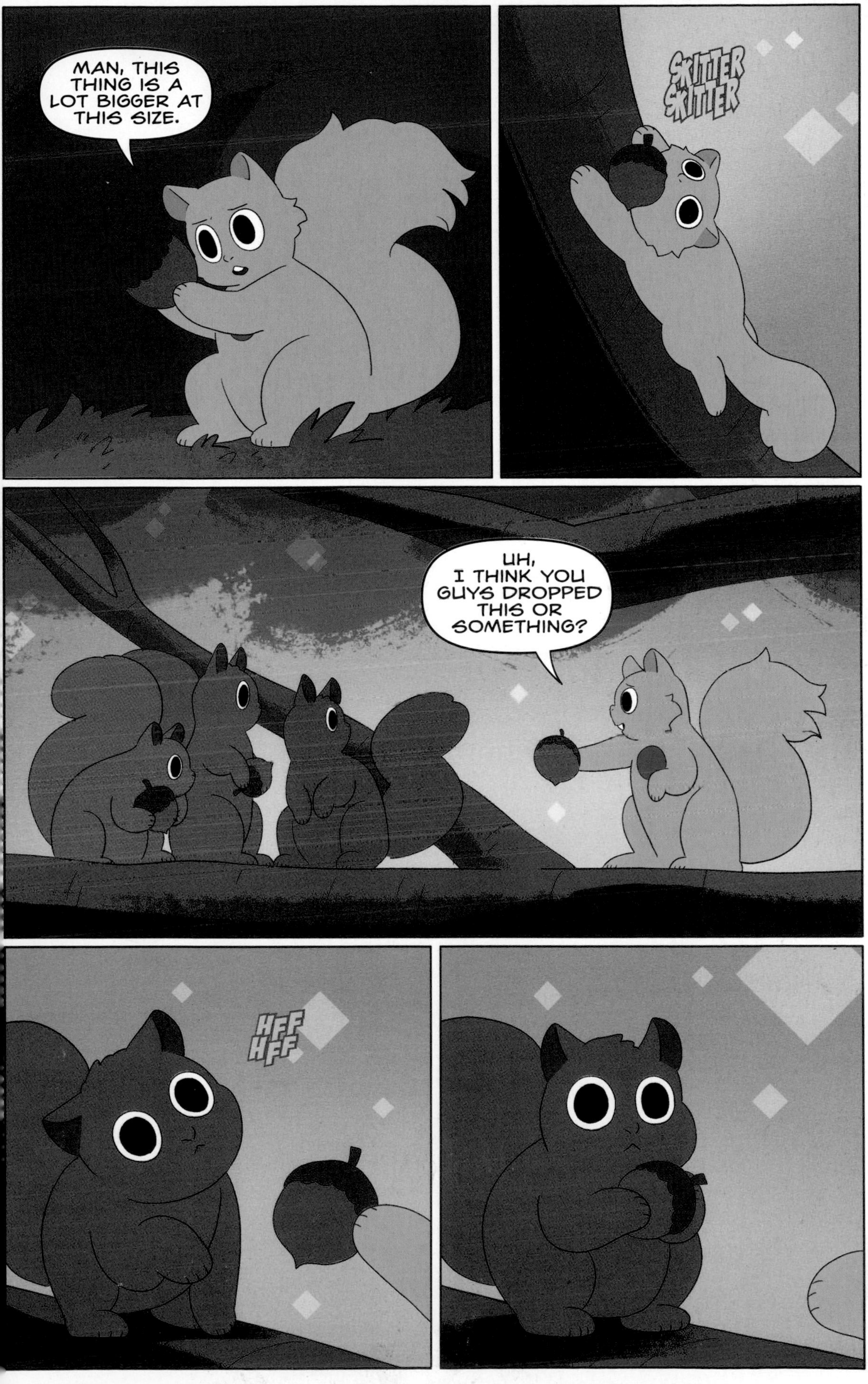
MAN, THIS THING IS A LOT BIGGER AT THIS SIZE.
SKITTER SKITTER
UH, I THINK YOU GUYS DROPPED THIS OR SOMETHING?
HFF HFF

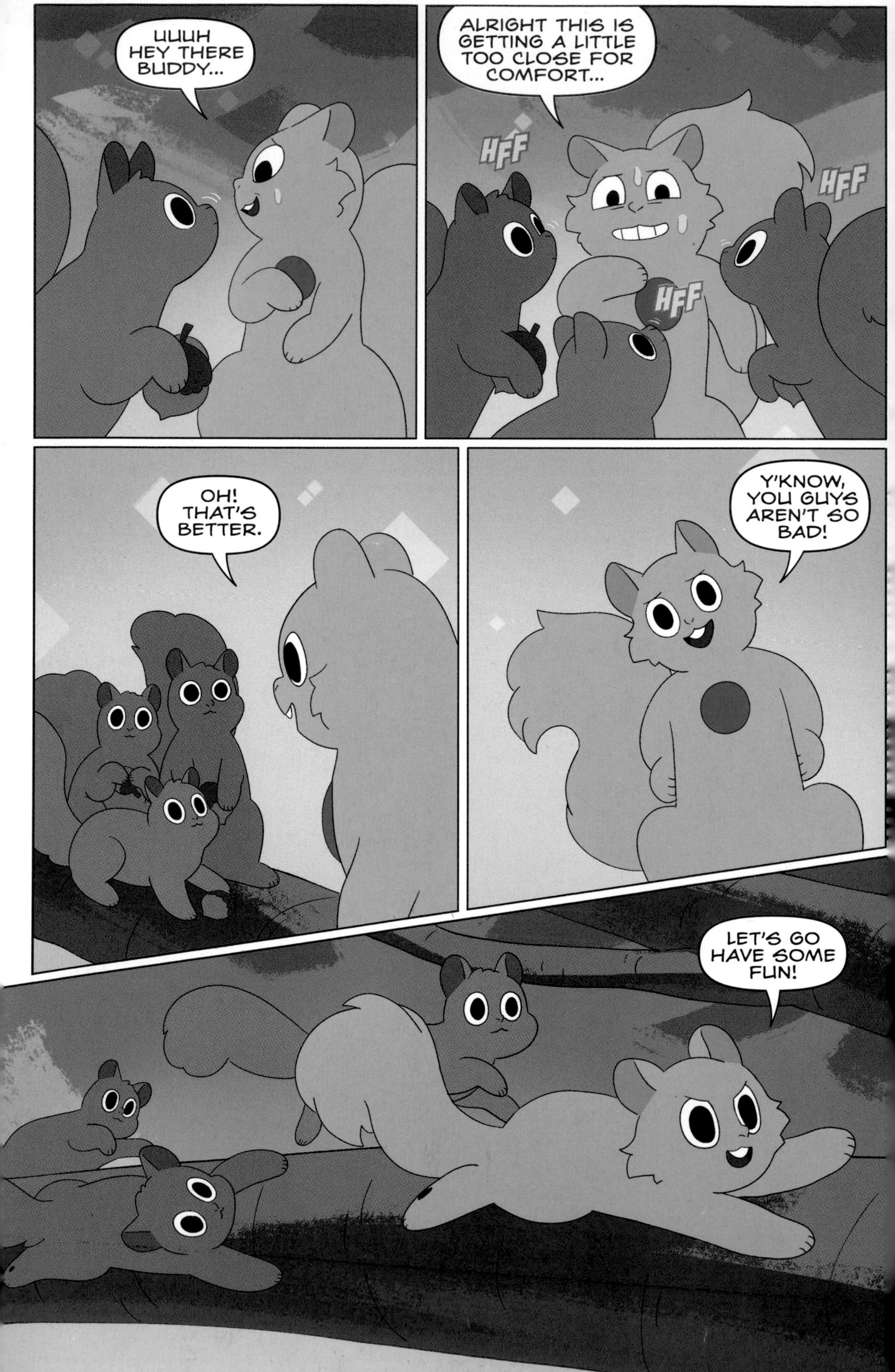
UUUH HEY THERE BUDDY...
ALRIGHT THIS IS GETTING A LITTLE TOO CLOSE FOR COMFORT...
HFF
HFF
HFF
OH! THAT'S BETTER.
Y'KNOW, YOU GUYS AREN'T SO BAD!
LET'S GO HAVE SOME FUN!

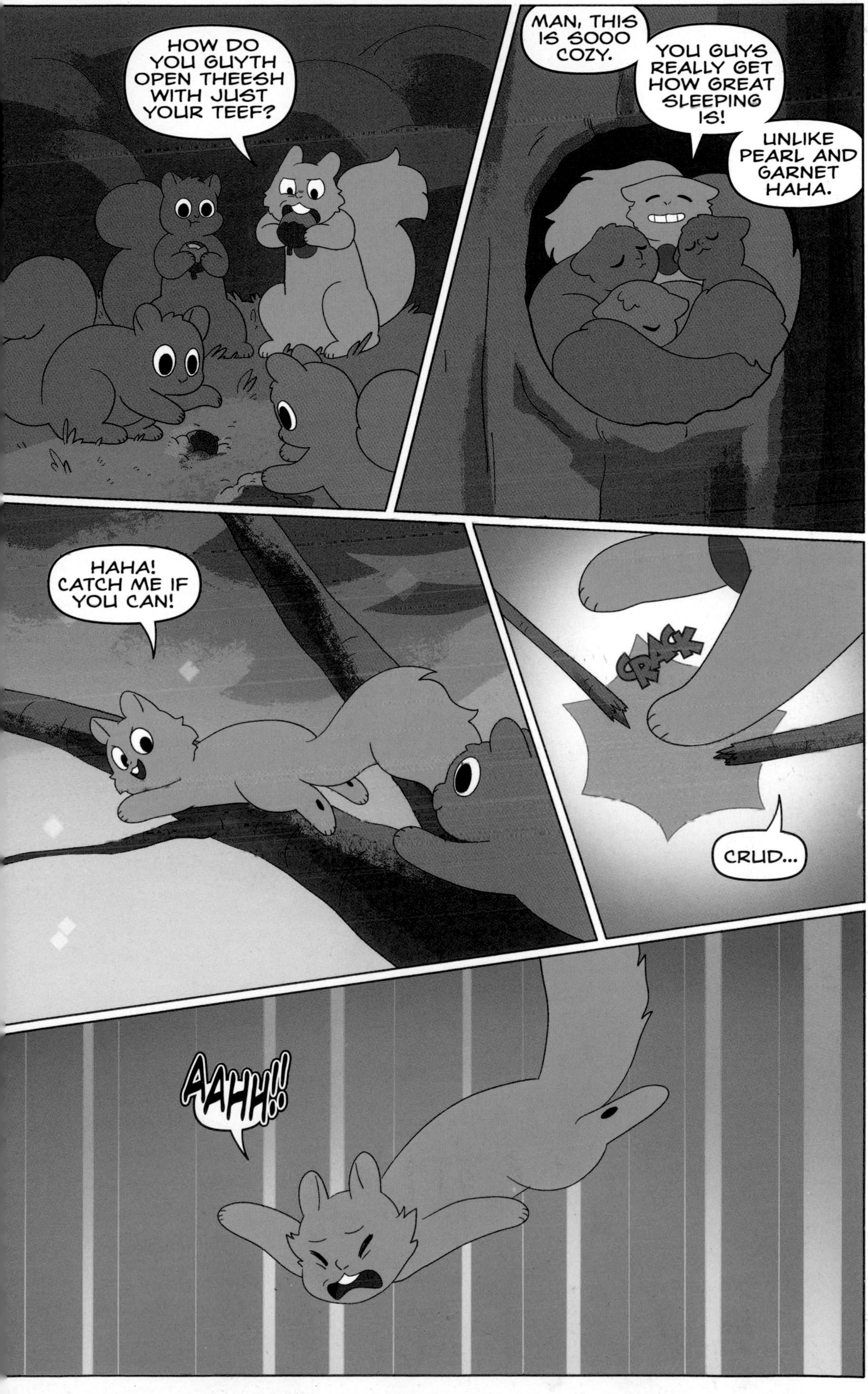
HOW DO YOU GUYTH OPEN THEESH WITH JUST YOUR TEEF?
MAN, THIS IS SOOO COZY.
YOU GUYS REALLY GET HOW GREAT SLEEPING IS!
UNLIKE PEARL AND GARNET HAHA.
HAHA! CATCH ME IF YOU CAN!
CRACK
CRUD...
AAHH!!

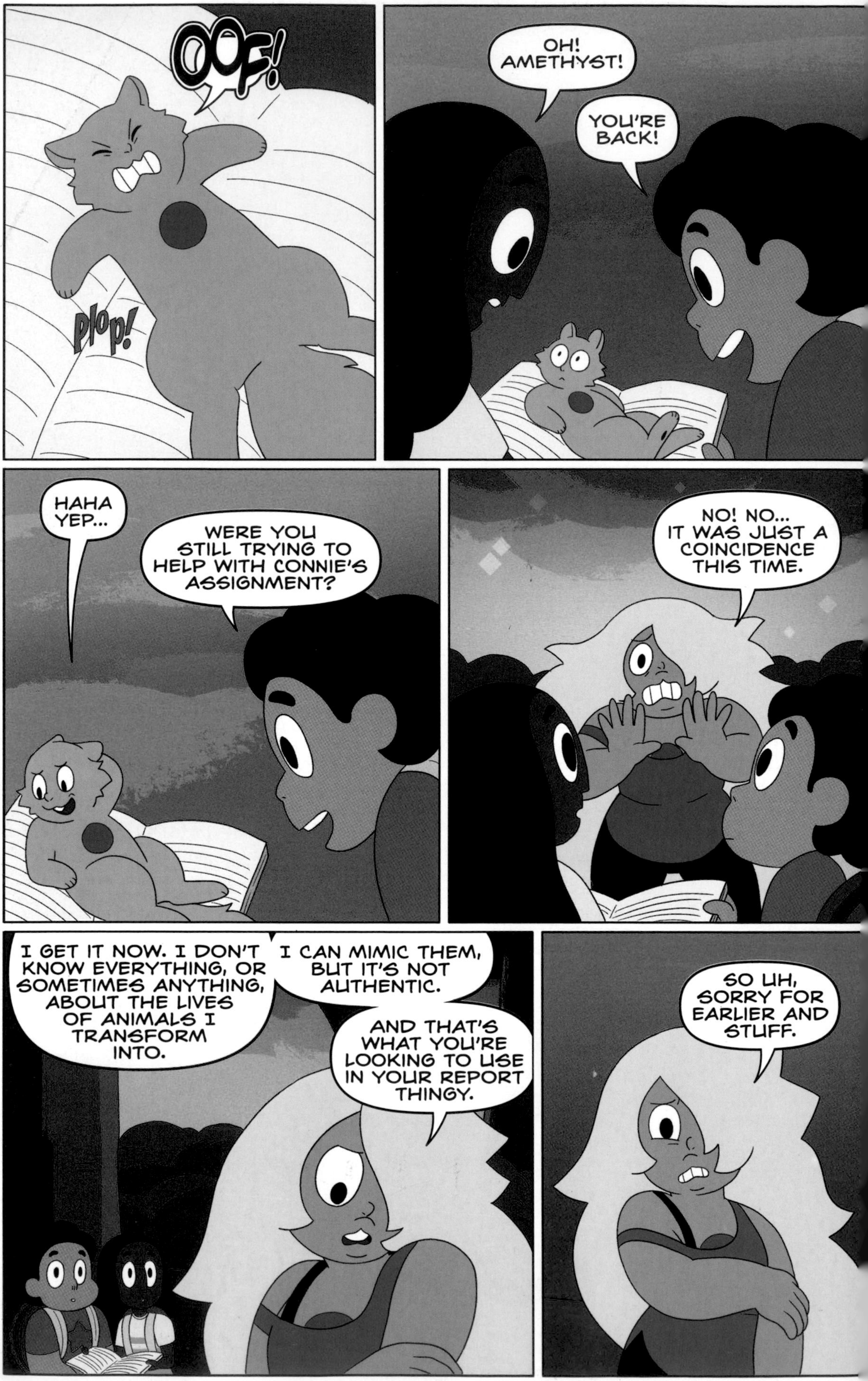
OOF!
PLOP!
OH! AMETHYST!
YOU'RE BACK!
HAHA YEP...
WERE YOU STILL TRYING TO HELP WITH CONNIE'S ASSIGNMENT?
NO! NO... IT WAS JUST A COINCIDENCE THIS TIME.
I GET IT NOW. I DON'T KNOW EVERYTHING, OR SOMETIMES ANYTHING, ABOUT THE LIVES OF ANIMALS I TRANSFORM INTO.
I CAN MIMIC THEM, BUT IT'S NOT AUTHENTIC.
AND THAT'S WHAT YOU'RE LOOKING TO USE IN YOUR REPORT THINGY.
SO UH, SORRY FOR EARLIER AND STUFF.

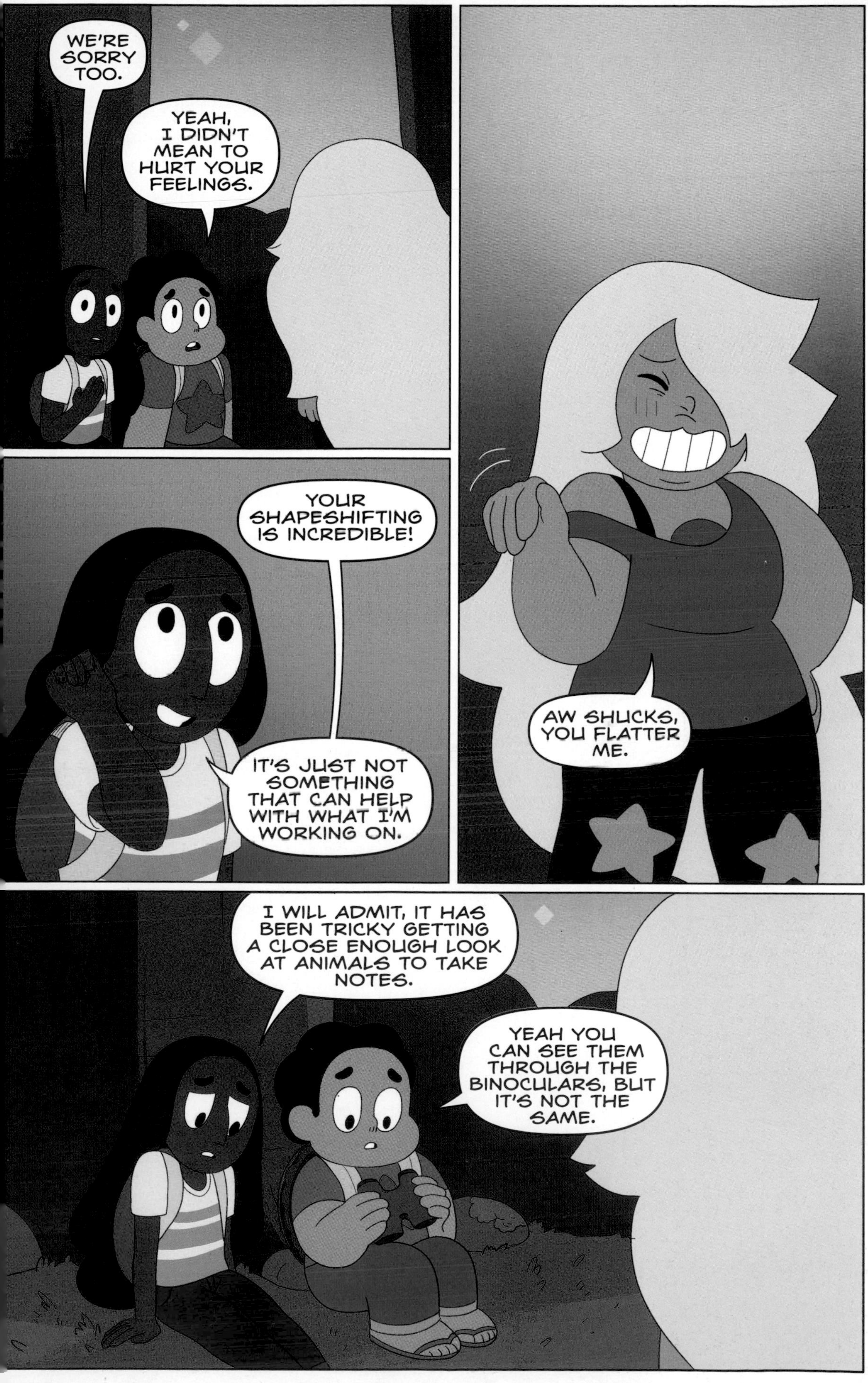
WE'RE SORRY TOO.
YEAH, I DIDN'T MEAN TO HURT YOUR FEELINGS.
YOUR SHAPESHIFTING IS INCREDIBLE!
IT'S JUST NOT SOMETHING THAT CAN HELP WITH WHAT I'M WORKING ON.
AW SHUCKS, YOU FLATTER ME.
I WILL ADMIT, IT HAS BEEN TRICKY GETTING A CLOSE ENOUGH LOOK AT ANIMALS TO TAKE NOTES.
YEAH YOU CAN SEE THEM THROUGH THE BINOCULARS, BUT IT'S NOT THE SAME.

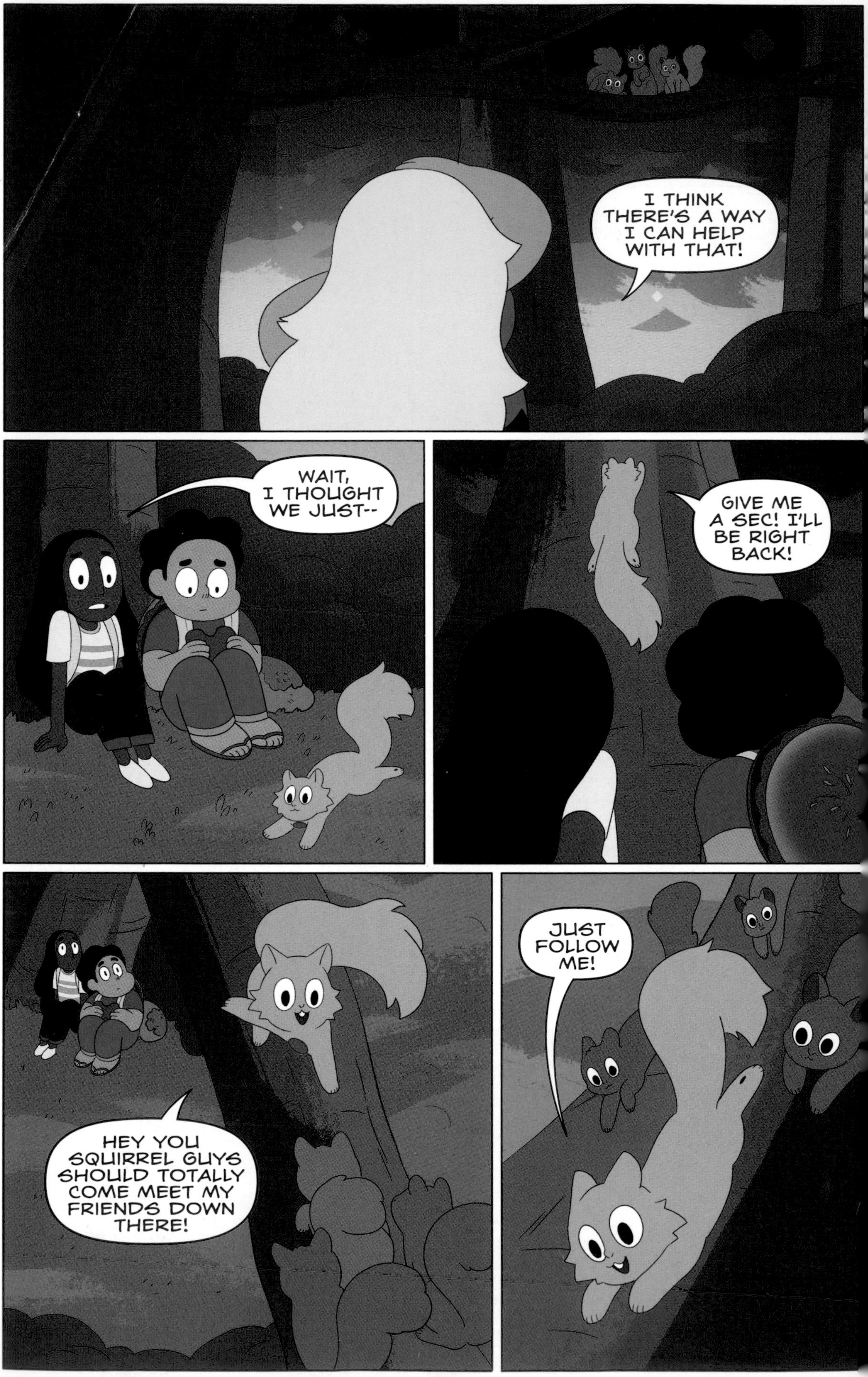
I THINK THERE'S A WAY I CAN HELP WITH THAT!
WAIT, I THOUGHT WE JUST--
GIVE ME A SEC! I'LL BE RIGHT BACK!
HEY YOU SQUIRREL GUYS SHOULD TOTALLY COME MEET MY FRIENDS DOWN THERE!
JUST FOLLOW ME!

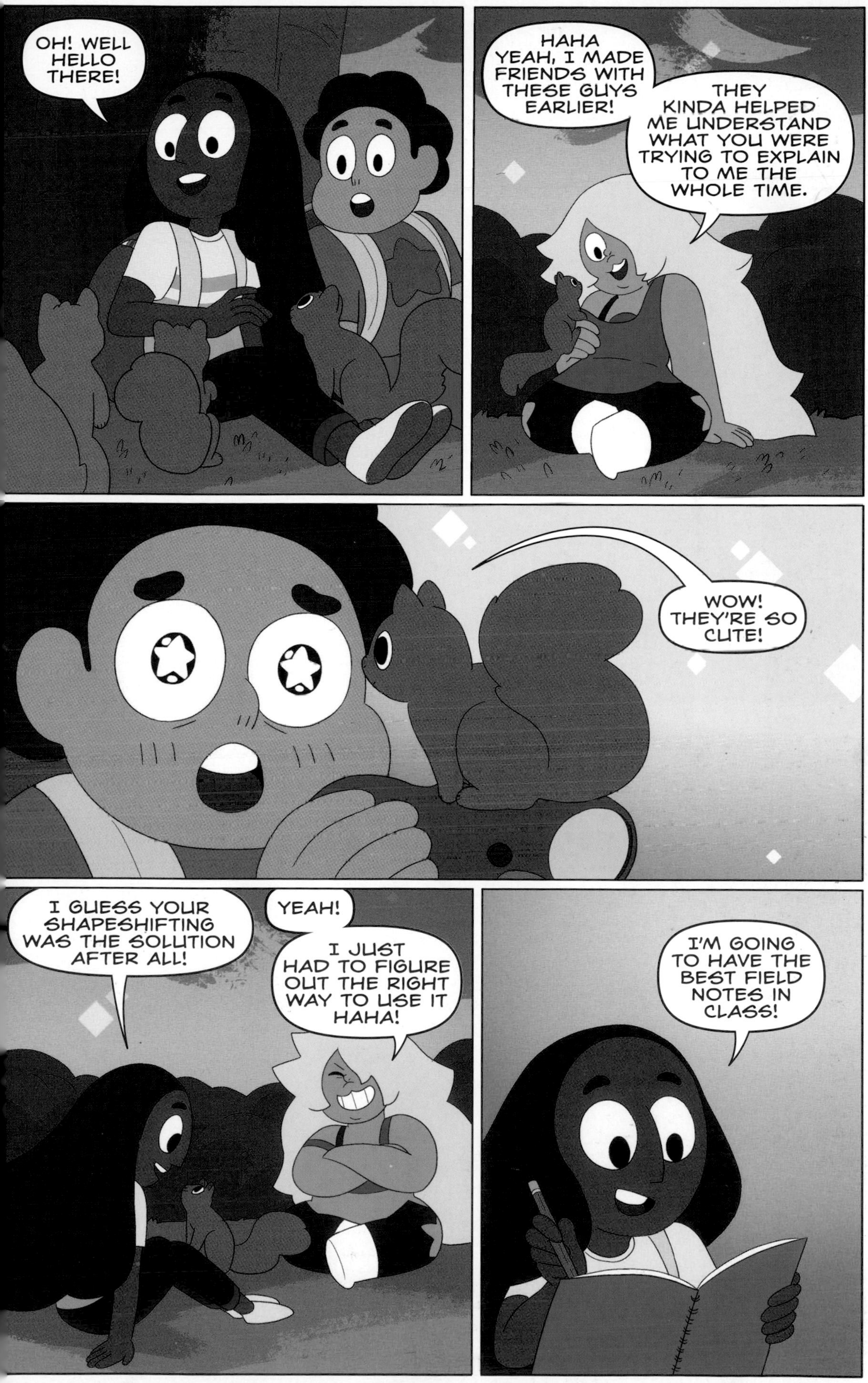
OH! WELL HELLO THERE!
HAHA YEAH, I MADE FRIENDS WITH THESE GUYS EARLIER!
THEY KINDA HELPED ME UNDERSTAND WHAT YOU WERE TRYING TO EXPLAIN TO ME THE WHOLE TIME.
WOW! THEY'RE SO CUTE!
I GUESS YOUR SHAPESHIFTING WAS THE SOLUTION AFTER ALL!
YEAH!
I JUST HAD TO FIGURE OUT THE RIGHT WAY TO USE IT HAHA!
I'M GOING TO HAVE THE BEST FIELD NOTES IN CLASS!

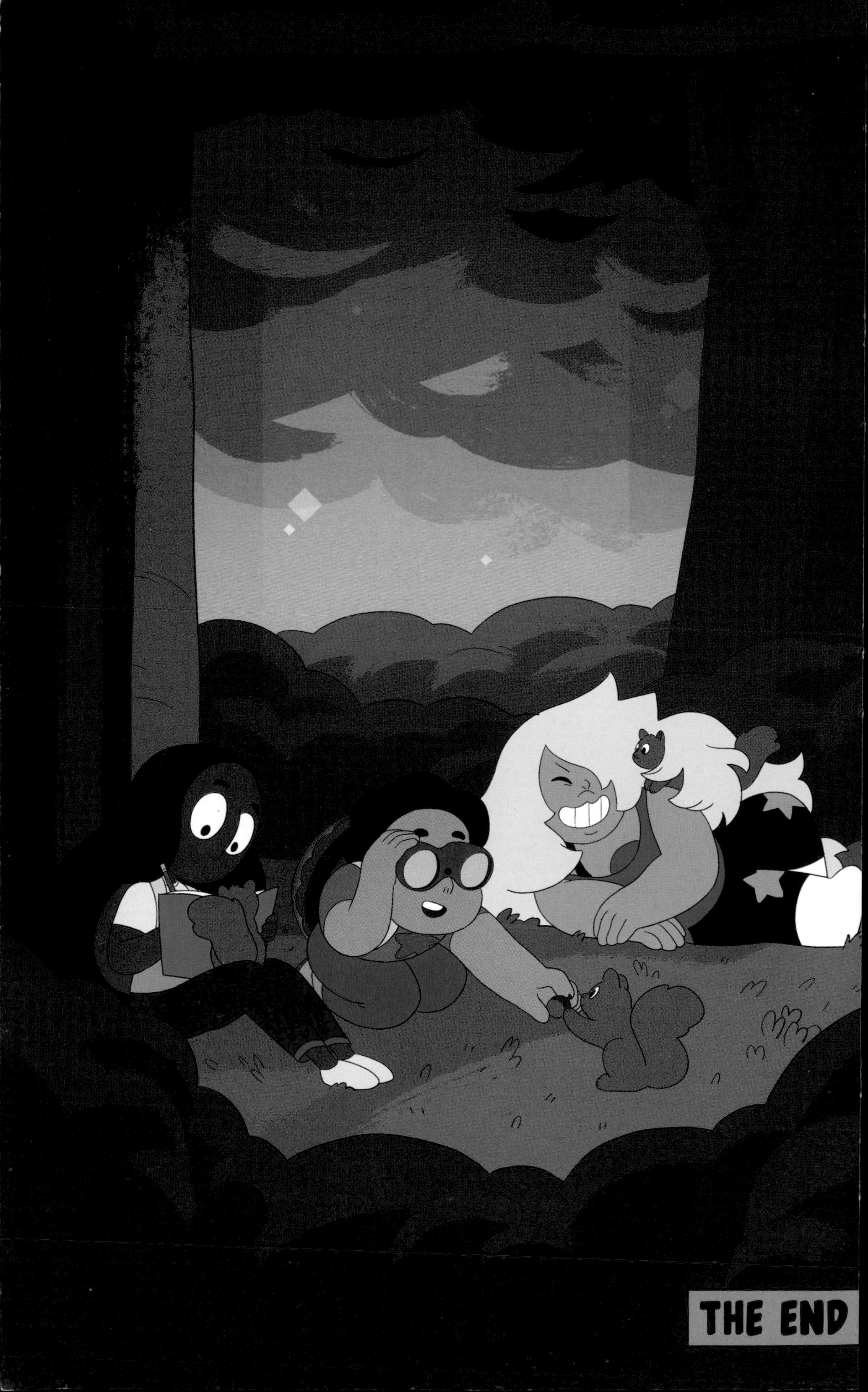
THE END

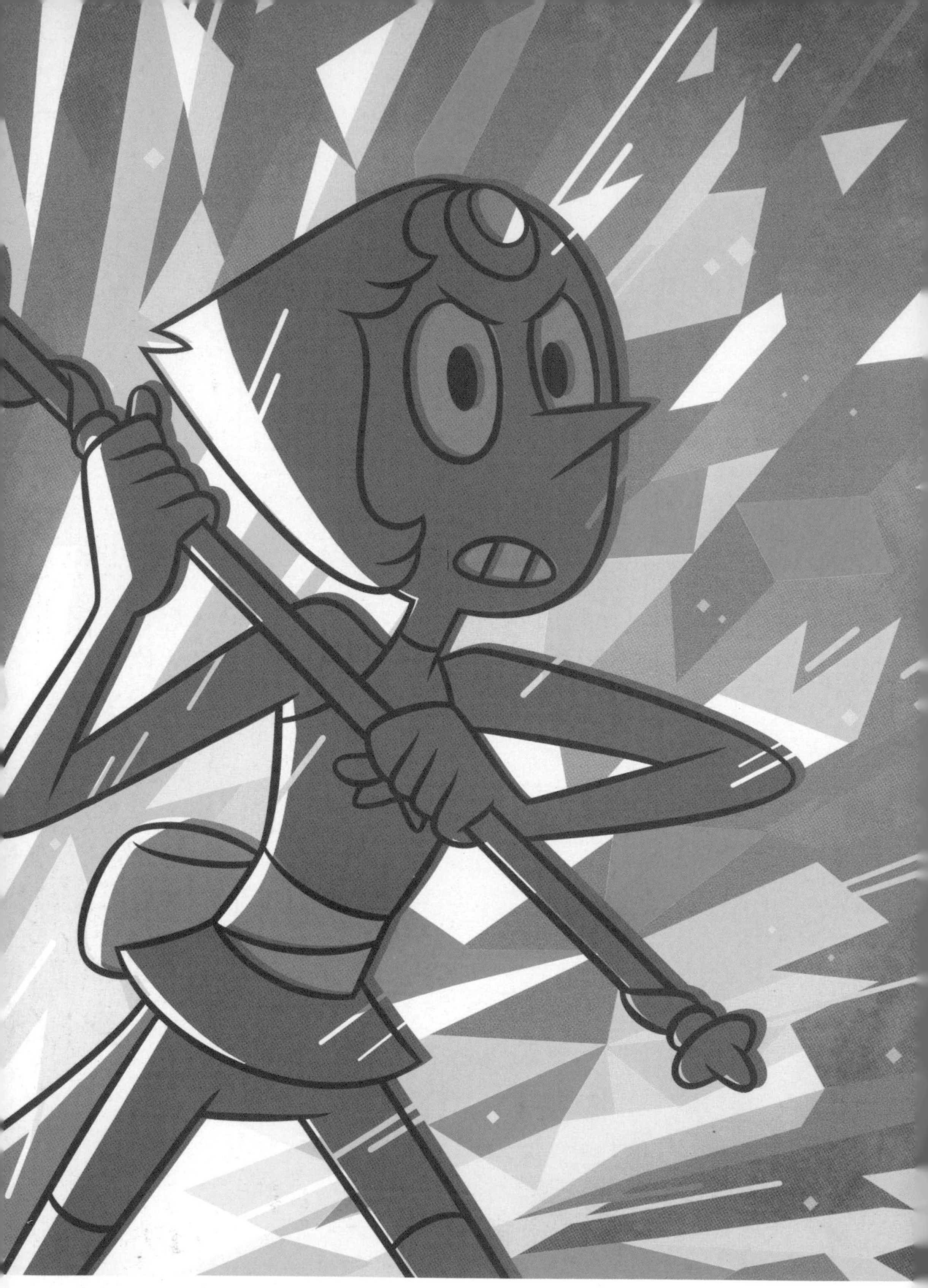

CHAPTER ELEVEN

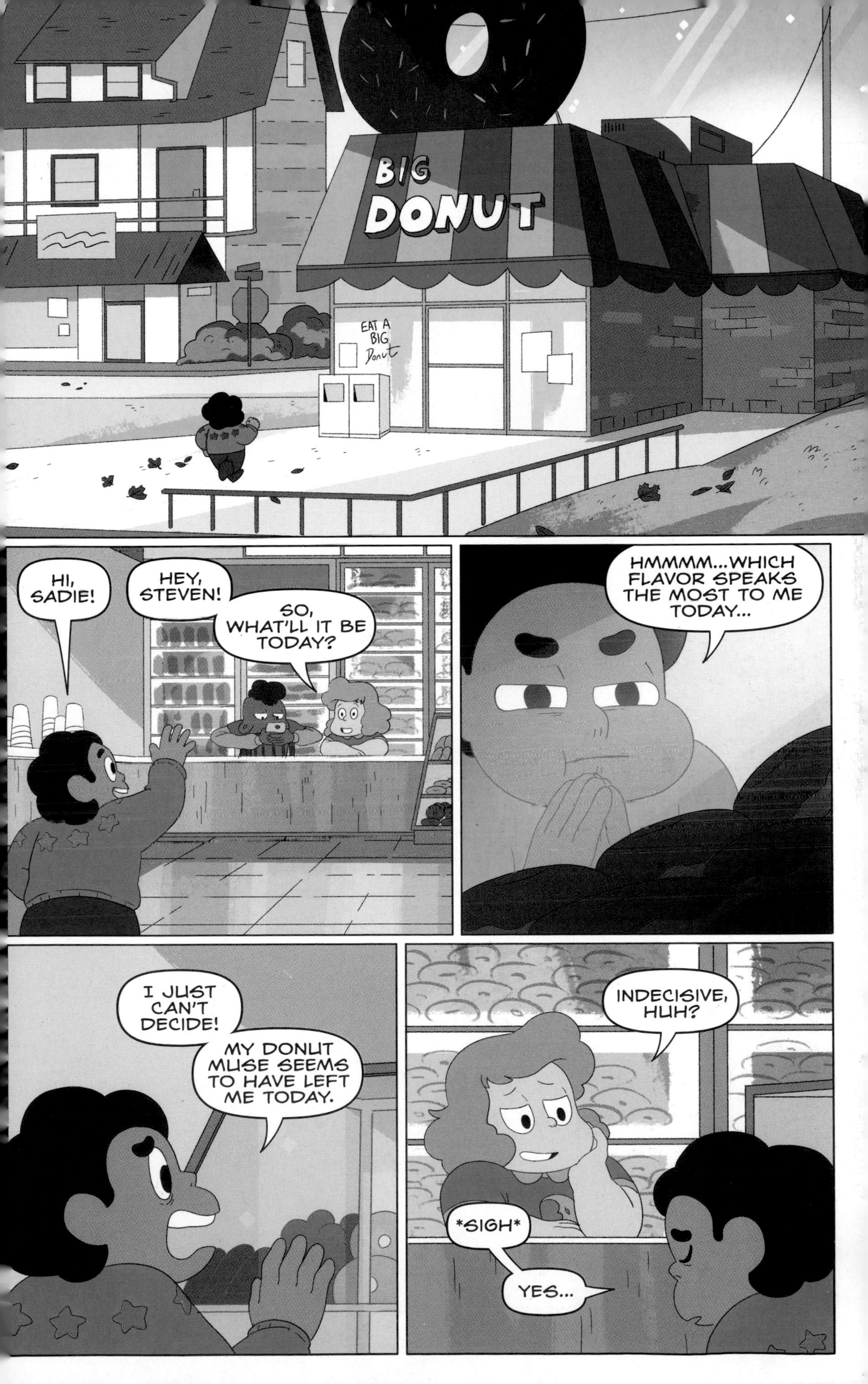
BIG DONUT
EAT A BIG Donut
HI, SADIE!
HEY, STEVEN!
SO, WHAT'LL IT BE TODAY?
HMMMM...WHICH FLAVOR SPEAKS THE MOST TO ME TODAY...
I JUST CAN'T DECIDE!
MY DONUT MUSE SEEMS TO HAVE LEFT ME TODAY.
INDECISIVE, HUH?
SIGH
YES...

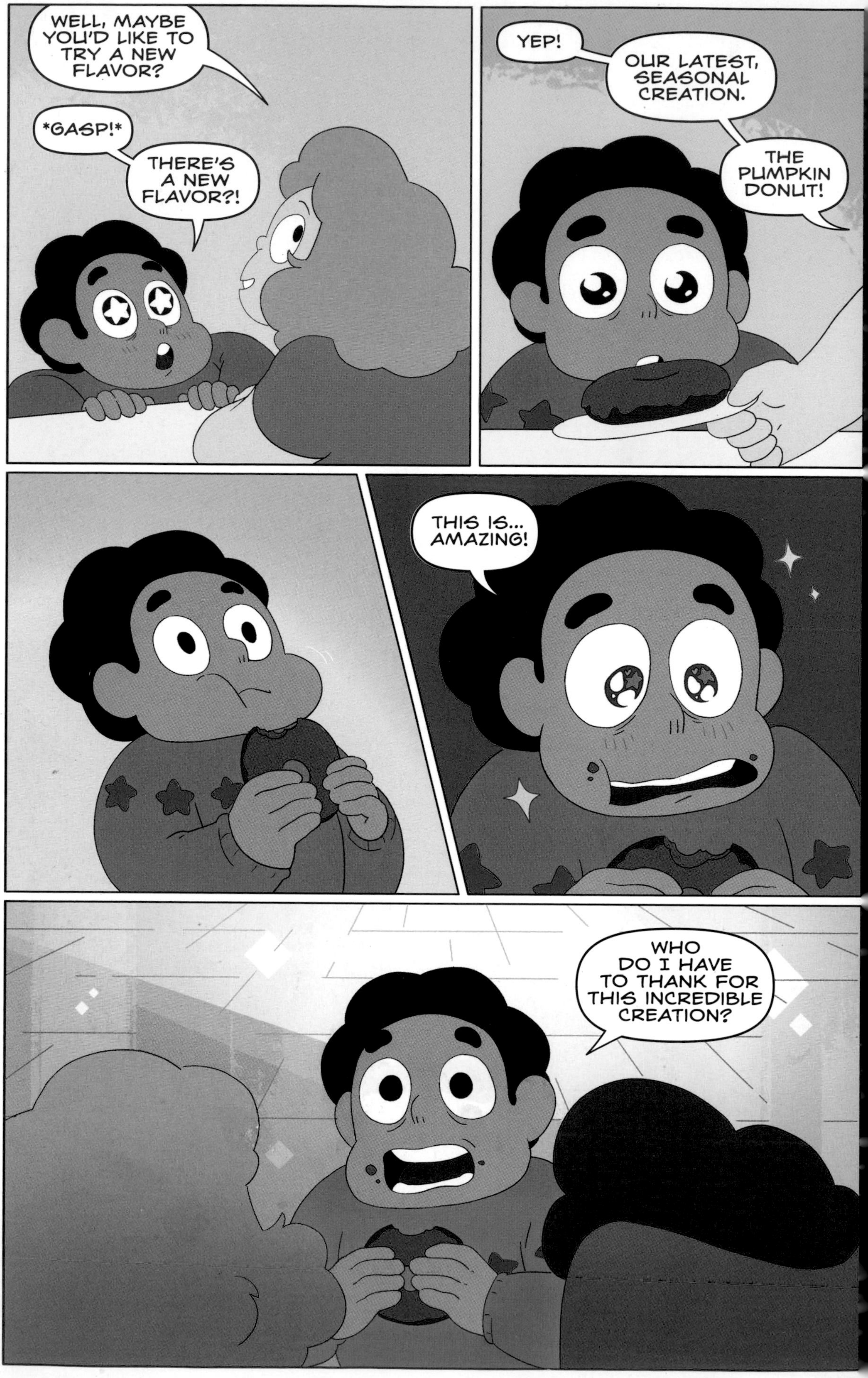
WELL, MAYBE YOU'D LIKE TO TRY A NEW FLAVOR?
GASP!
THERE'S A NEW FLAVOR?!
YEP!
OUR LATEST, SEASONAL CREATION.
THE PUMPKIN DONUT!
THIS IS... AMAZING!
WHO DO I HAVE TO THANK FOR THIS INCREDIBLE CREATION?

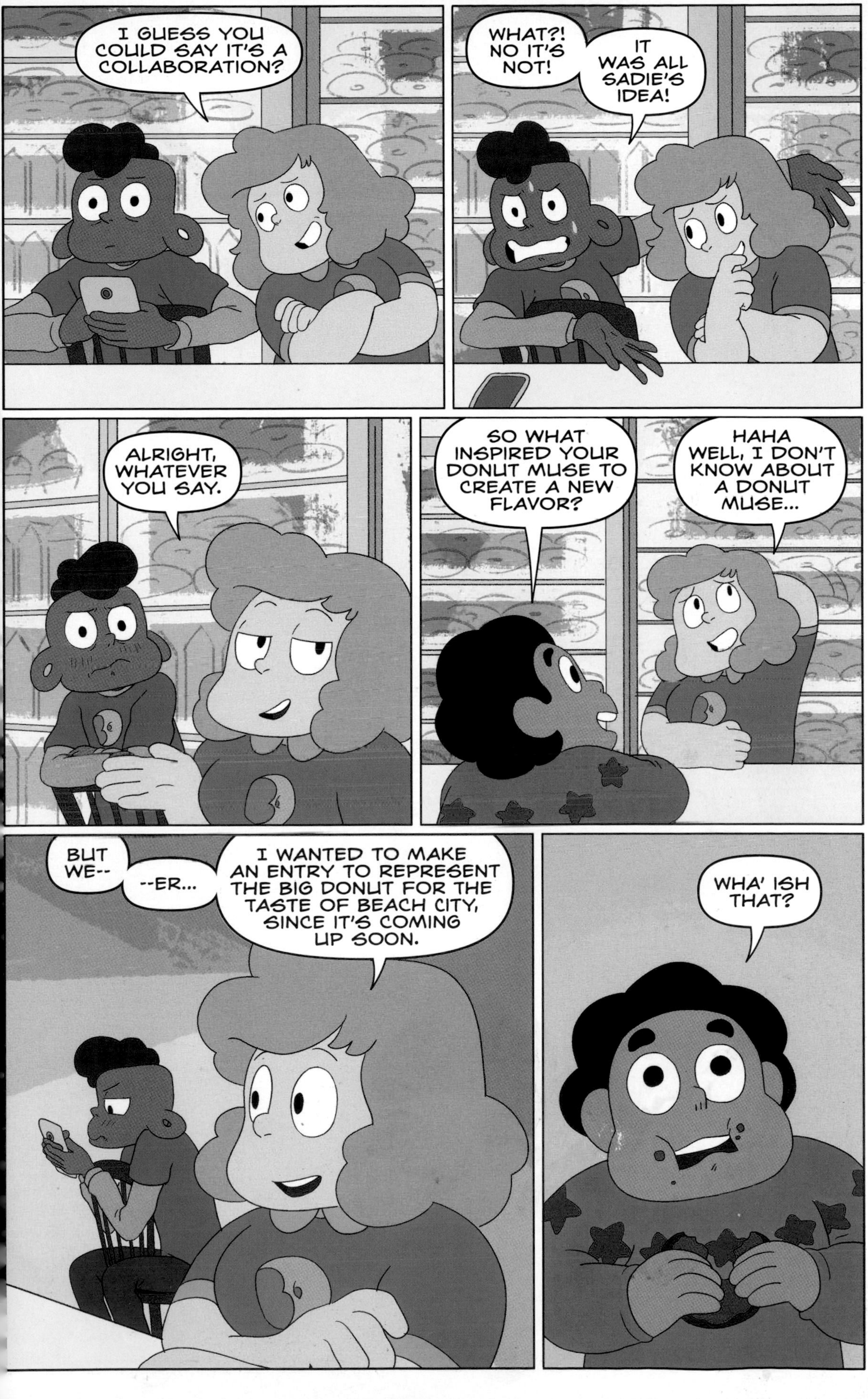
I GUESS YOU COULD SAY IT'S A COLLABORATION?
WHAT?! NO IT'S NOT!
IT WAS ALL SADIE'S IDEA!
ALRIGHT, WHATEVER YOU SAY.
SO WHAT INSPIRED YOUR DONUT MUSE TO CREATE A NEW FLAVOR?
HAHA WELL, I DON'T KNOW ABOUT A DONUT MUSE...
BUT WE--
--ER...
I WANTED TO MAKE AN ENTRY TO REPRESENT THE BIG DONUT FOR THE TASTE OF BEACH CITY, SINCE IT'S COMING UP SOON.
WHA' ISH THAT?

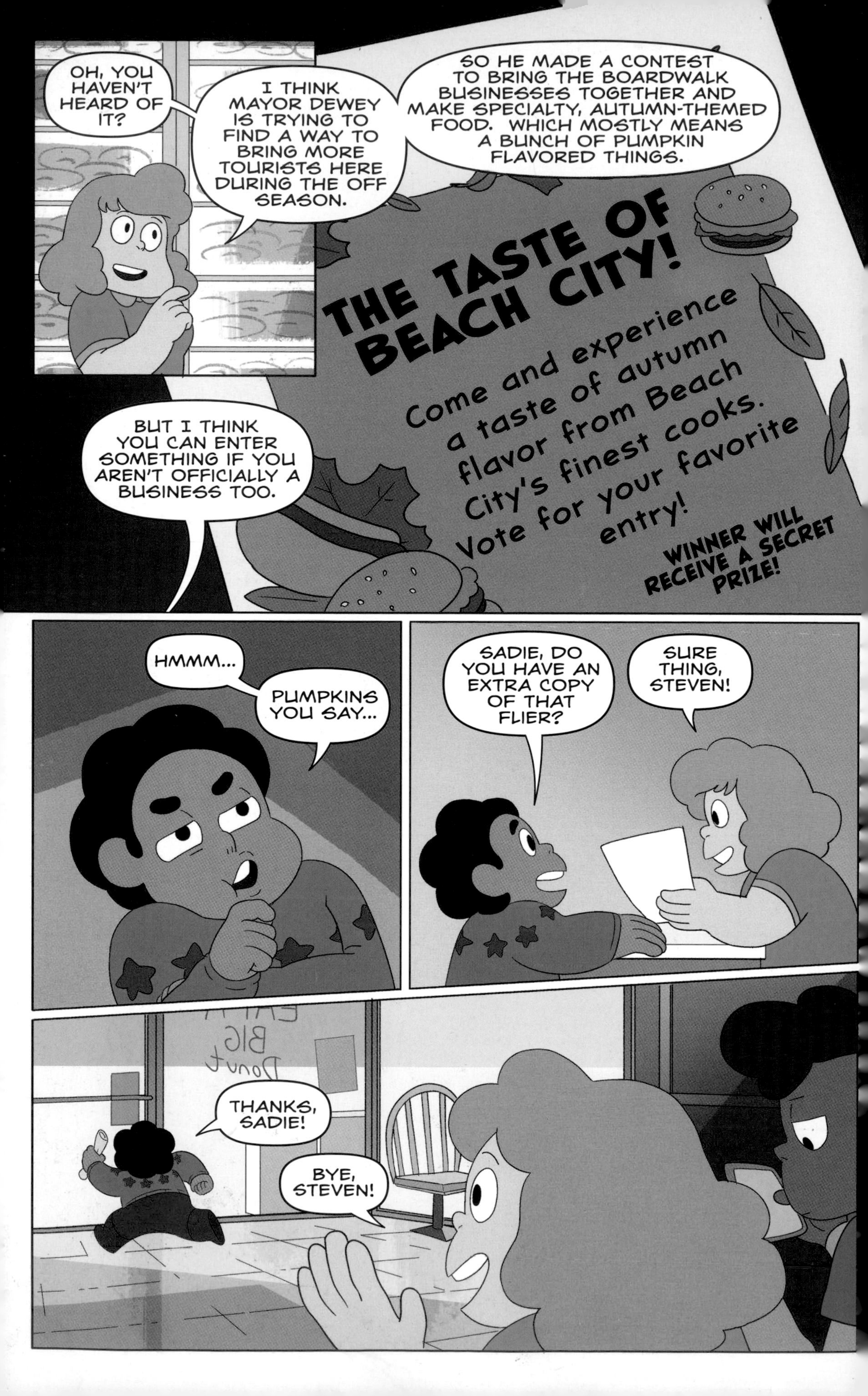

OH, YOU HAVEN'T HEARD OF IT?
I THINK MAYOR DEWEY IS TRYING TO FIND A WAY TO BRING MORE TOURISTS HERE DURING THE OFF SEASON.
SO HE MADE A CONTEST TO BRING THE BOARDWALK BUSINESSES TOGETHER AND MAKE SPECIALTY, AUTUMN-THEMED FOOD. WHICH MOSTLY MEANS A BUNCH OF PUMPKIN FLAVORED THINGS.
THE TASTE OF BEACH CITY!
Come and experience a taste of autumn flavor from Beach City's finest cooks. Vote for your favorite entry!
WINNER WILL RECEIVE A SECRET PRIZE!
BUT I THINK YOU CAN ENTER SOMETHING IF YOU AREN'T OFFICIALLY A BUSINESS TOO.
HMMM...
PUMPKINS YOU SAY...
SADIE, DO YOU HAVE AN EXTRA COPY OF THAT FLIER?
SURE THING, STEVEN!
THANKS, SADIE!
BYE, STEVEN!

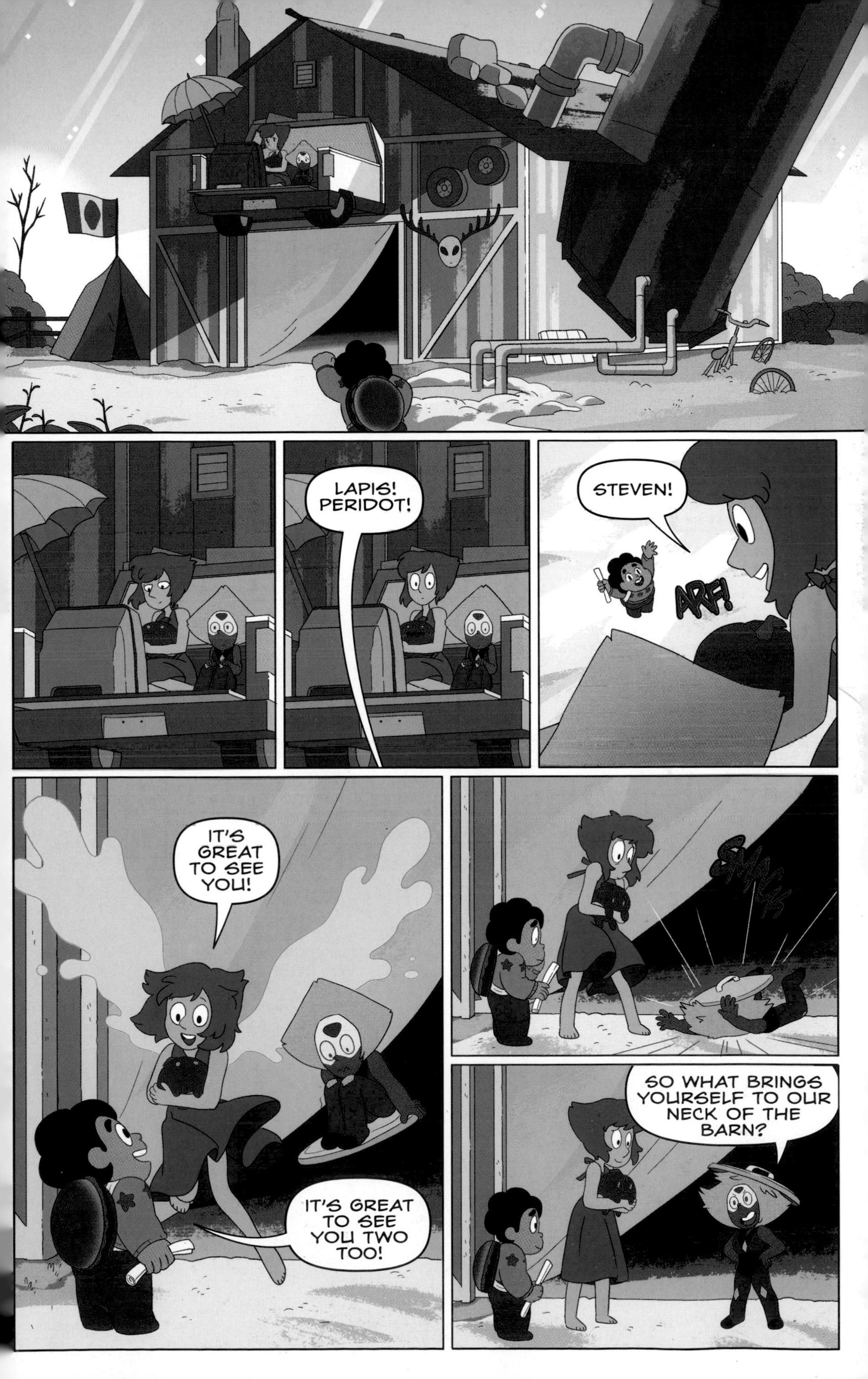
LAPIS! PERIDOT!
STEVEN!
ARF!
IT'S GREAT TO SEE YOU!
IT'S GREAT TO SEE YOU TWO TOO!
SMACK
SO WHAT BRINGS YOURSELF TO OUR NECK OF THE BARN?

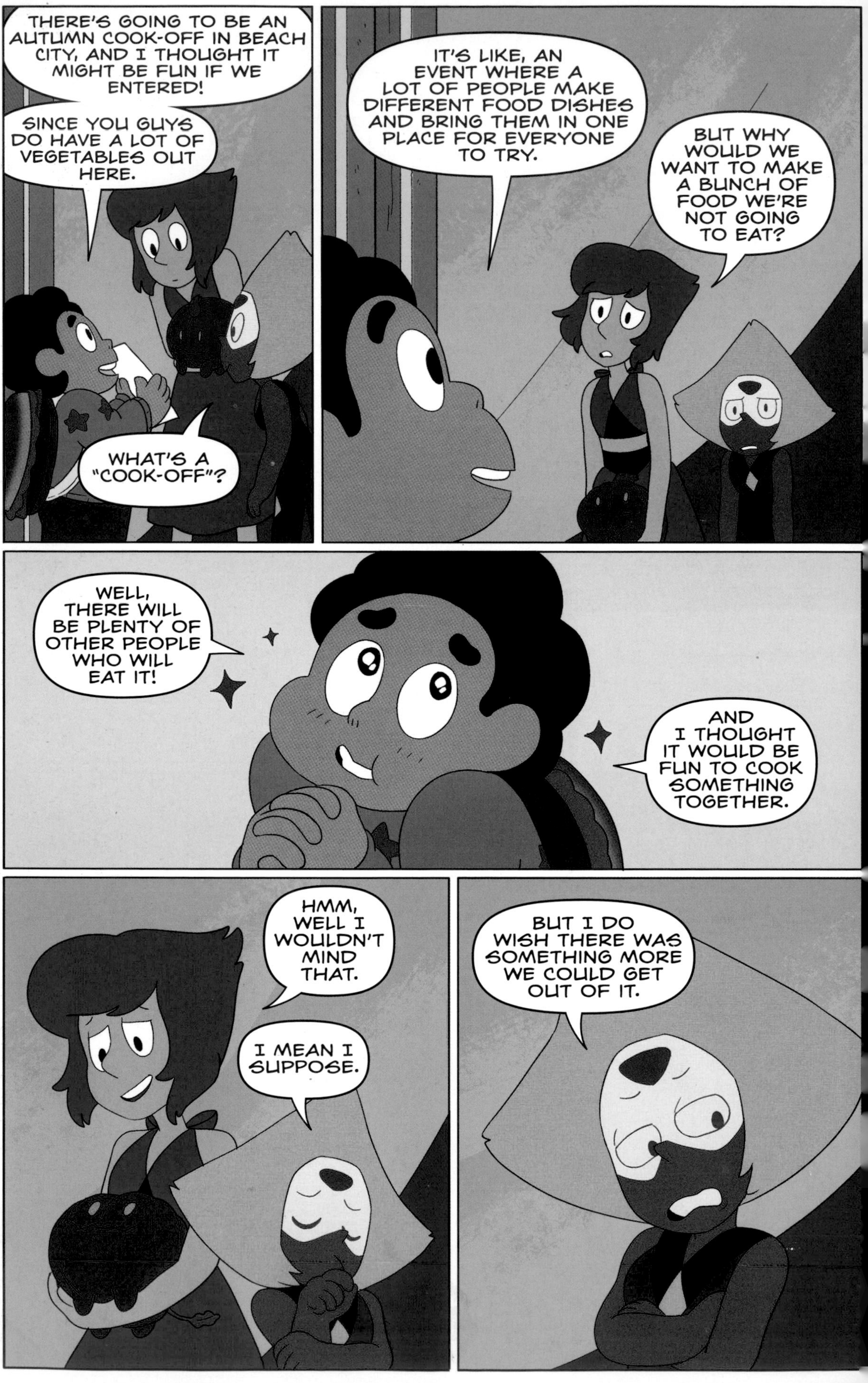
THERE'S GOING TO BE AN AUTUMN COOK-OFF IN BEACH CITY, AND I THOUGHT IT MIGHT BE FUN IF WE ENTERED!
SINCE YOU GUYS DO HAVE A LOT OF VEGETABLES OUT HERE.
WHAT'S A "COOK-OFF"?
IT'S LIKE, AN EVENT WHERE A LOT OF PEOPLE MAKE DIFFERENT FOOD DISHES AND BRING THEM IN ONE PLACE FOR EVERYONE TO TRY.
BUT WHY WOULD WE WANT TO MAKE A BUNCH OF FOOD WE'RE NOT GOING TO EAT?
WELL, THERE WILL BE PLENTY OF OTHER PEOPLE WHO WILL EAT IT!
AND I THOUGHT IT WOULD BE FUN TO COOK SOMETHING TOGETHER.
HMM, WELL I WOULDN'T MIND THAT.
I MEAN I SUPPOSE.
BUT I DO WISH THERE WAS SOMETHING MORE WE COULD GET OUT OF IT.

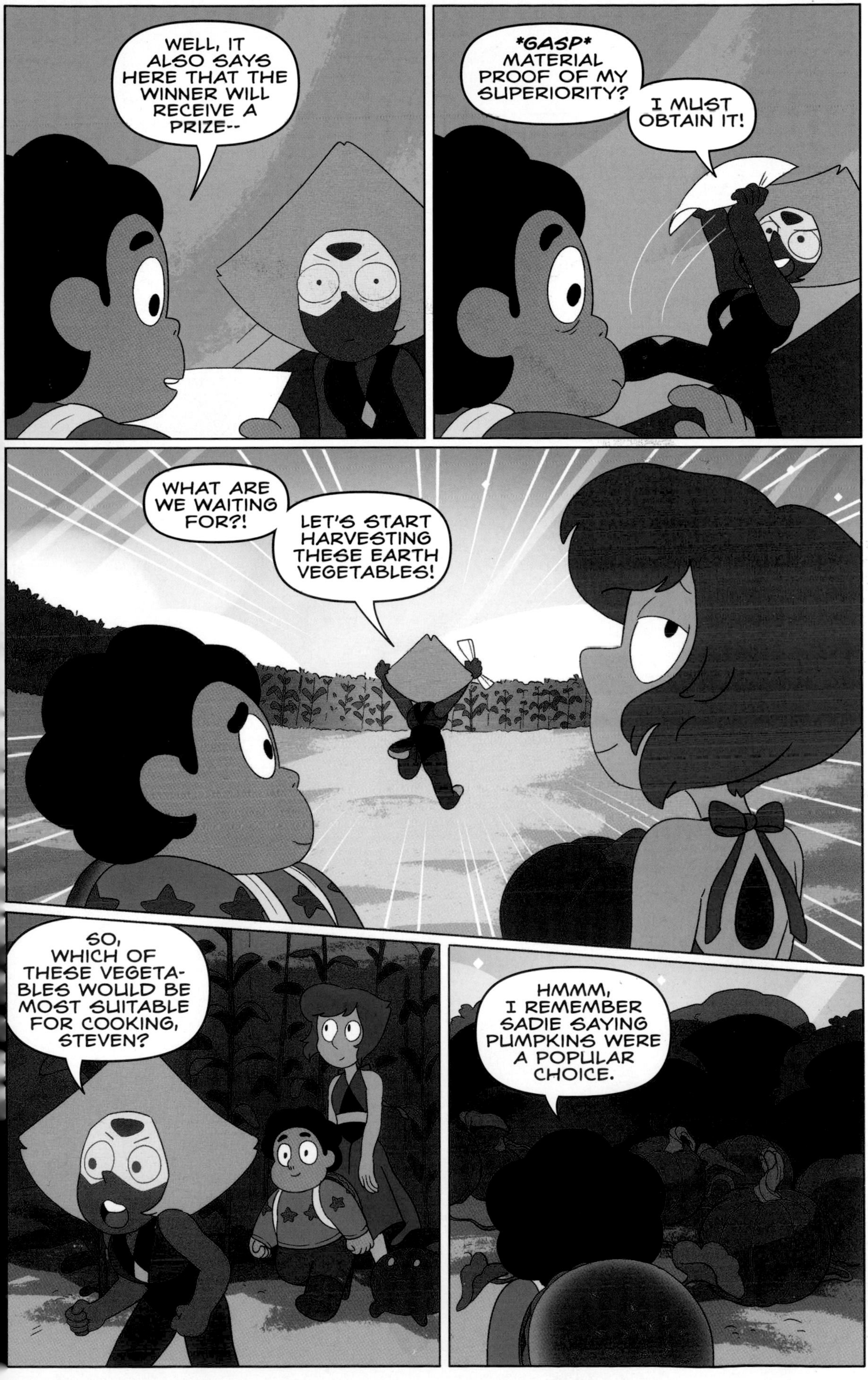
WELL, IT ALSO SAYS HERE THAT THE WINNER WILL RECEIVE A PRIZE--
GASP MATERIAL PROOF OF MY SUPERIORITY?
I MUST OBTAIN IT!
WHAT ARE WE WAITING FOR?!
LET'S START HARVESTING THESE EARTH VEGETABLES!
SO, WHICH OF THESE VEGETA-BLES WOULD BE MOST SUITABLE FOR COOKING, STEVEN?
HMMM, I REMEMBER SADIE SAYING PUMPKINS WERE A POPULAR CHOICE.

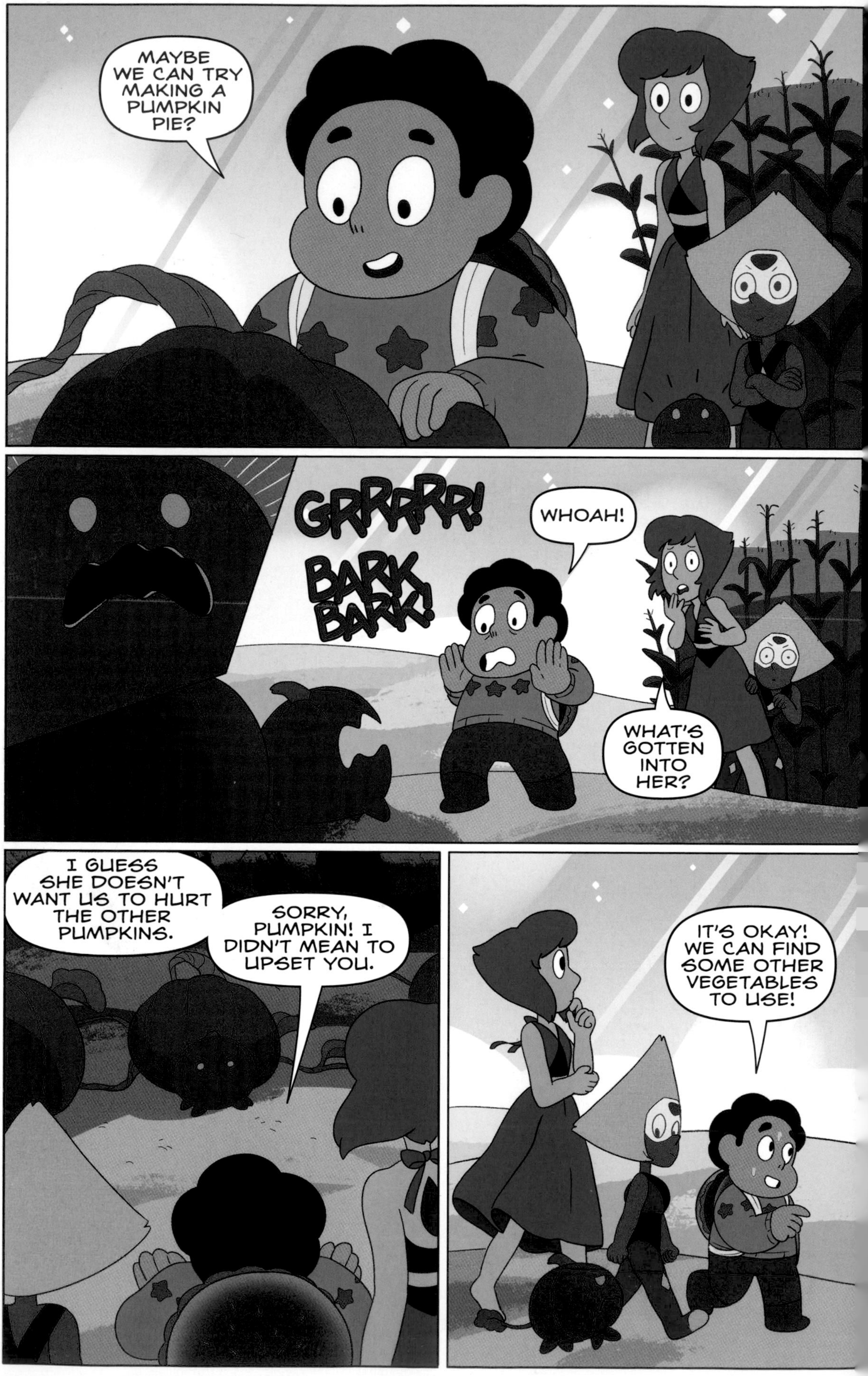

MAYBE WE CAN TRY MAKING A PUMPKIN PIE?
GRRRRR!
BARK BARK!
WHOAH!
WHAT'S GOTTEN INTO HER?
I GUESS SHE DOESN'T WANT US TO HURT THE OTHER PUMPKINS.
SORRY, PUMPKIN! I DIDN'T MEAN TO UPSET YOU.
IT'S OKAY! WE CAN FIND SOME OTHER VEGETABLES TO USE!

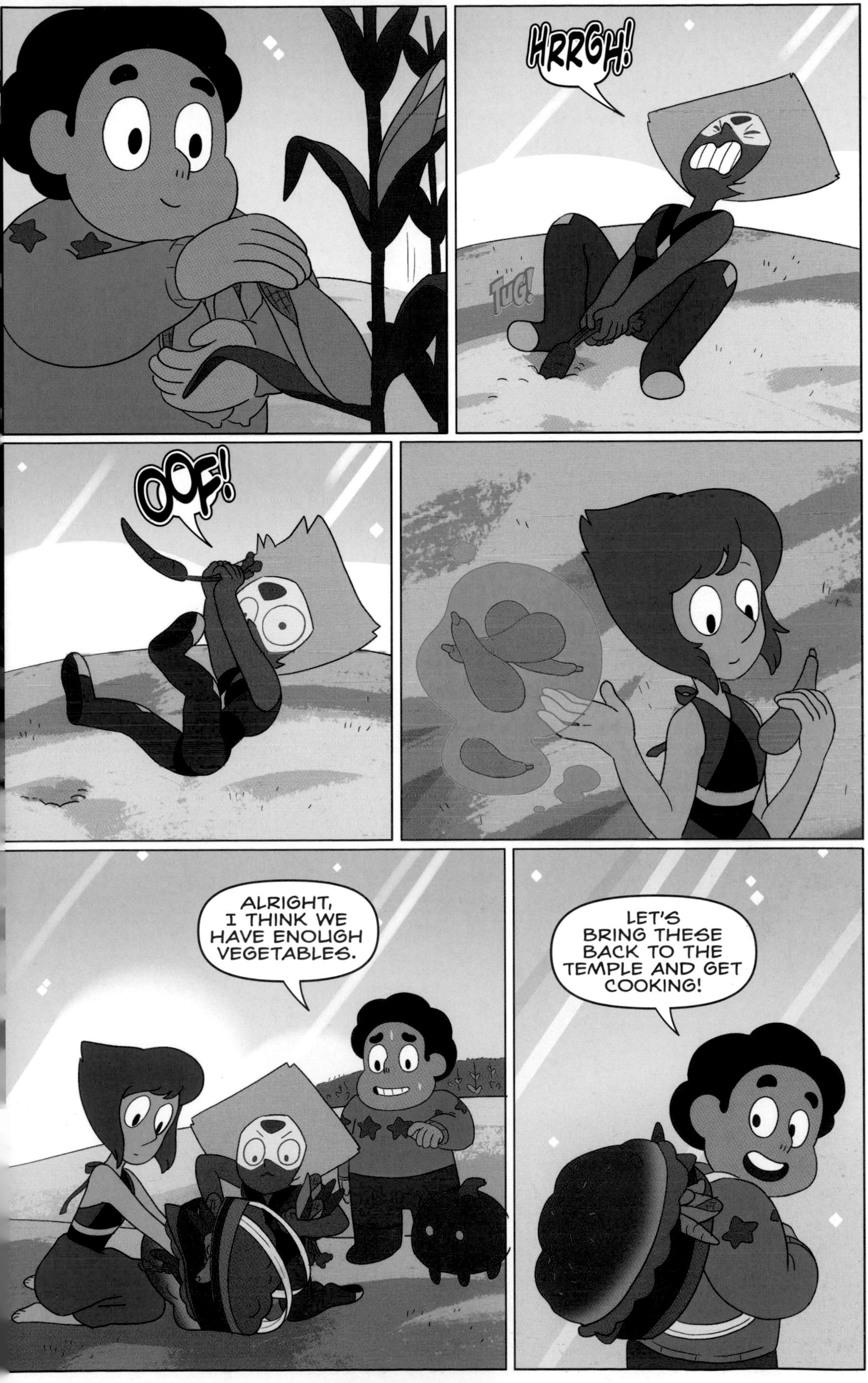
HRRGH!
TUG!
OOF!
ALRIGHT, I THINK WE HAVE ENOUGH VEGETABLES.
LET'S BRING THESE BACK TO THE TEMPLE AND GET COOKING!

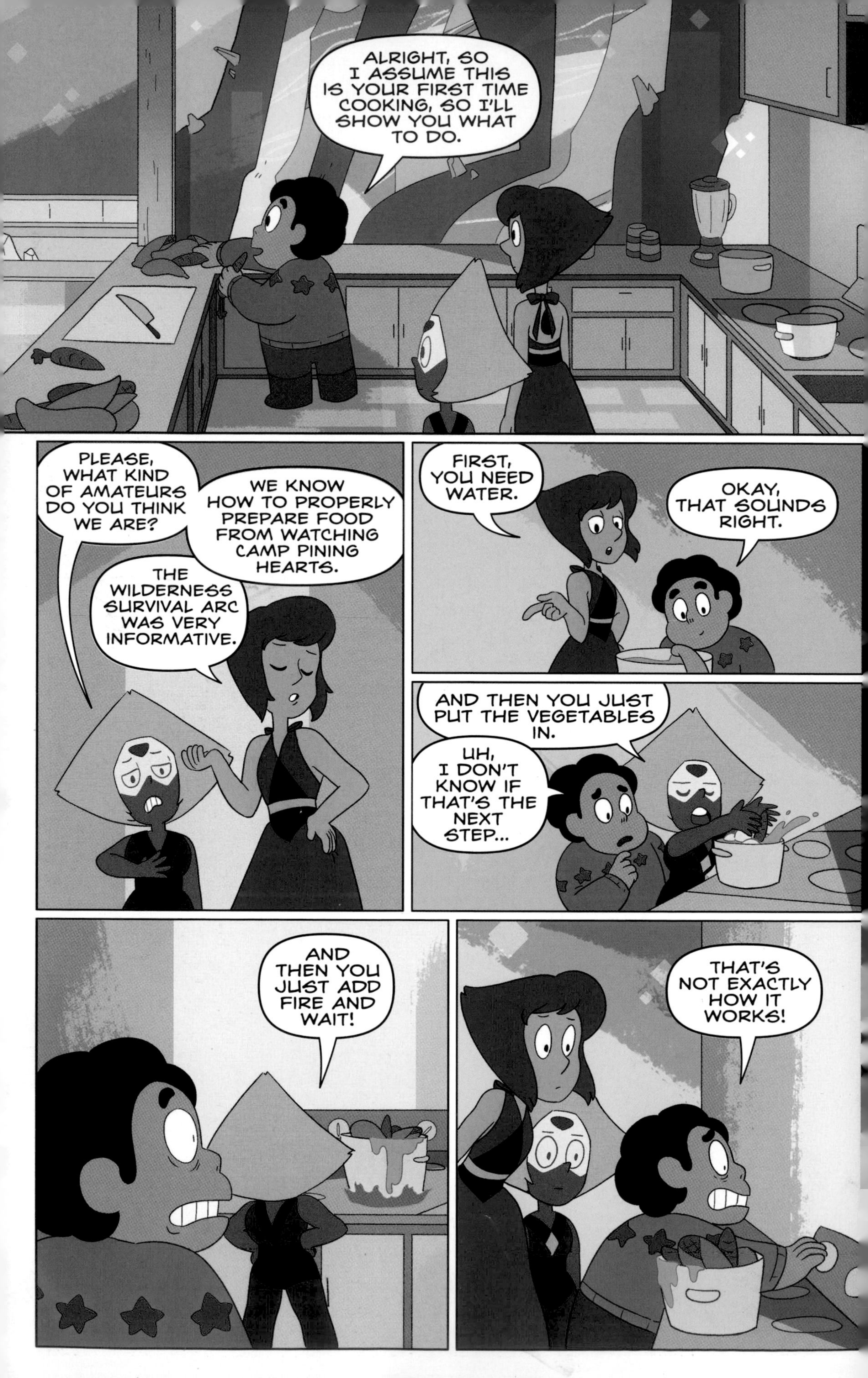
ALRIGHT, SO I ASSUME THIS IS YOUR FIRST TIME COOKING, SO I'LL SHOW YOU WHAT TO DO.
PLEASE, WHAT KIND OF AMATEURS DO YOU THINK WE ARE?
WE KNOW HOW TO PROPERLY PREPARE FOOD FROM WATCHING CAMP PINING HEARTS.
THE WILDERNESS SURVIVAL ARC WAS VERY INFORMATIVE.
FIRST, YOU NEED WATER.
OKAY, THAT SOUNDS RIGHT.
AND THEN YOU JUST PUT THE VEGETABLES IN.
UH, I DON'T KNOW IF THAT'S THE NEXT STEP...
AND THEN YOU JUST ADD FIRE AND WAIT!
THAT'S NOT EXACTLY HOW IT WORKS!

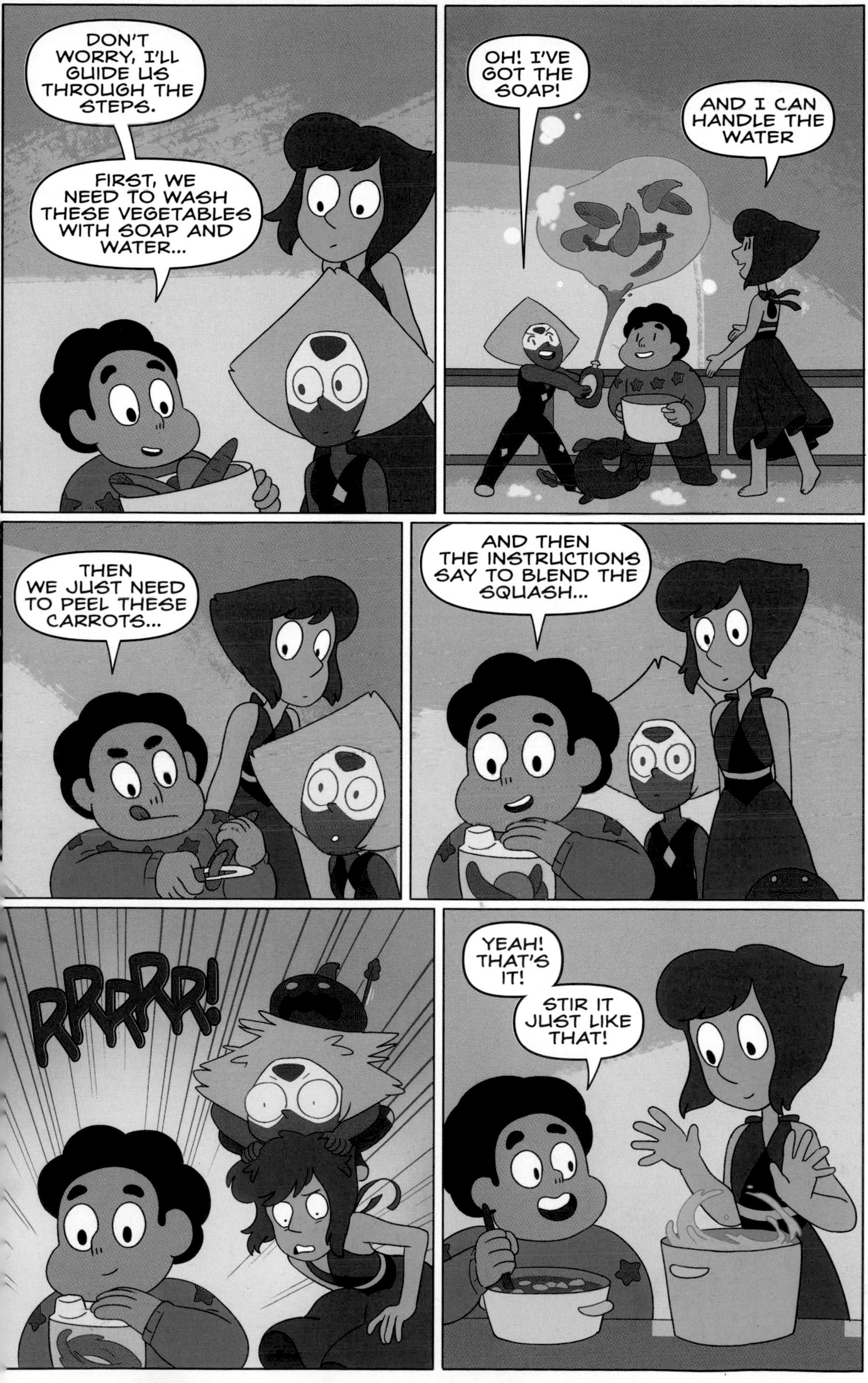

DON'T WORRY, I'LL GUIDE US THROUGH THE STEPS.
FIRST, WE NEED TO WASH THESE VEGETABLES WITH SOAP AND WATER...
OH! I'VE GOT THE SOAP!
AND I CAN HANDLE THE WATER
THEN WE JUST NEED TO PEEL THESE CARROTS...
AND THEN THE INSTRUCTIONS SAY TO BLEND THE SQUASH...
RRRRR!
YEAH! THAT'S IT!
STIR IT JUST LIKE THAT!

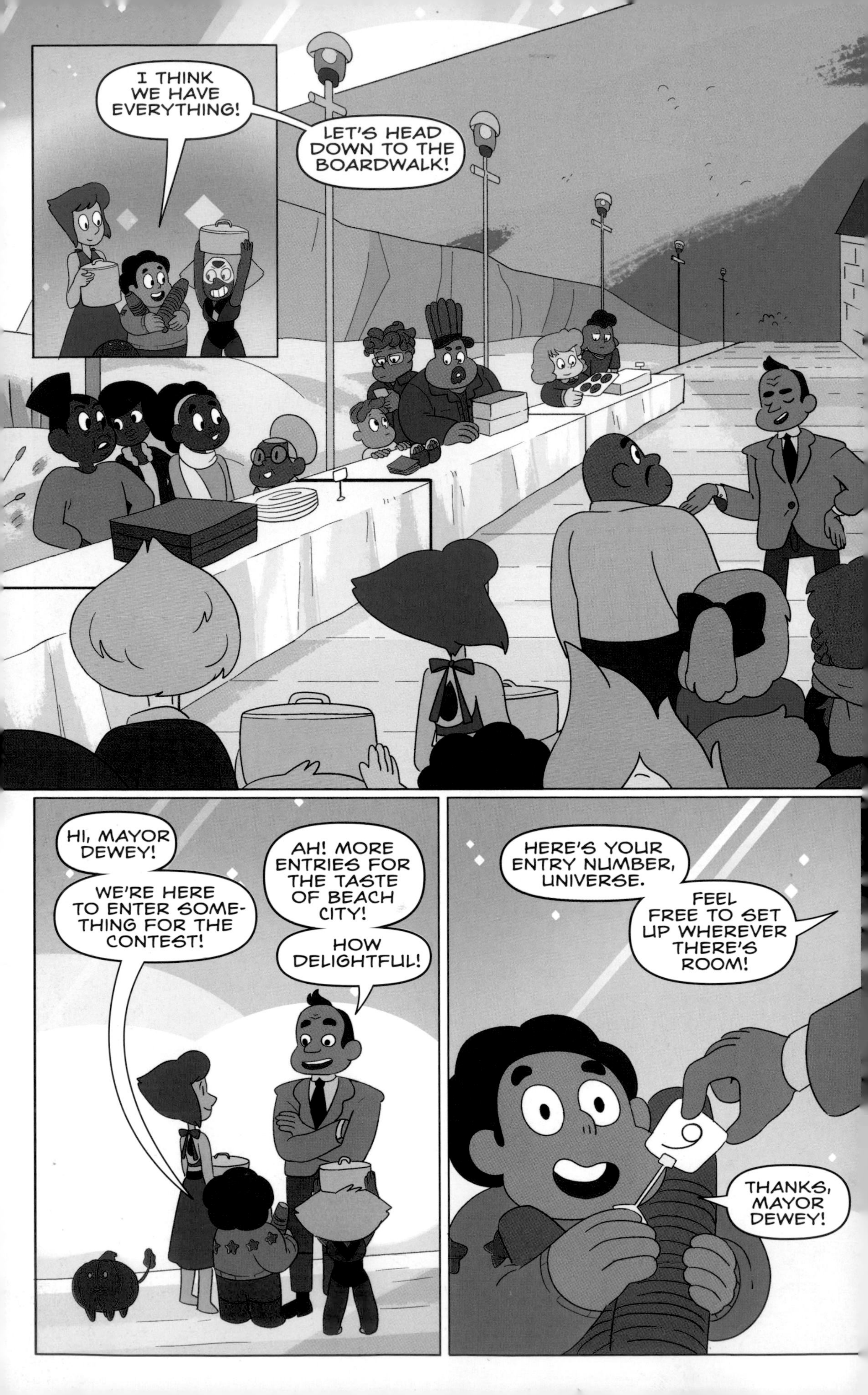
I THINK WE HAVE EVERYTHING!
LET'S HEAD DOWN TO THE BOARDWALK!
HI, MAYOR DEWEY!
WE'RE HERE TO ENTER SOME-THING FOR THE CONTEST!
AH! MORE ENTRIES FOR THE TASTE OF BEACH CITY!
HOW DELIGHTFUL!
HERE'S YOUR ENTRY NUMBER, UNIVERSE.
FEEL FREE TO SET UP WHEREVER THERE'S ROOM!
9
THANKS, MAYOR DEWEY!

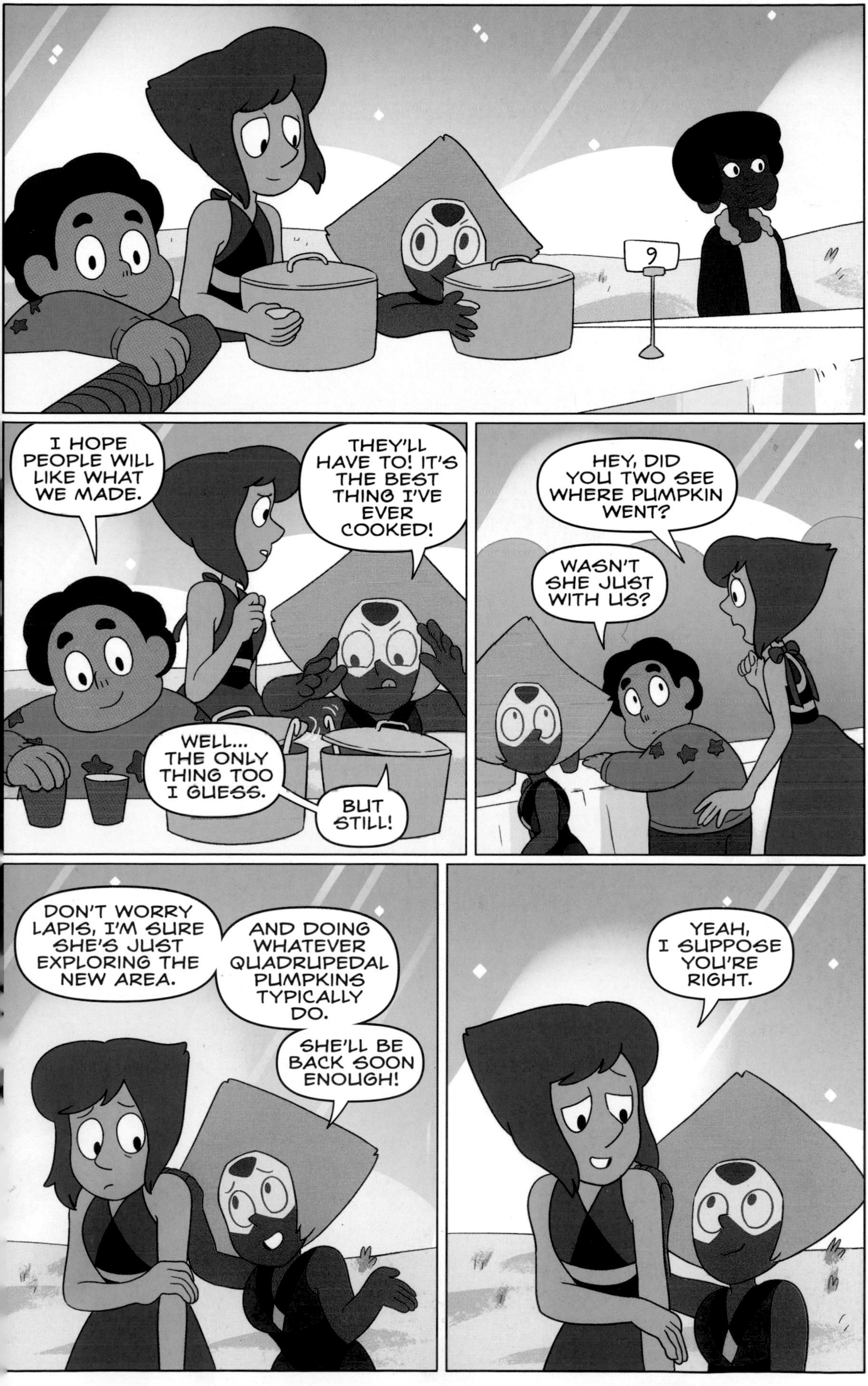
9
I HOPE PEOPLE WILL LIKE WHAT WE MADE.
THEY'LL HAVE TO! IT'S THE BEST THING I'VE EVER COOKED!
WELL... THE ONLY THING TOO I GUESS.
BUT STILL!
HEY, DID YOU TWO SEE WHERE PUMPKIN WENT?
WASN'T SHE JUST WITH US?
DON'T WORRY LAPIS, I'M SURE SHE'S JUST EXPLORING THE NEW AREA.
AND DOING WHATEVER QUADRUPEDAL PUMPKINS TYPICALLY DO.
SHE'LL BE BACK SOON ENOUGH!
YEAH, I SUPPOSE YOU'RE RIGHT.

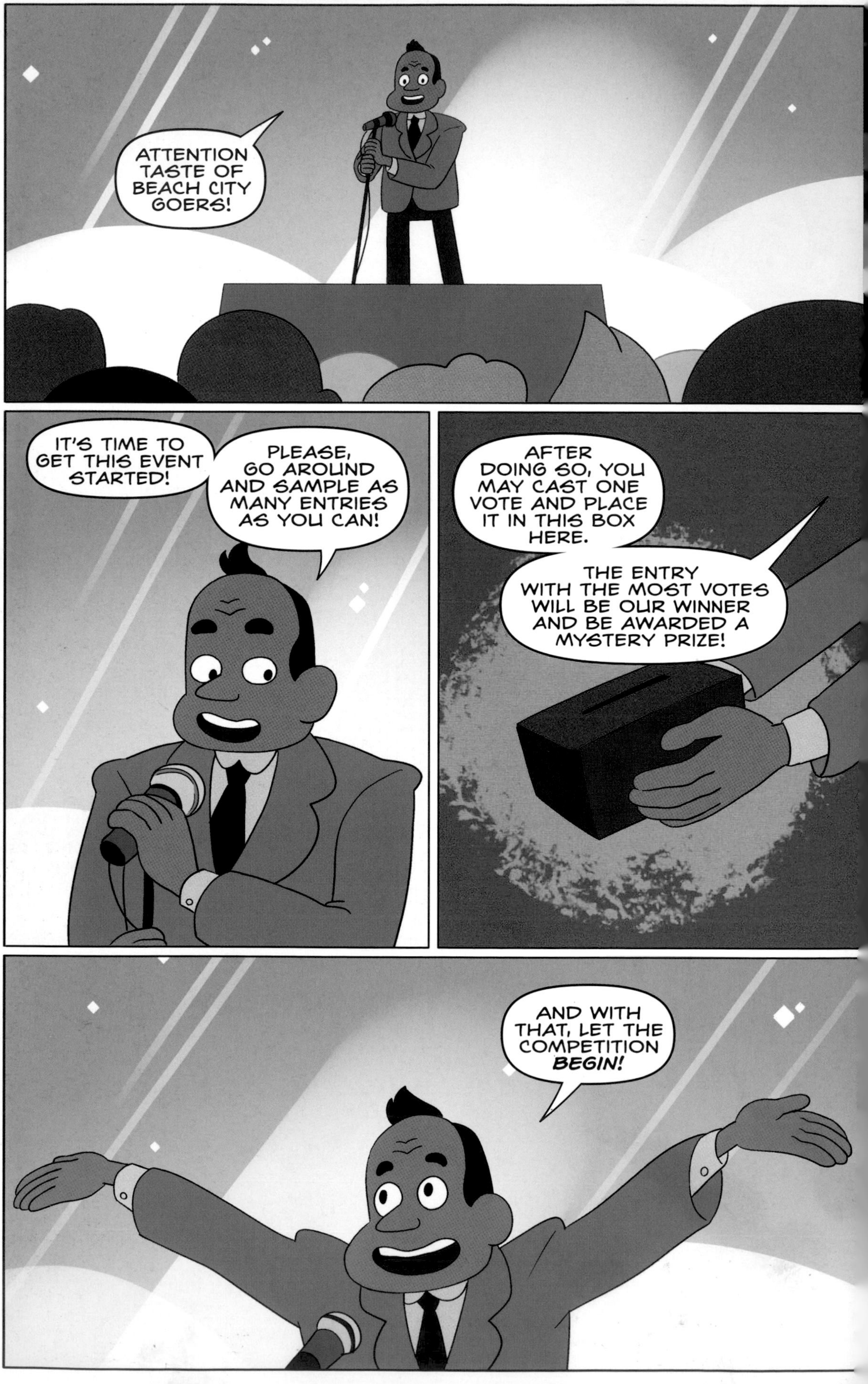
ATTENTION TASTE OF BEACH CITY GOERS!
IT'S TIME TO GET THIS EVENT STARTED!
PLEASE, GO AROUND AND SAMPLE AS MANY ENTRIES AS YOU CAN!
AFTER DOING SO, YOU MAY CAST ONE VOTE AND PLACE IT IN THIS BOX HERE.
THE ENTRY WITH THE MOST VOTES WILL BE OUR WINNER AND BE AWARDED A MYSTERY PRIZE!
AND WITH THAT, LET THE COMPETITION *BEGIN!*

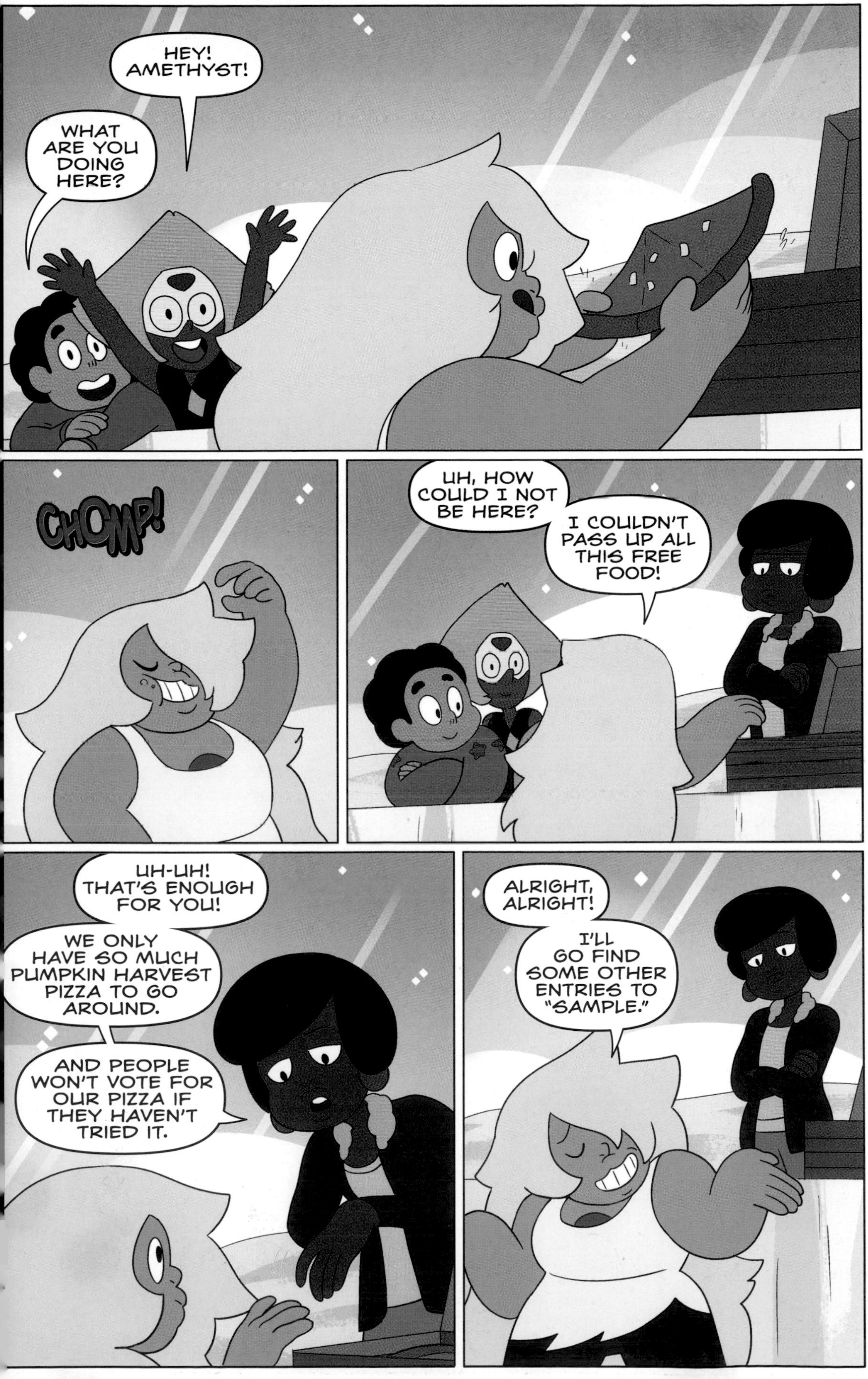
HEY! AMETHYST!
WHAT ARE YOU DOING HERE?
CHOMP!
UH, HOW COULD I NOT BE HERE?
I COULDN'T PASS UP ALL THIS FREE FOOD!
UH-UH! THAT'S ENOUGH FOR YOU!
WE ONLY HAVE SO MUCH PUMPKIN HARVEST PIZZA TO GO AROUND.
AND PEOPLE WON'T VOTE FOR OUR PIZZA IF THEY HAVEN'T TRIED IT.
ALRIGHT, ALRIGHT!
I'LL GO FIND SOME OTHER ENTRIES TO "SAMPLE."

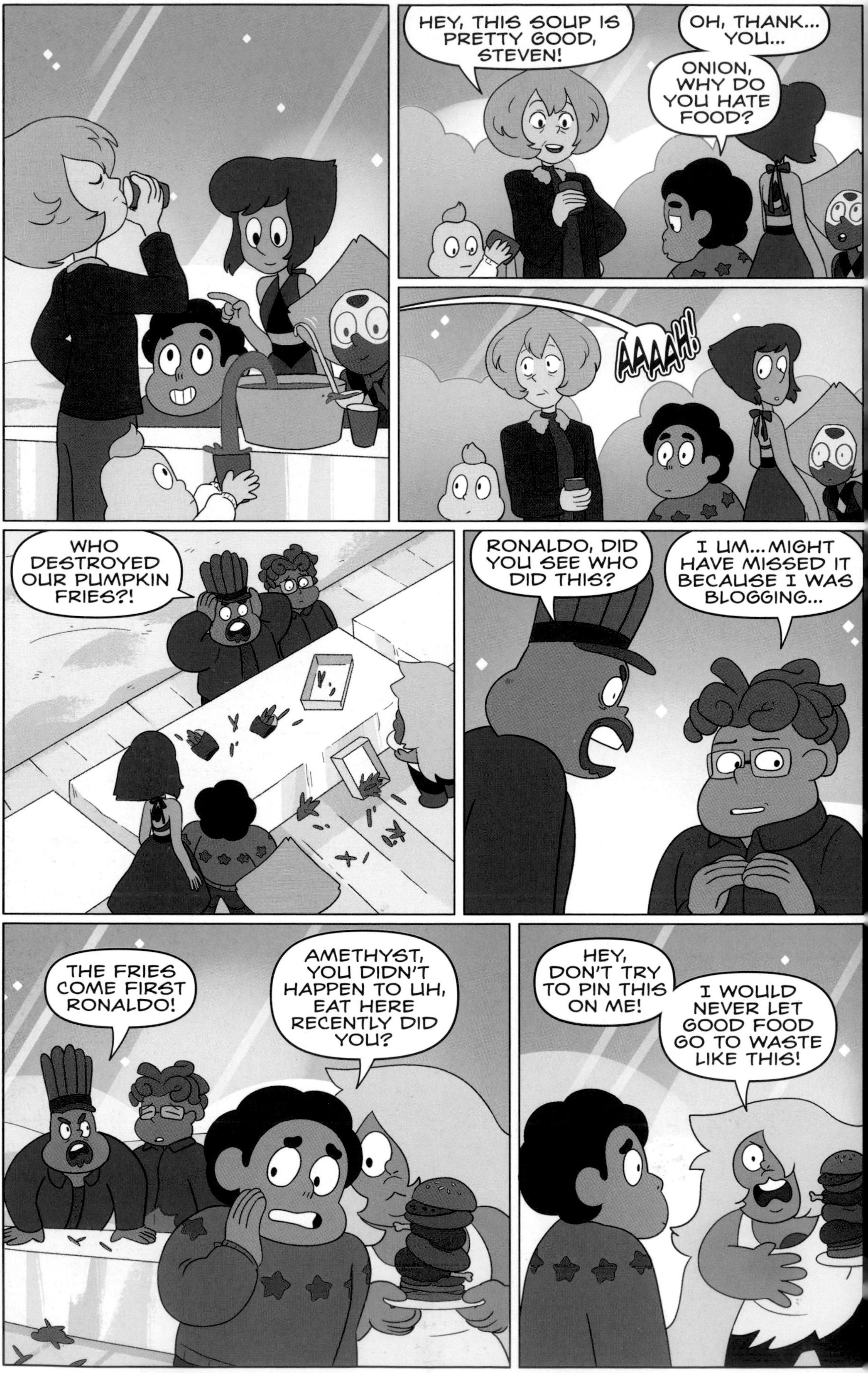
HEY, THIS SOUP IS PRETTY GOOD, STEVEN!
OH, THANK... YOU...
ONION, WHY DO YOU HATE FOOD?
AAAAH!
WHO DESTROYED OUR PUMPKIN FRIES?!
RONALDO, DID YOU SEE WHO DID THIS?
I UM...MIGHT HAVE MISSED IT BECAUSE I WAS BLOGGING...
THE FRIES COME FIRST RONALDO!
AMETHYST, YOU DIDN'T HAPPEN TO UH, EAT HERE RECENTLY DID YOU?
HEY, DON'T TRY TO PIN THIS ON ME!
I WOULD NEVER LET GOOD FOOD GO TO WASTE LIKE THIS!

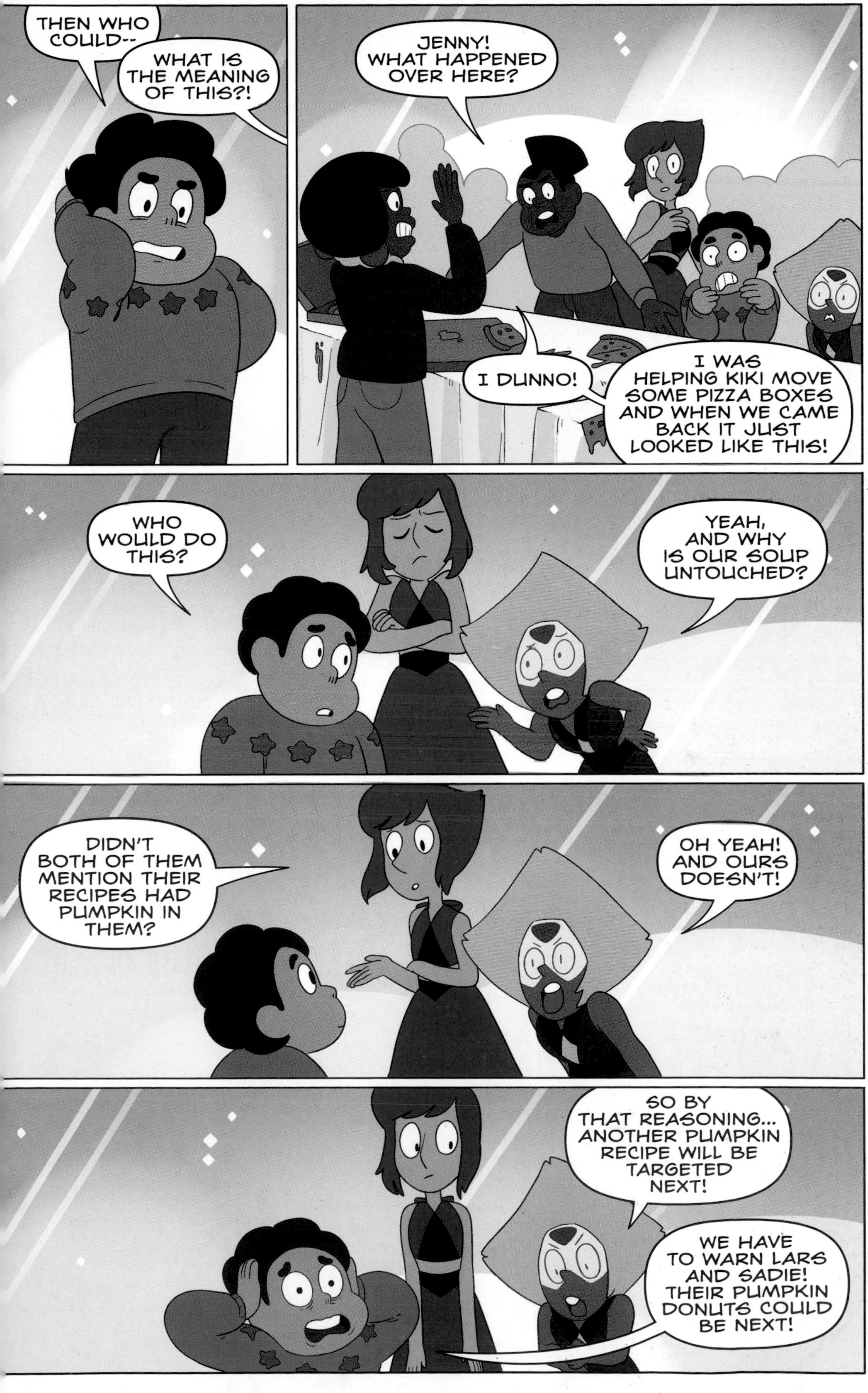
THEN WHO COULD--
WHAT IS THE MEANING OF THIS?!
JENNY! WHAT HAPPENED OVER HERE?
I DUNNO!
I WAS HELPING KIKI MOVE SOME PIZZA BOXES AND WHEN WE CAME BACK IT JUST LOOKED LIKE THIS!
WHO WOULD DO THIS?
YEAH, AND WHY IS OUR SOUP UNTOUCHED?
DIDN'T BOTH OF THEM MENTION THEIR RECIPES HAD PUMPKIN IN THEM?
OH YEAH! AND OURS DOESN'T!
SO BY THAT REASONING... ANOTHER PUMPKIN RECIPE WILL BE TARGETED NEXT!
WE HAVE TO WARN LARS AND SADIE! THEIR PUMPKIN DONUTS COULD BE NEXT!

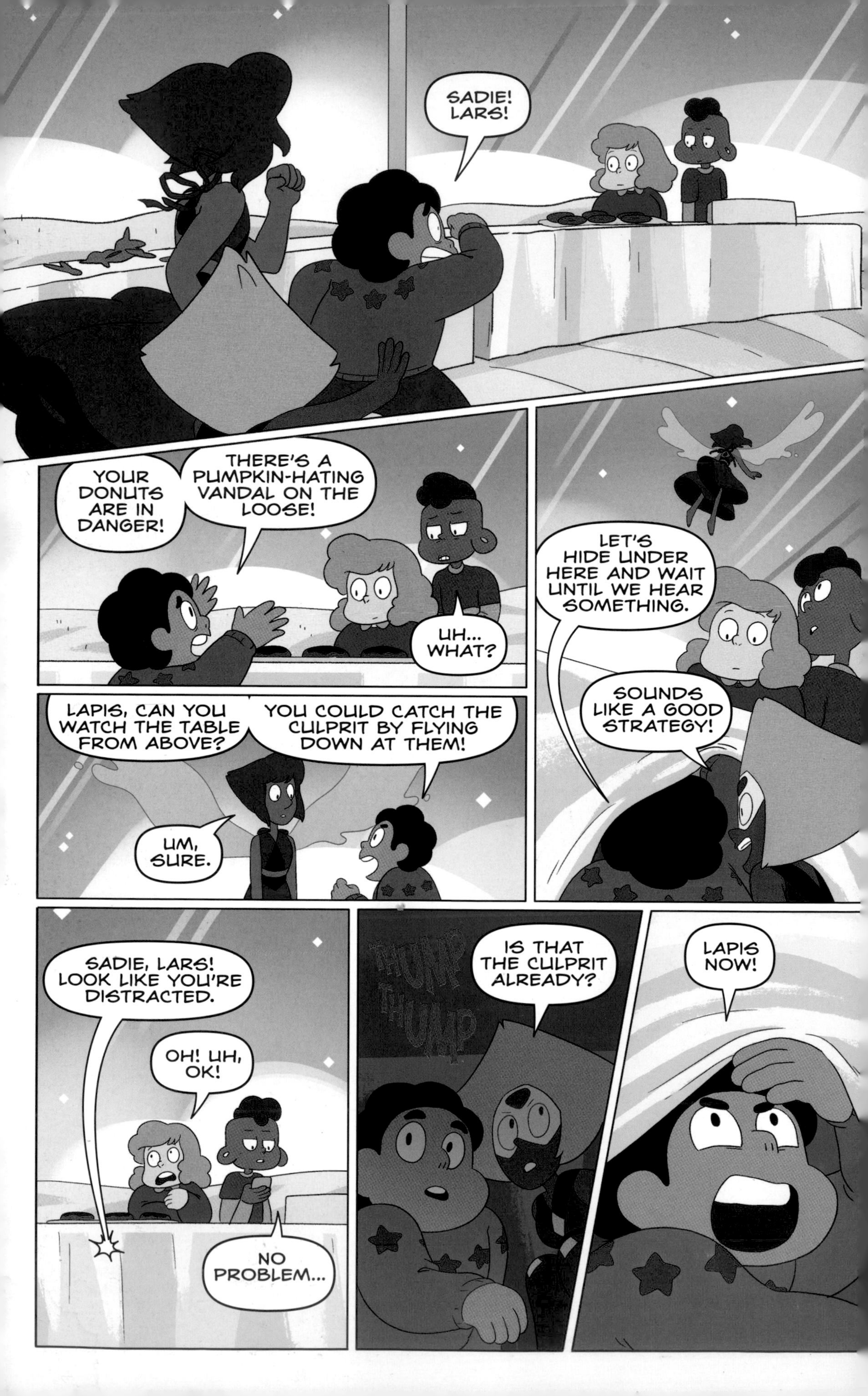

SADIE! LARS!
YOUR DONUTS ARE IN DANGER!
THERE'S A PUMPKIN-HATING VANDAL ON THE LOOSE!
UH... WHAT?
LET'S HIDE UNDER HERE AND WAIT UNTIL WE HEAR SOMETHING.
SOUNDS LIKE A GOOD STRATEGY!
LAPIS, CAN YOU WATCH THE TABLE FROM ABOVE?
YOU COULD CATCH THE CULPRIT BY FLYING DOWN AT THEM!
UM, SURE.
SADIE, LARS! LOOK LIKE YOU'RE DISTRACTED.
OH! UH, OK!
NO PROBLEM...
THUMP THUMP
IS THAT THE CULPRIT ALREADY?
LAPIS NOW!

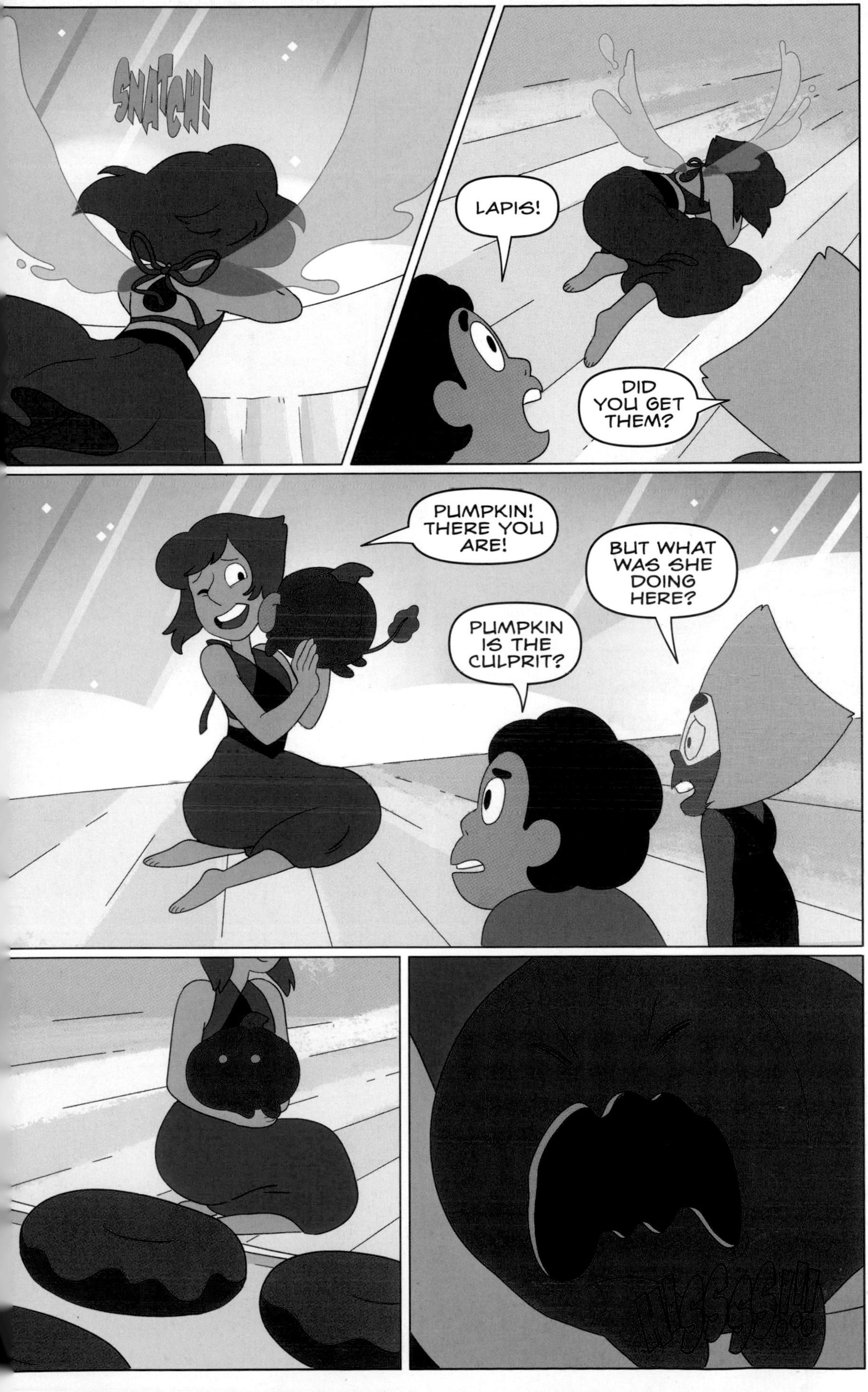
SNATCH!
LAPIS!
DID YOU GET THEM?
PUMPKIN! THERE YOU ARE!
BUT WHAT WAS SHE DOING HERE?
PUMPKIN IS THE CULPRIT?

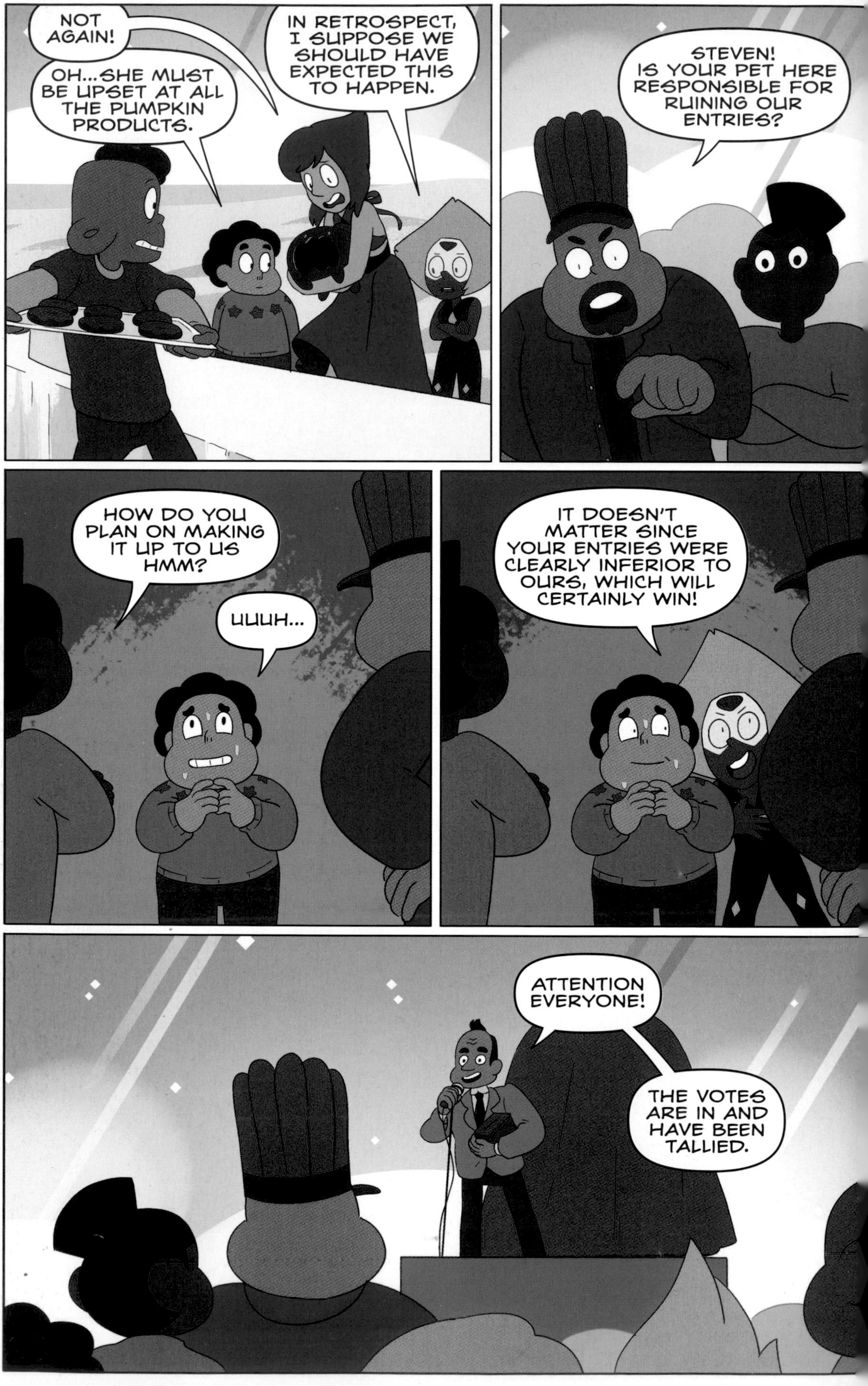
NOT AGAIN!
OH...SHE MUST BE UPSET AT ALL THE PUMPKIN PRODUCTS.
IN RETROSPECT, I SUPPOSE WE SHOULD HAVE EXPECTED THIS TO HAPPEN.
STEVEN! IS YOUR PET HERE RESPONSIBLE FOR RUINING OUR ENTRIES?
HOW DO YOU PLAN ON MAKING IT UP TO US HMM?
UUUH...
IT DOESN'T MATTER SINCE YOUR ENTRIES WERE CLEARLY INFERIOR TO OURS, WHICH WILL CERTAINLY WIN!
ATTENTION EVERYONE!
THE VOTES ARE IN AND HAVE BEEN TALLIED.

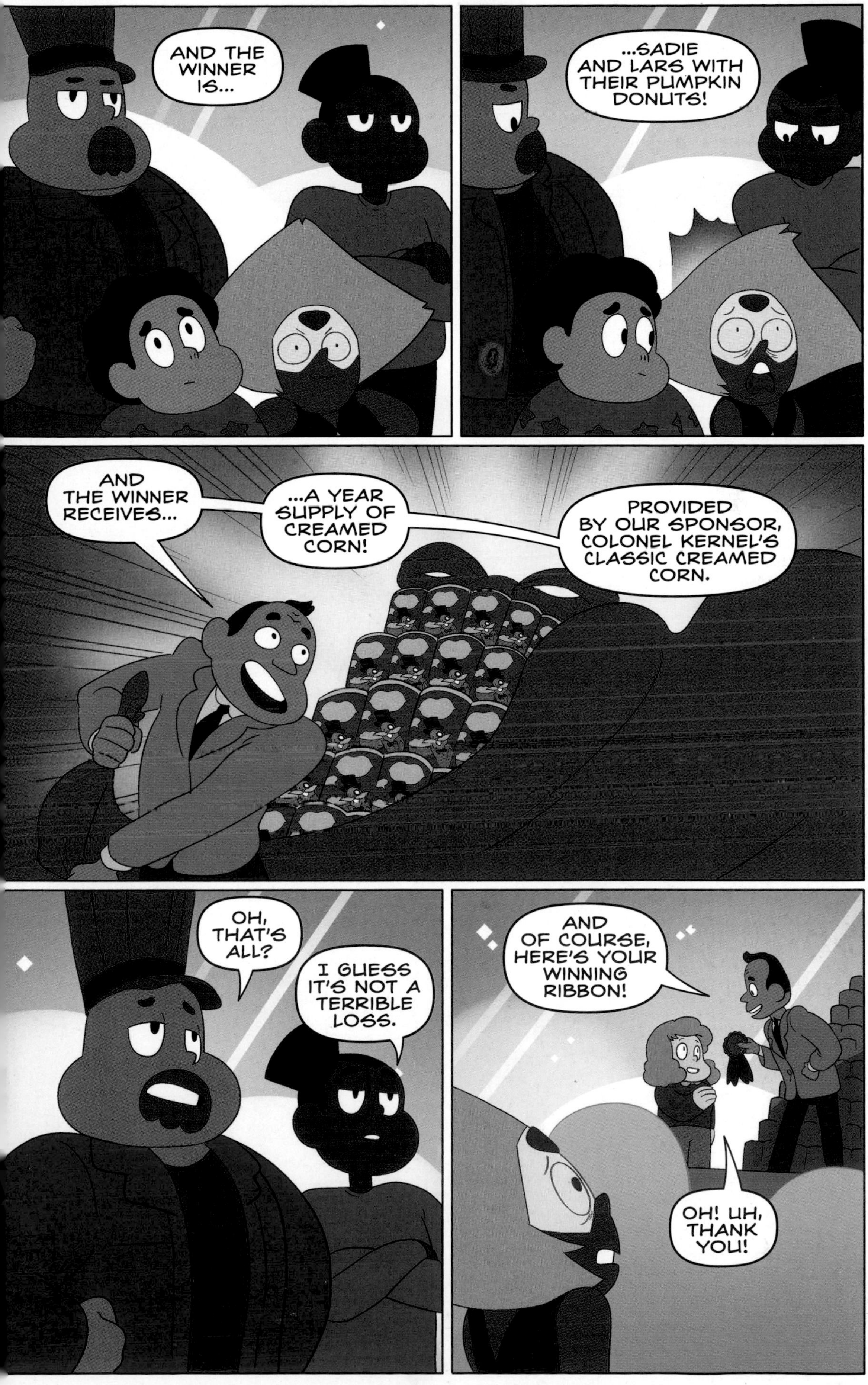
AND THE WINNER IS...
...SADIE AND LARS WITH THEIR PUMPKIN DONUTS!
AND THE WINNER RECEIVES...
...A YEAR SUPPLY OF CREAMED CORN!
PROVIDED BY OUR SPONSOR, COLONEL KERNEL'S CLASSIC CREAMED CORN.
OH, THAT'S ALL?
I GUESS IT'S NOT A TERRIBLE LOSS.
AND OF COURSE, HERE'S YOUR WINNING RIBBON!
OH! UH, THANK YOU!

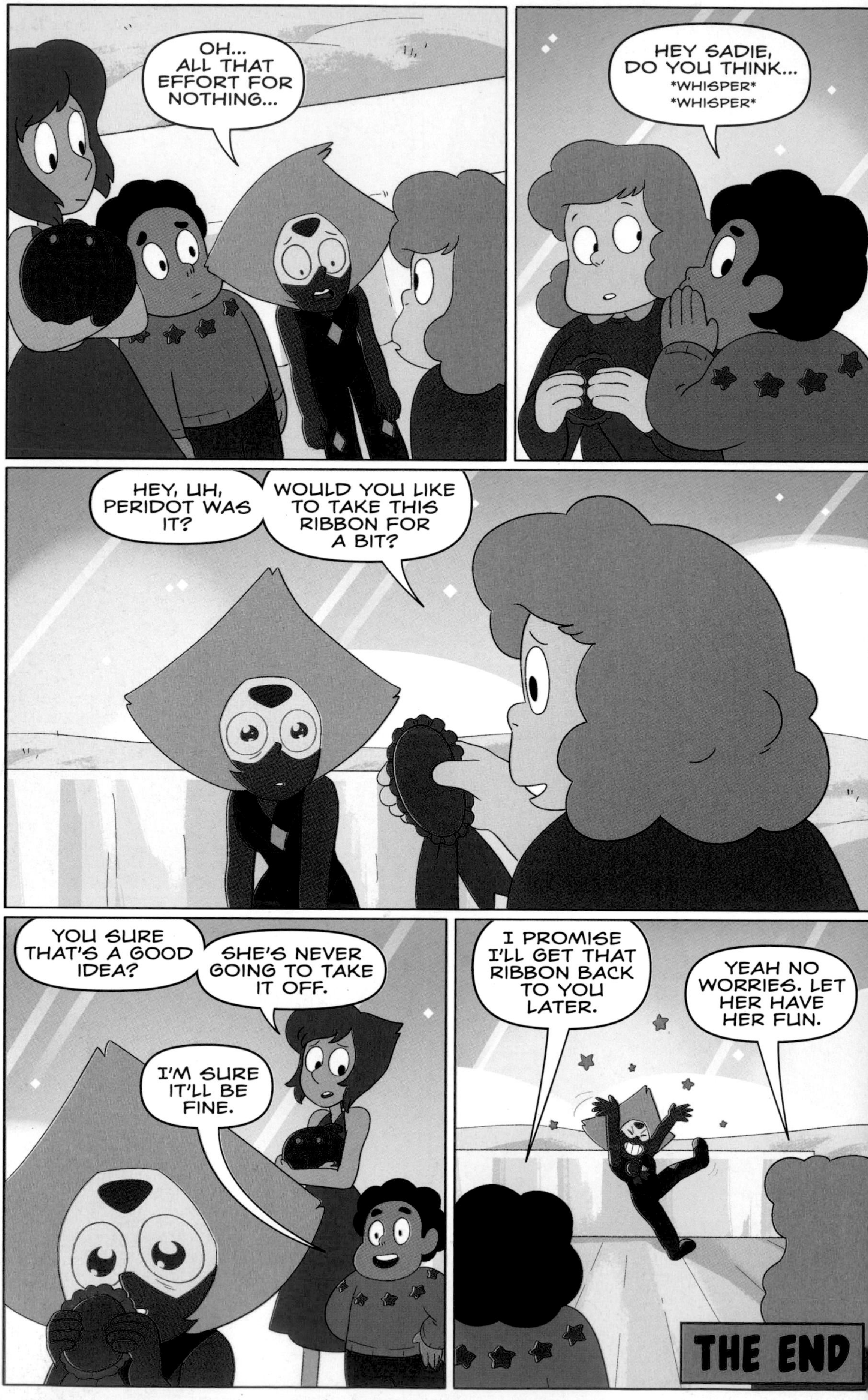
OH... ALL THAT EFFORT FOR NOTHING...
HEY SADIE, DO YOU THINK... *WHISPER* *WHISPER*
HEY, UH, PERIDOT WAS IT?
WOULD YOU LIKE TO TAKE THIS RIBBON FOR A BIT?
YOU SURE THAT'S A GOOD IDEA?
SHE'S NEVER GOING TO TAKE IT OFF.
I'M SURE IT'LL BE FINE.
I PROMISE I'LL GET THAT RIBBON BACK TO YOU LATER.
YEAH NO WORRIES. LET HER HAVE HER FUN.
THE END

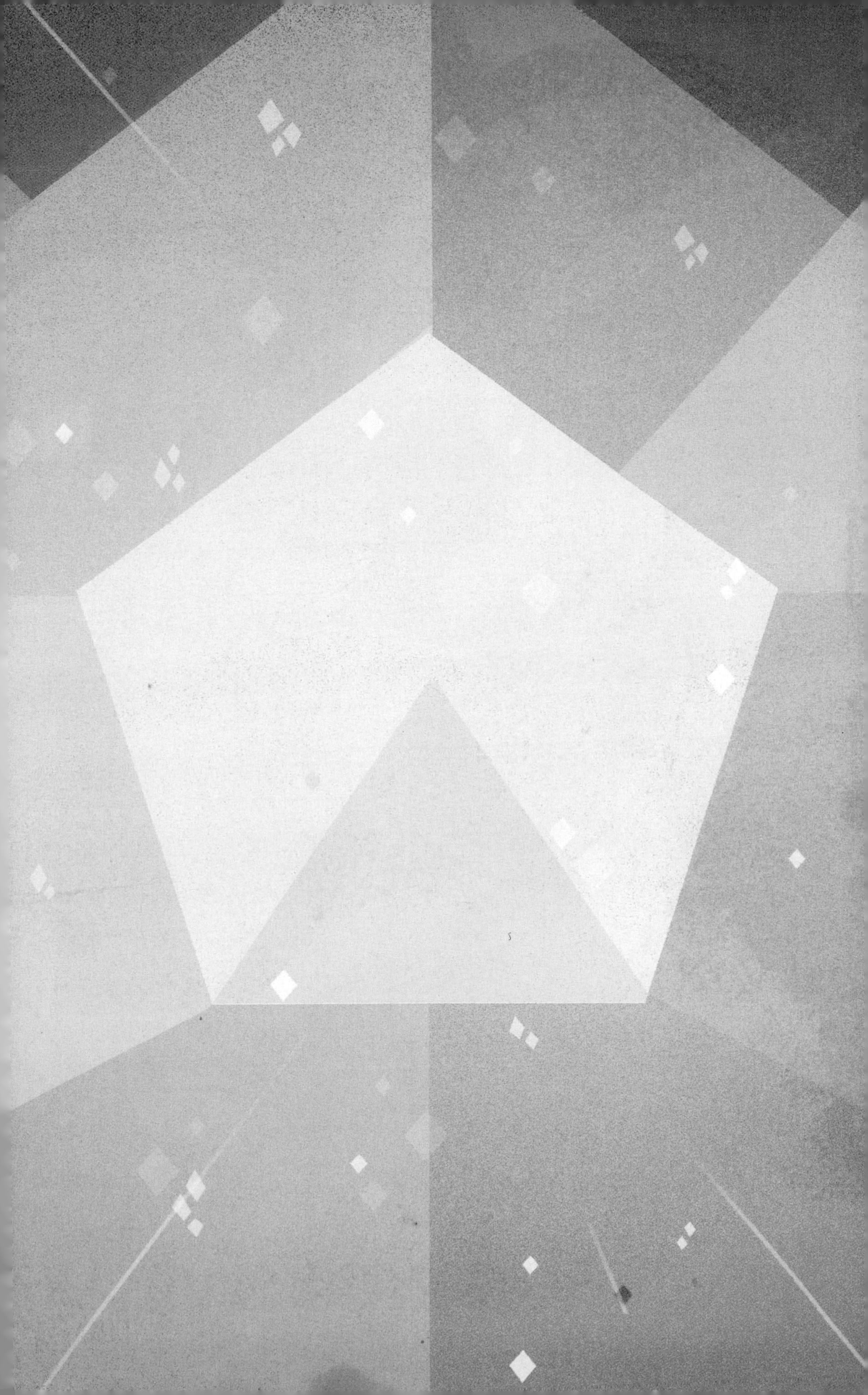

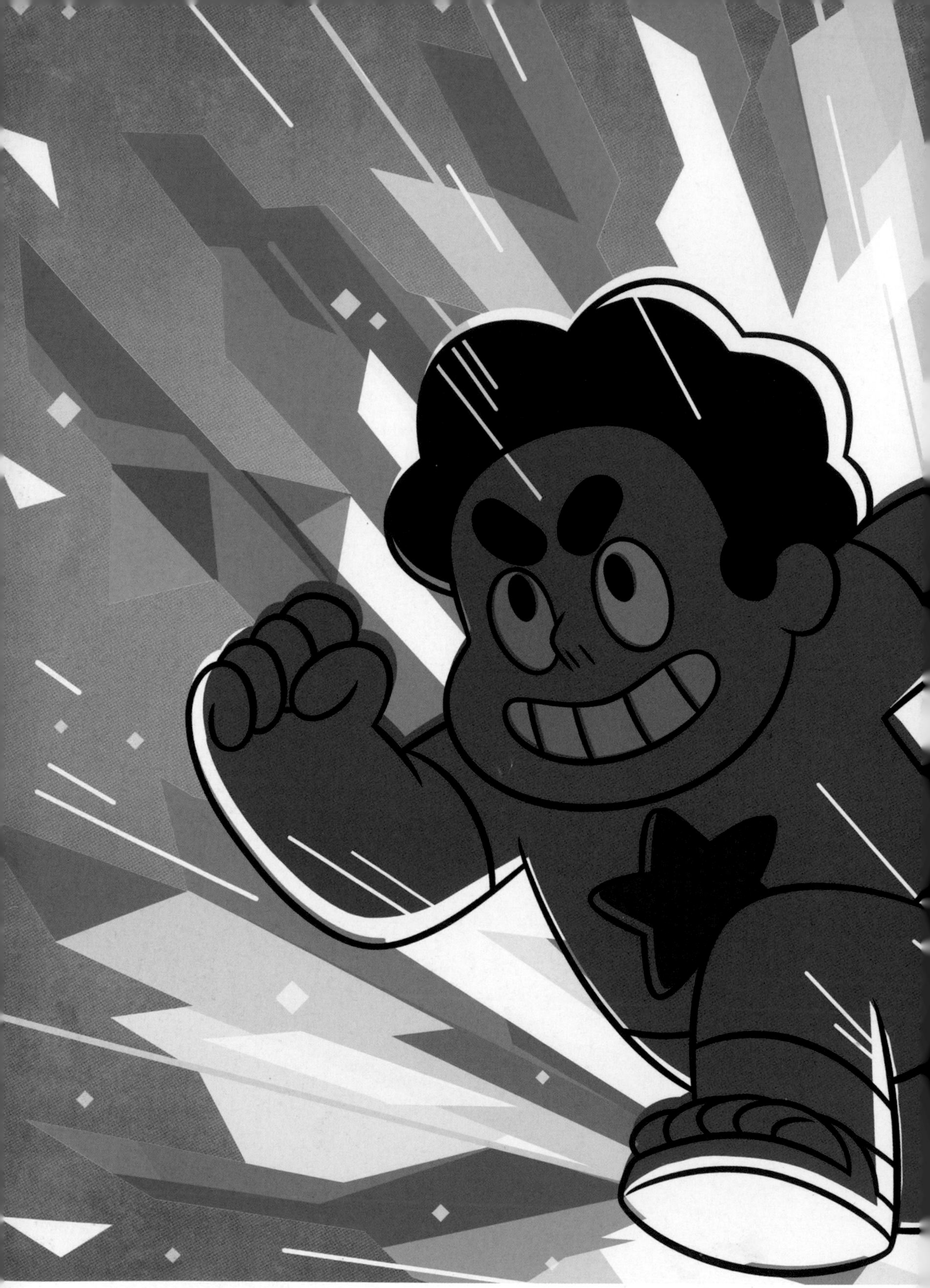

CHAPTER TWELVE

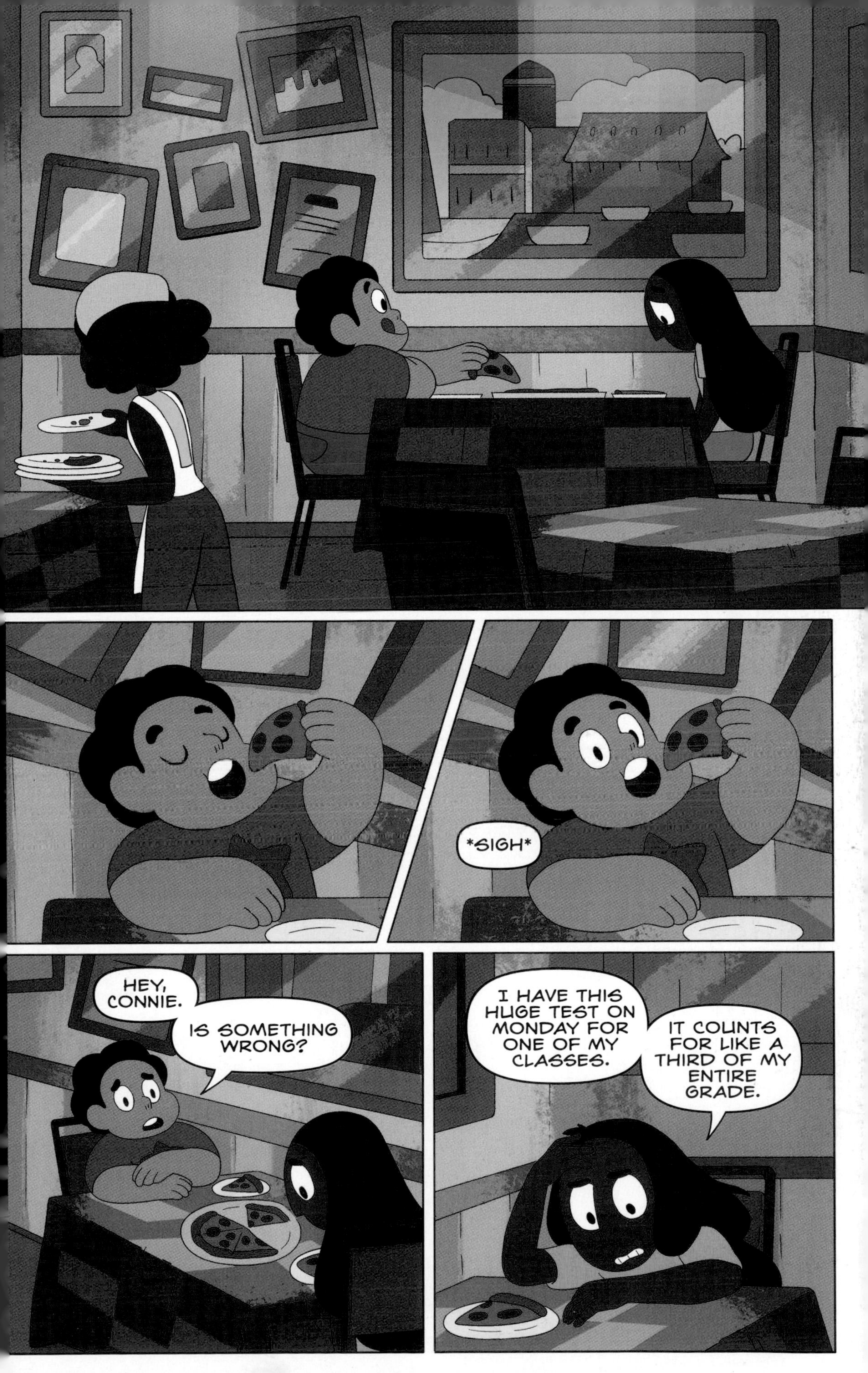
SIGH
HEY, CONNIE.
IS SOMETHING WRONG?
I HAVE THIS HUGE TEST ON MONDAY FOR ONE OF MY CLASSES.
IT COUNTS FOR LIKE A THIRD OF MY ENTIRE GRADE.

OH, ARE YOU WORRIED BECAUSE YOU HAVEN'T STUDIED FOR IT YET?
NO!
I'VE SPENT THE WHOLE WEEK STUDYING FOR IT! BUT I STILL FEEL LIKE I'M NOT READY!
LIKE, WHAT IF THERE'S SOMETHING I MISSED?
CONNIE, I'M SURE YOU'LL DO FINE.
YOU'RE REALLY SMART, AND YOU WORK HARD!
HMMM... MAYBE.
I JUST CAN'T HELP BUT FEEL STRESSED ABOUT IT.
WELL...MAYBE WE CAN DO SOMETHING TO HELP YOU RELAX.
WHAT DO YOU HAVE IN MIND?
LET'S HAVE A SLUMBER PARTY AT MY HOUSE TOMORROW!
WE'LL HAVE SUCH A GOOD TIME THAT YOU'LL FORGET ALL ABOUT THE TEST!
AND THEN, YOU'LL STILL HAVE THE NEXT DAY TO GET SOME LAST-MINUTE STUDYING IN IF YOU WANT.
THAT...
...SOUNDS LIKE A GREAT IDEA, ACTUALLY!

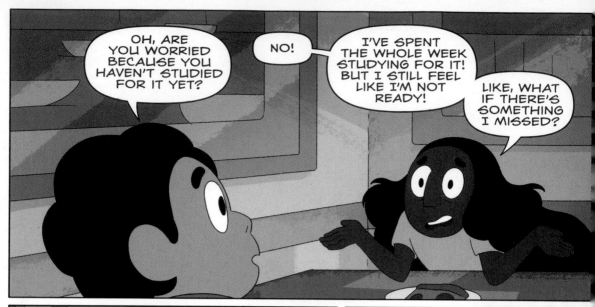

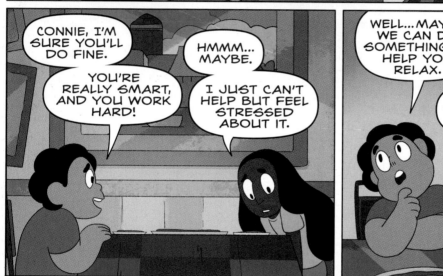

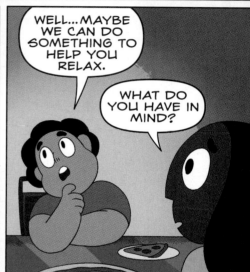

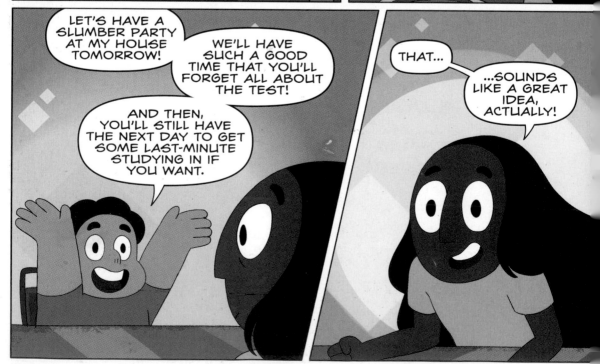

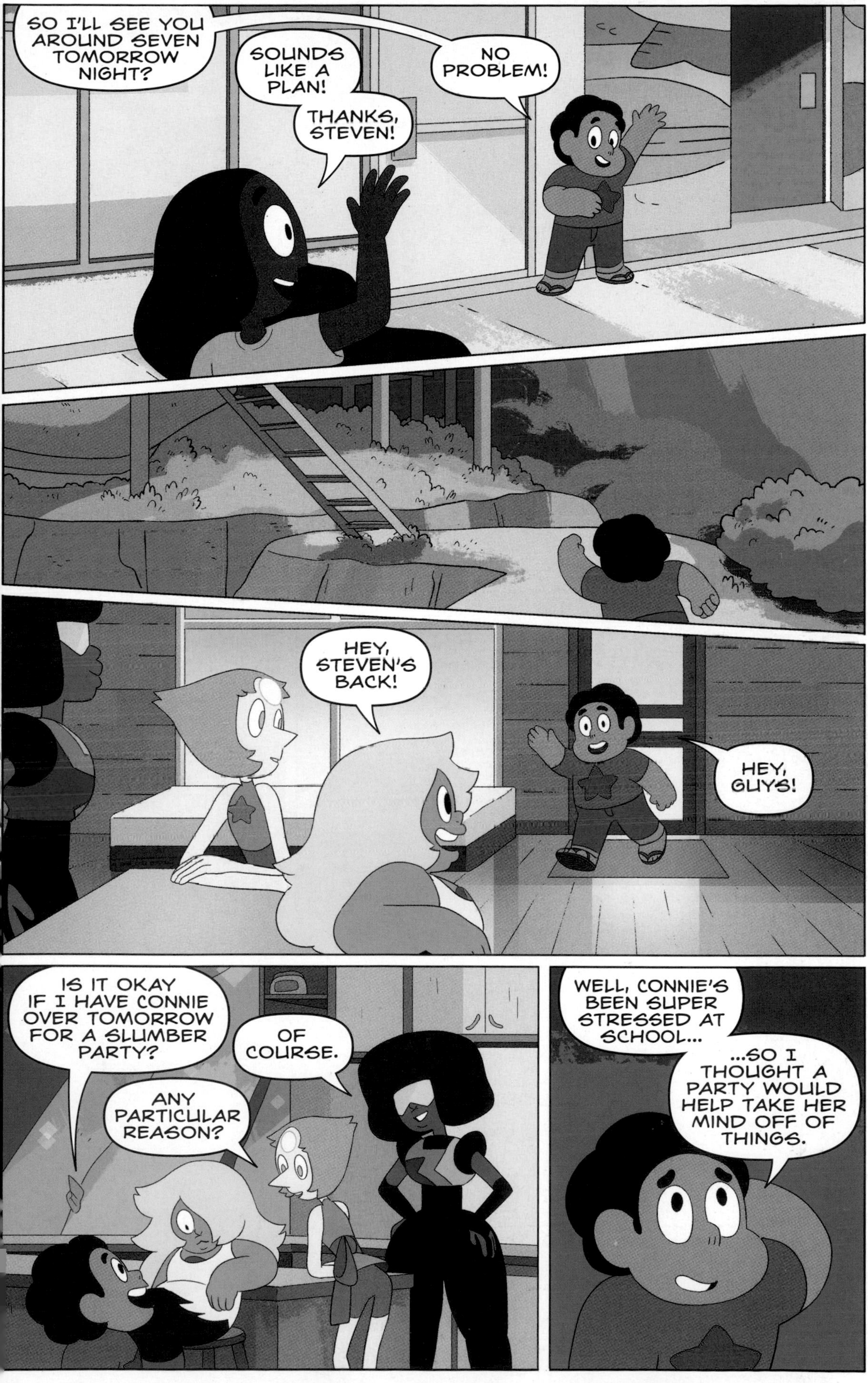
SO I'LL SEE YOU AROUND SEVEN TOMORROW NIGHT?
SOUNDS LIKE A PLAN!
THANKS, STEVEN!
NO PROBLEM!
HEY, STEVEN'S BACK!
HEY, GUYS!
IS IT OKAY IF I HAVE CONNIE OVER TOMORROW FOR A SLUMBER PARTY?
OF COURSE.
ANY PARTICULAR REASON?
WELL, CONNIE'S BEEN SUPER STRESSED AT SCHOOL...
...SO I THOUGHT A PARTY WOULD HELP TAKE HER MIND OFF OF THINGS.

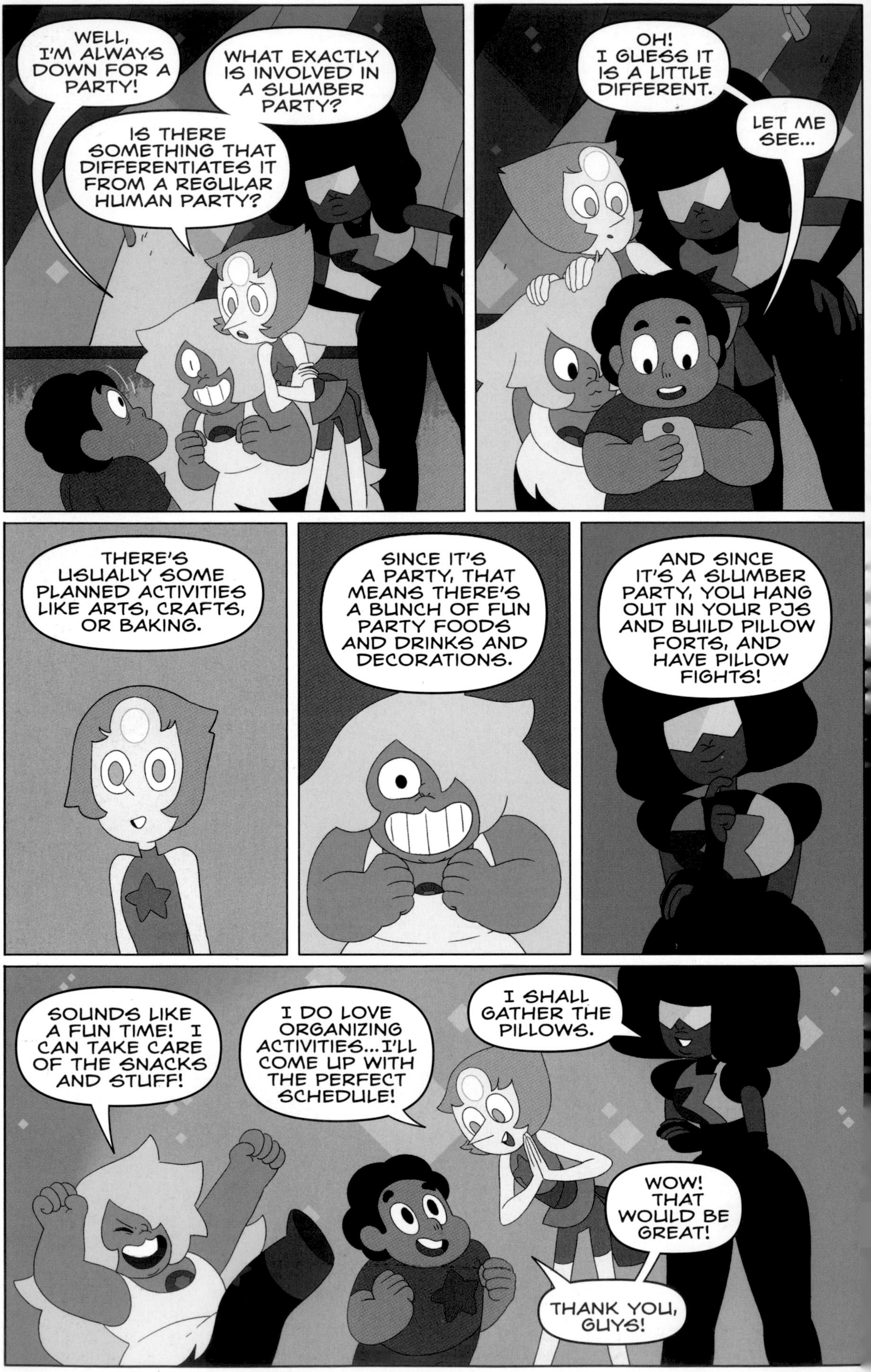

WELL, I'M ALWAYS DOWN FOR A PARTY!
WHAT EXACTLY IS INVOLVED IN A SLUMBER PARTY?
IS THERE SOMETHING THAT DIFFERENTIATES IT FROM A REGULAR HUMAN PARTY?
OH! I GUESS IT IS A LITTLE DIFFERENT.
LET ME SEE...
THERE'S USUALLY SOME PLANNED ACTIVITIES LIKE ARTS, CRAFTS, OR BAKING.
SINCE IT'S A PARTY, THAT MEANS THERE'S A BUNCH OF FUN PARTY FOODS AND DRINKS AND DECORATIONS.
AND SINCE IT'S A SLUMBER PARTY, YOU HANG OUT IN YOUR PJS AND BUILD PILLOW FORTS, AND HAVE PILLOW FIGHTS!
SOUNDS LIKE A FUN TIME! I CAN TAKE CARE OF THE SNACKS AND STUFF!
I DO LOVE ORGANIZING ACTIVITIES...I'LL COME UP WITH THE PERFECT SCHEDULE!
I SHALL GATHER THE PILLOWS.
WOW! THAT WOULD BE GREAT!
THANK YOU, GUYS!

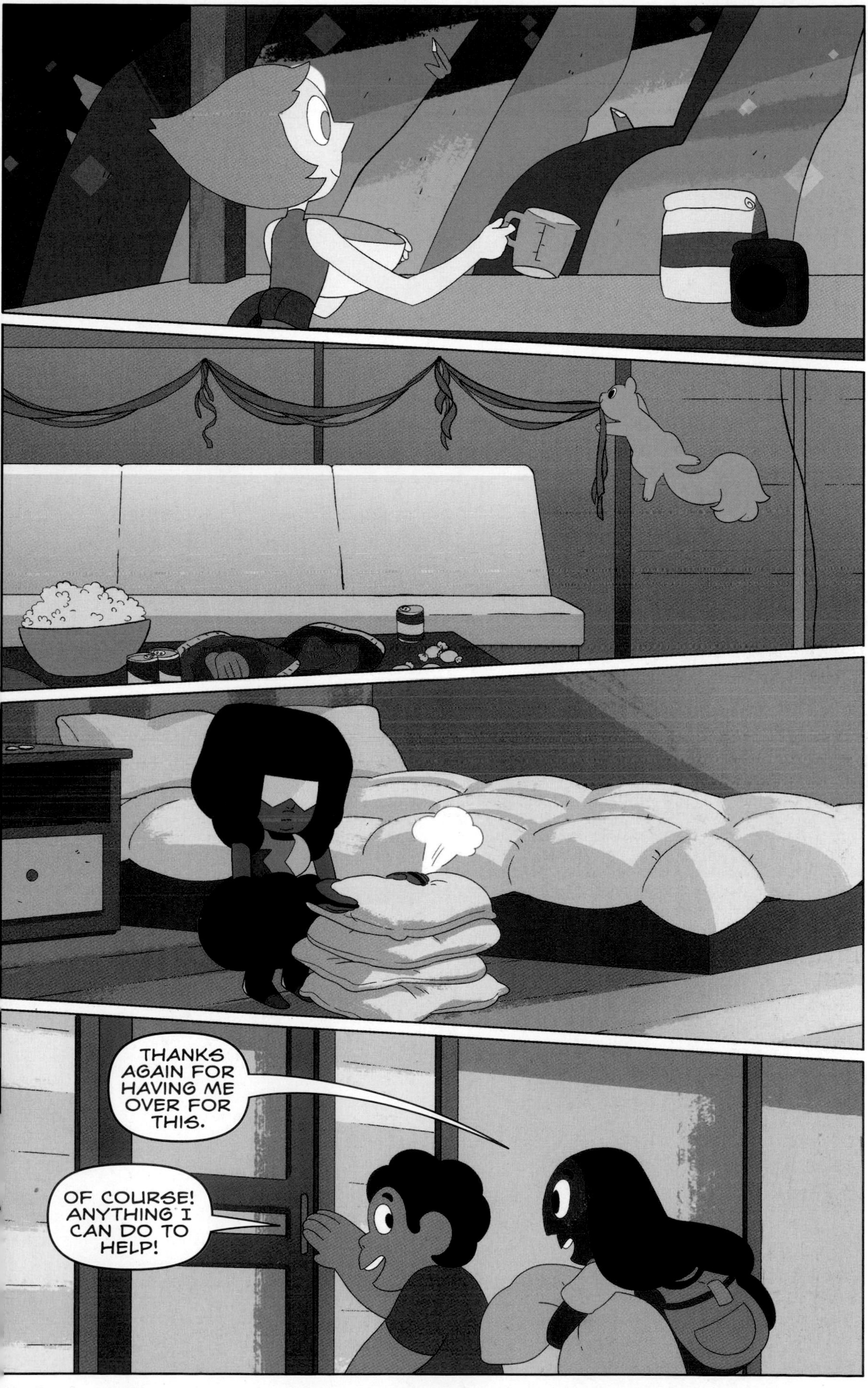
THANKS AGAIN FOR HAVING ME OVER FOR THIS.
OF COURSE! ANYTHING I CAN DO TO HELP!

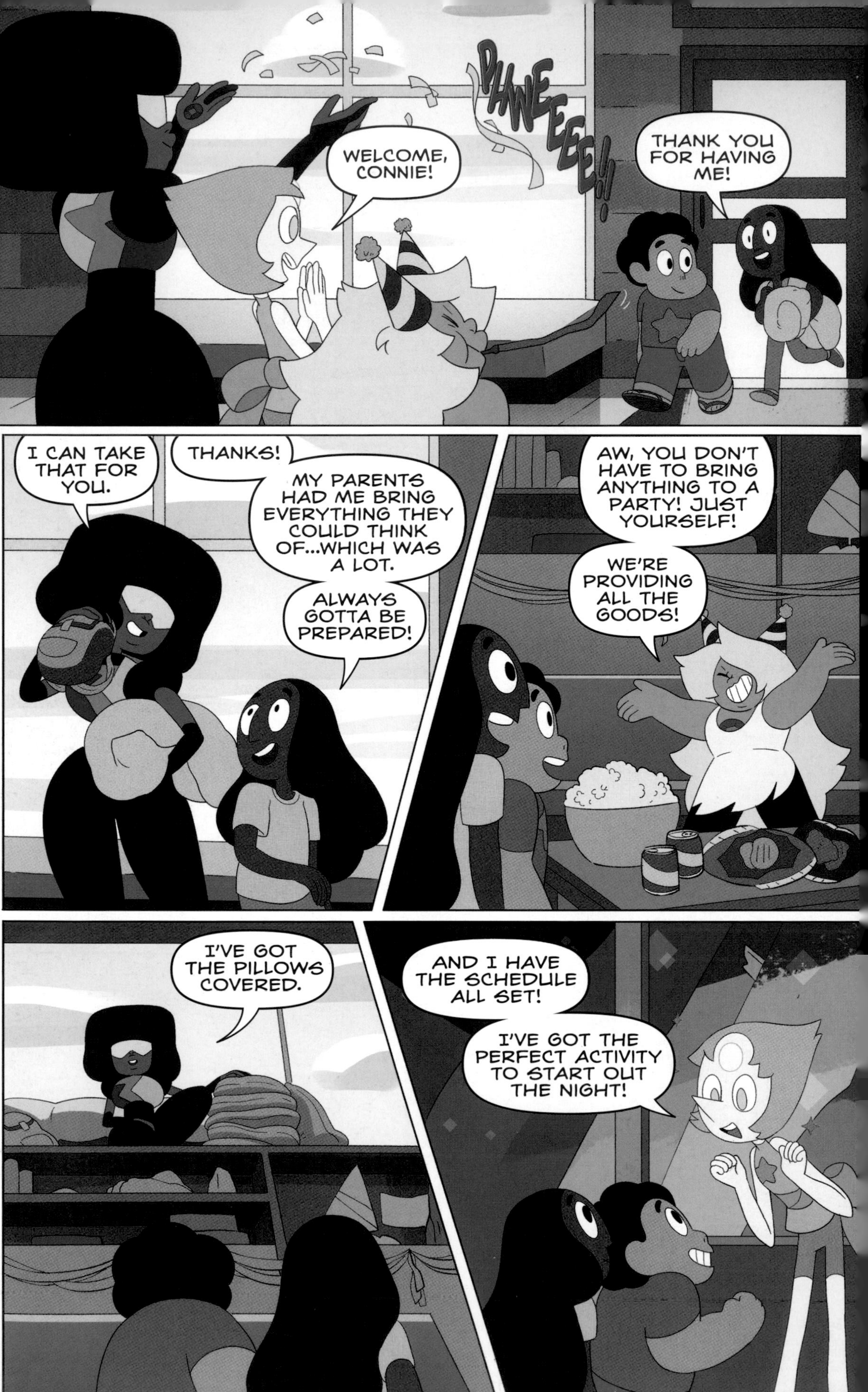
WELCOME, CONNIE!
PHWEEEEE!!
THANK YOU FOR HAVING ME!
I CAN TAKE THAT FOR YOU.
THANKS!
MY PARENTS HAD ME BRING EVERYTHING THEY COULD THINK OF...WHICH WAS A LOT.
ALWAYS GOTTA BE PREPARED!
AW, YOU DON'T HAVE TO BRING ANYTHING TO A PARTY! JUST YOURSELF!
WE'RE PROVIDING ALL THE GOODS!
I'VE GOT THE PILLOWS COVERED.
AND I HAVE THE SCHEDULE ALL SET!
I'VE GOT THE PERFECT ACTIVITY TO START OUT THE NIGHT!

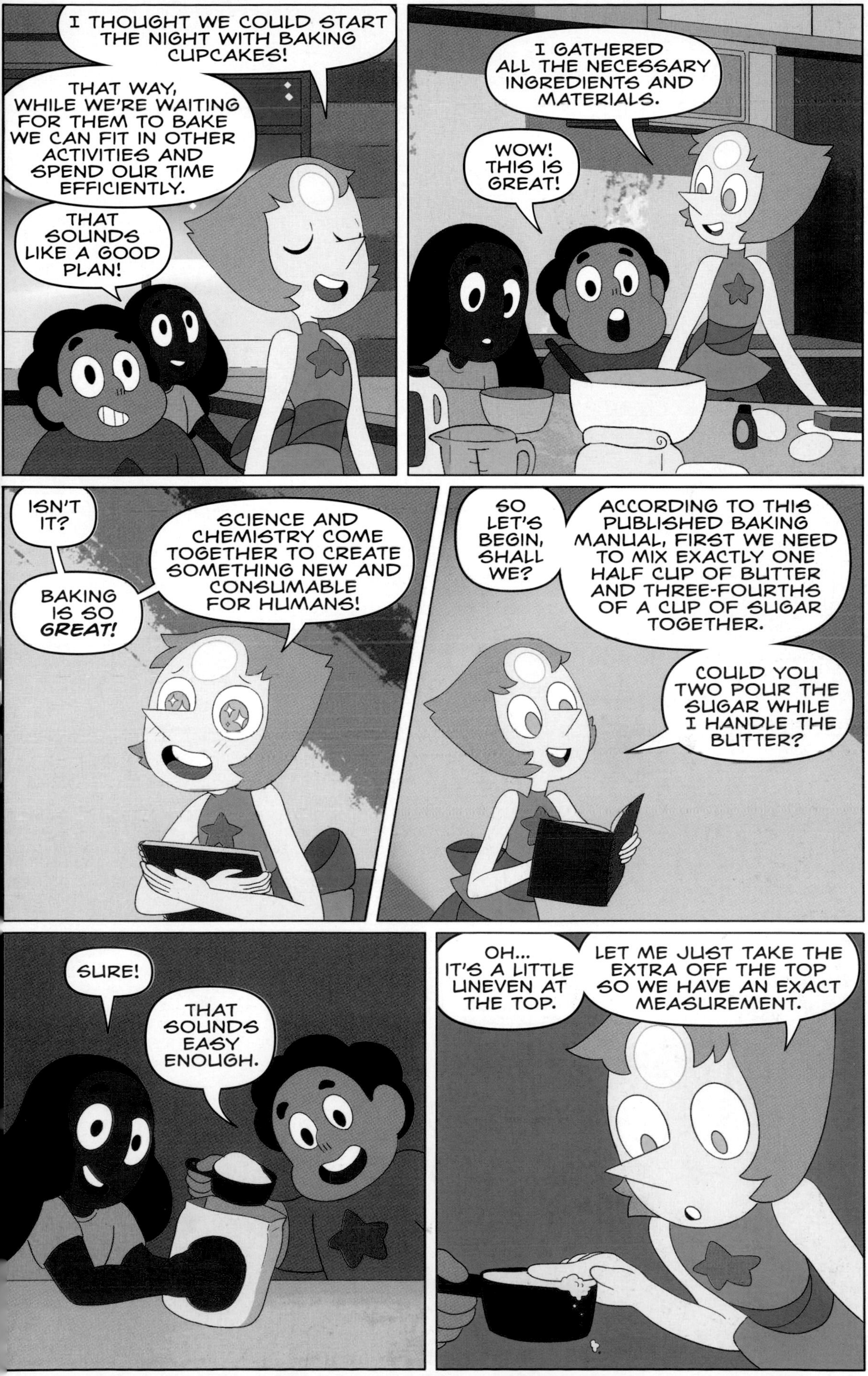
I THOUGHT WE COULD START THE NIGHT WITH BAKING CUPCAKES!
THAT WAY, WHILE WE'RE WAITING FOR THEM TO BAKE WE CAN FIT IN OTHER ACTIVITIES AND SPEND OUR TIME EFFICIENTLY.
THAT SOUNDS LIKE A GOOD PLAN!
I GATHERED ALL THE NECESSARY INGREDIENTS AND MATERIALS.
WOW! THIS IS GREAT!
ISN'T IT?
BAKING IS SO GREAT!
SCIENCE AND CHEMISTRY COME TOGETHER TO CREATE SOMETHING NEW AND CONSUMABLE FOR HUMANS!
SO LET'S BEGIN, SHALL WE?
ACCORDING TO THIS PUBLISHED BAKING MANUAL, FIRST WE NEED TO MIX EXACTLY ONE HALF CUP OF BUTTER AND THREE-FOURTHS OF A CUP OF SUGAR TOGETHER.
COULD YOU TWO POUR THE SUGAR WHILE I HANDLE THE BUTTER?
SURE!
THAT SOUNDS EASY ENOUGH.
OH... IT'S A LITTLE UNEVEN AT THE TOP.
LET ME JUST TAKE THE EXTRA OFF THE TOP SO WE HAVE AN EXACT MEASUREMENT.

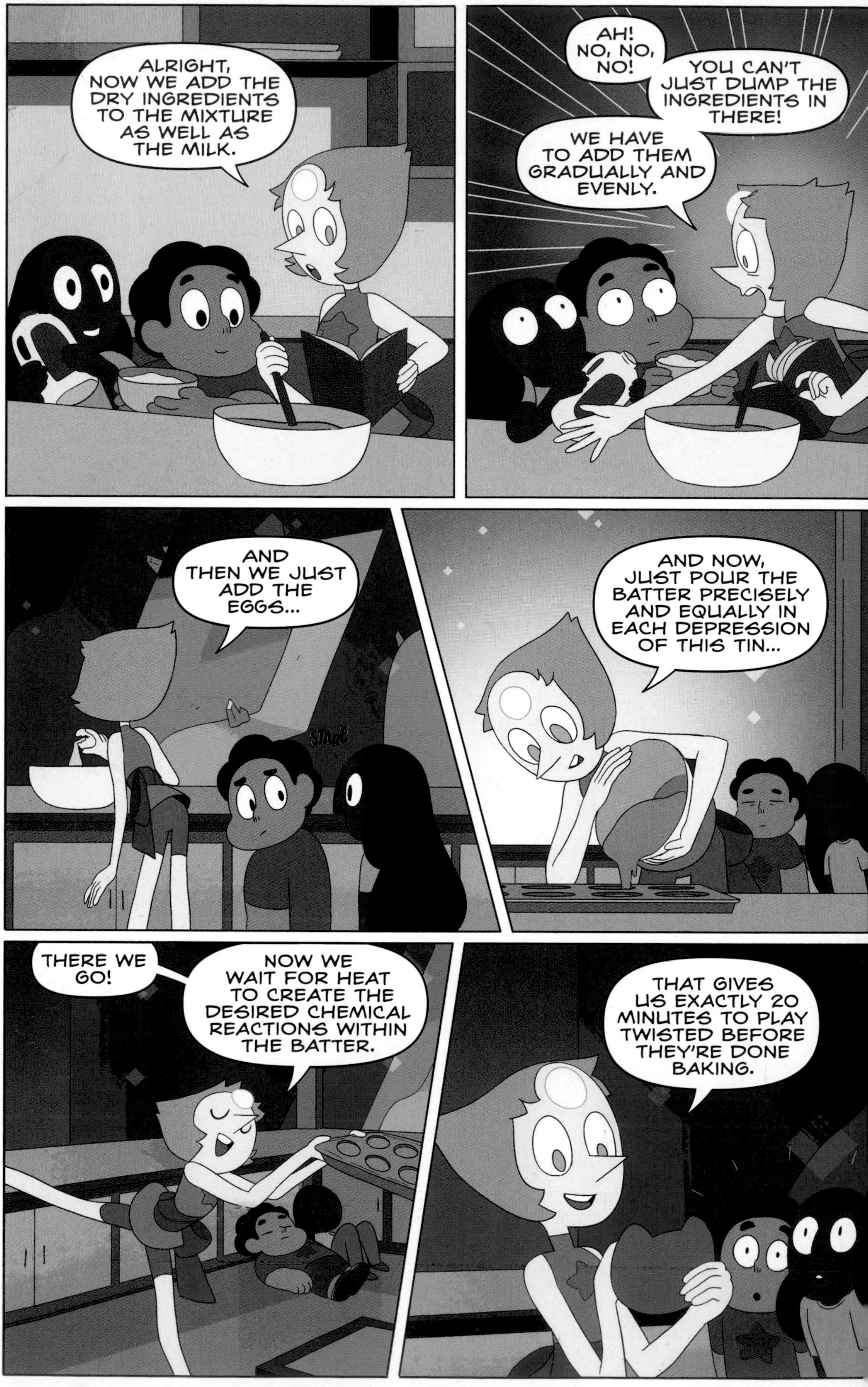
ALRIGHT, NOW WE ADD THE DRY INGREDIENTS TO THE MIXTURE AS WELL AS THE MILK.
AH! NO, NO, NO!
YOU CAN'T JUST DUMP THE INGREDIENTS IN THERE!
WE HAVE TO ADD THEM GRADUALLY AND EVENLY.
AND THEN WE JUST ADD THE EGGS...
STARE
AND NOW, JUST POUR THE BATTER PRECISELY AND EQUALLY IN EACH DEPRESSION OF THIS TIN...
THERE WE GO!
NOW WE WAIT FOR HEAT TO CREATE THE DESIRED CHEMICAL REACTIONS WITHIN THE BATTER.
THAT GIVES US EXACTLY 20 MINUTES TO PLAY TWISTED BEFORE THEY'RE DONE BAKING.

I DID SOME RESEARCH AND FOUND THAT THIS "TWISTED" IS A POPULAR FUN GAME CHILDREN USUALLY ENJOY.
HAHA, I'M IN! LOOKS LIKE FUN!
I'M ALWAYS UP FOR A CHALLENGE.
SO, ACCORDING TO THE SPINNING ARROW, THE FIRST MOVE WILL BE RIGHT FOOT ON PINK!
WELL, THAT'S NOT SO BAD.
NEXT IS LEFT HAND ON BLUE!
STILL PRETTY EASY.

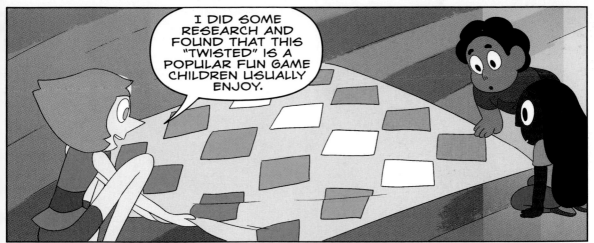

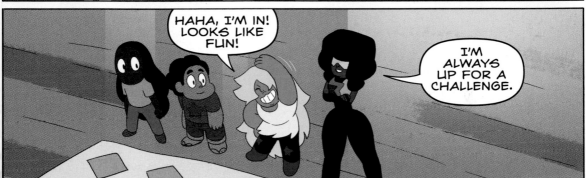

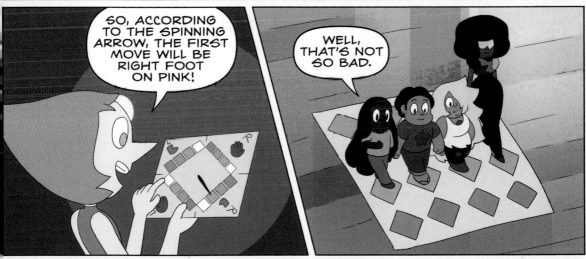

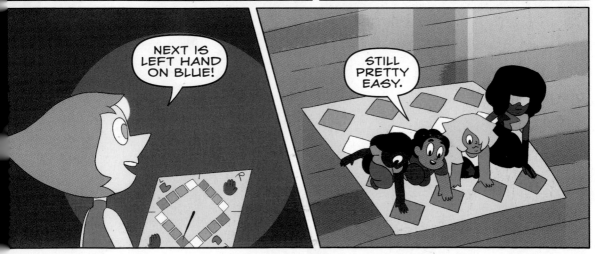

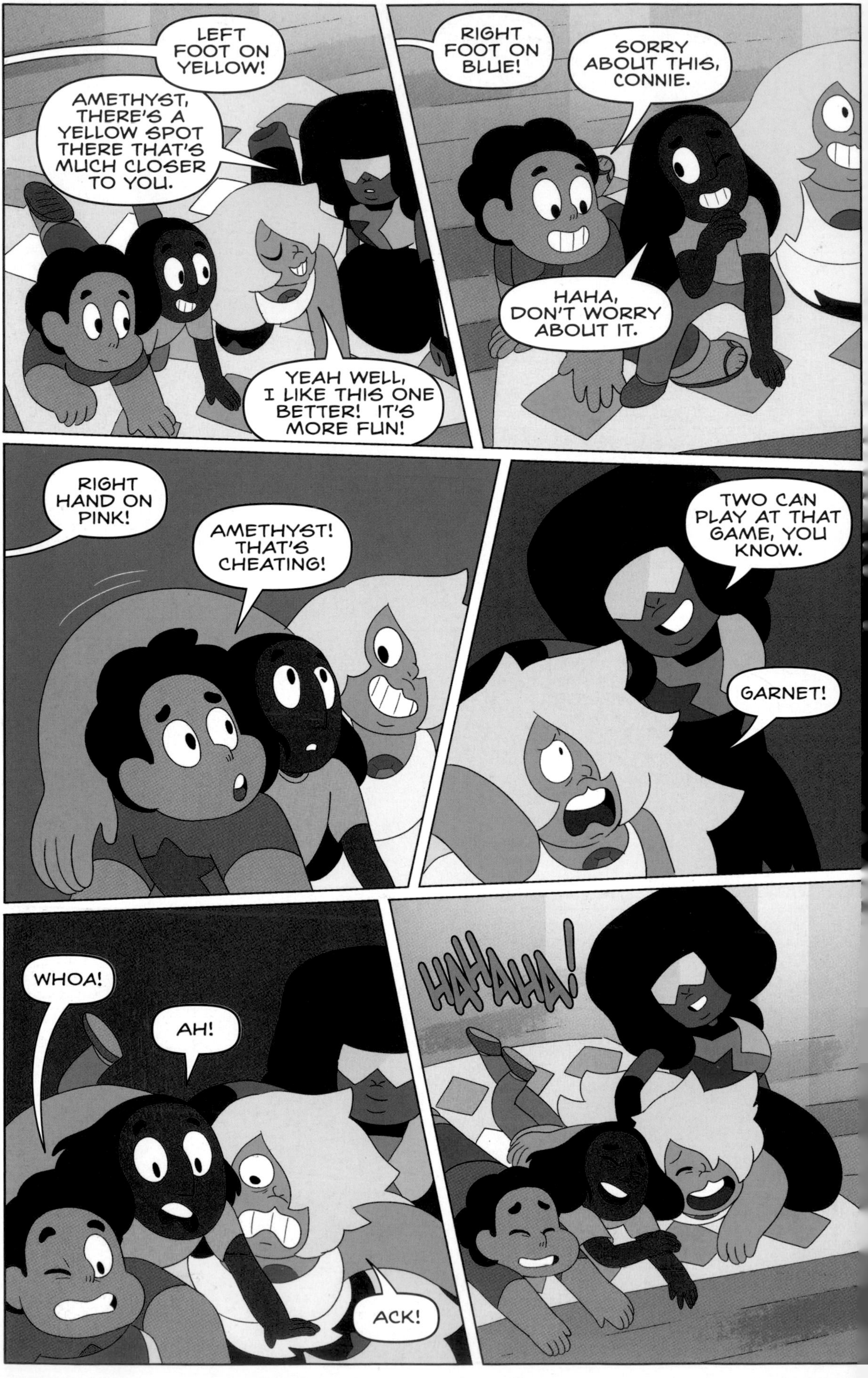
LEFT FOOT ON YELLOW!
AMETHYST, THERE'S A YELLOW SPOT THERE THAT'S MUCH CLOSER TO YOU.
YEAH WELL, I LIKE THIS ONE BETTER! IT'S MORE FUN!
RIGHT FOOT ON BLUE!
SORRY ABOUT THIS, CONNIE.
HAHA, DON'T WORRY ABOUT IT.
RIGHT HAND ON PINK!
AMETHYST! THAT'S CHEATING!
TWO CAN PLAY AT THAT GAME, YOU KNOW.
GARNET!
WHOA!
AH!
ACK!
HAHAHA!

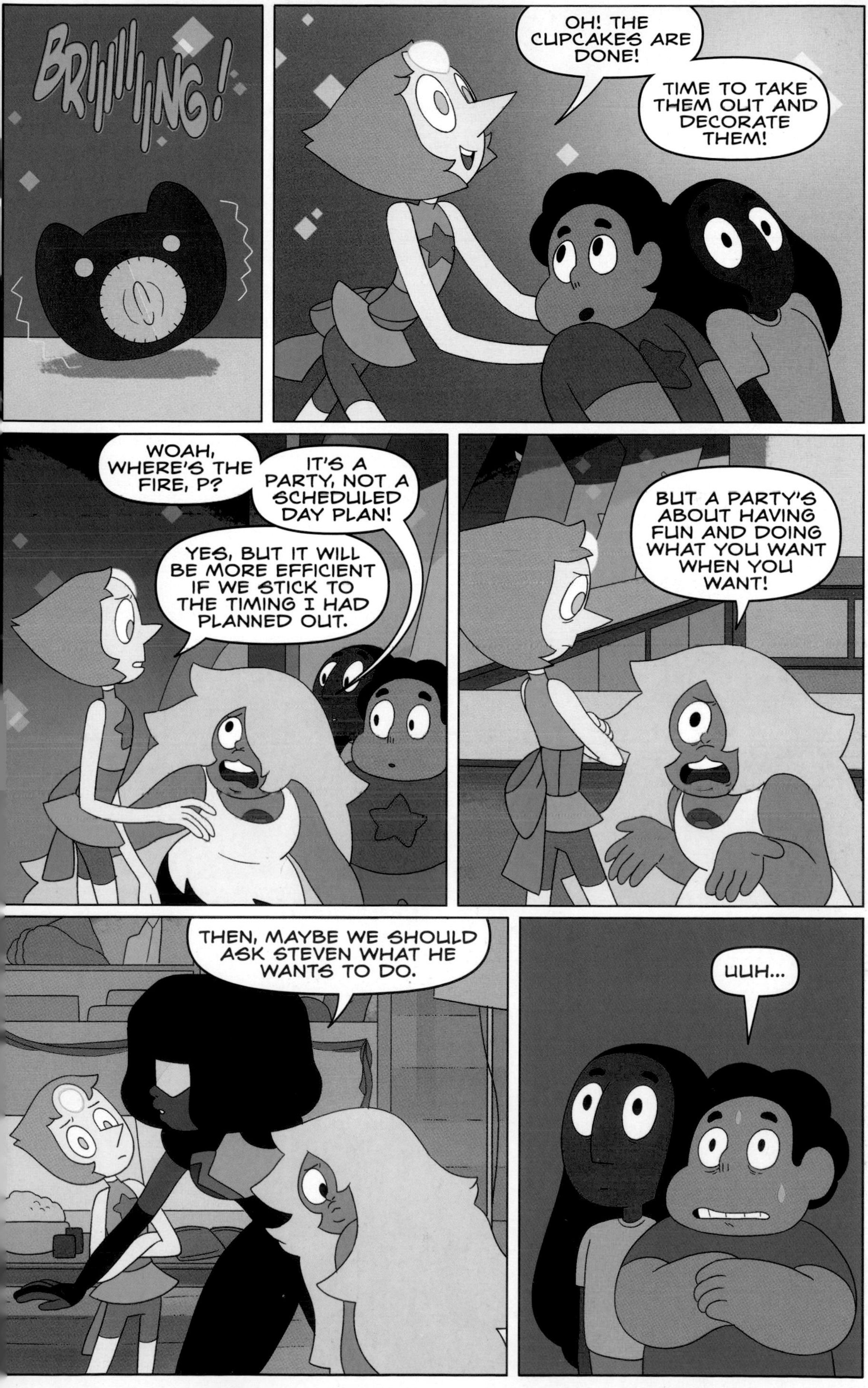
BRIIIIING!
OH! THE CUPCAKES ARE DONE!
TIME TO TAKE THEM OUT AND DECORATE THEM!
WOAH, WHERE'S THE FIRE, P?
IT'S A PARTY, NOT A SCHEDULED DAY PLAN!
YES, BUT IT WILL BE MORE EFFICIENT IF WE STICK TO THE TIMING I HAD PLANNED OUT.
BUT A PARTY'S ABOUT HAVING FUN AND DOING WHAT YOU WANT WHEN YOU WANT!
THEN, MAYBE WE SHOULD ASK STEVEN WHAT HE WANTS TO DO.
UUH...

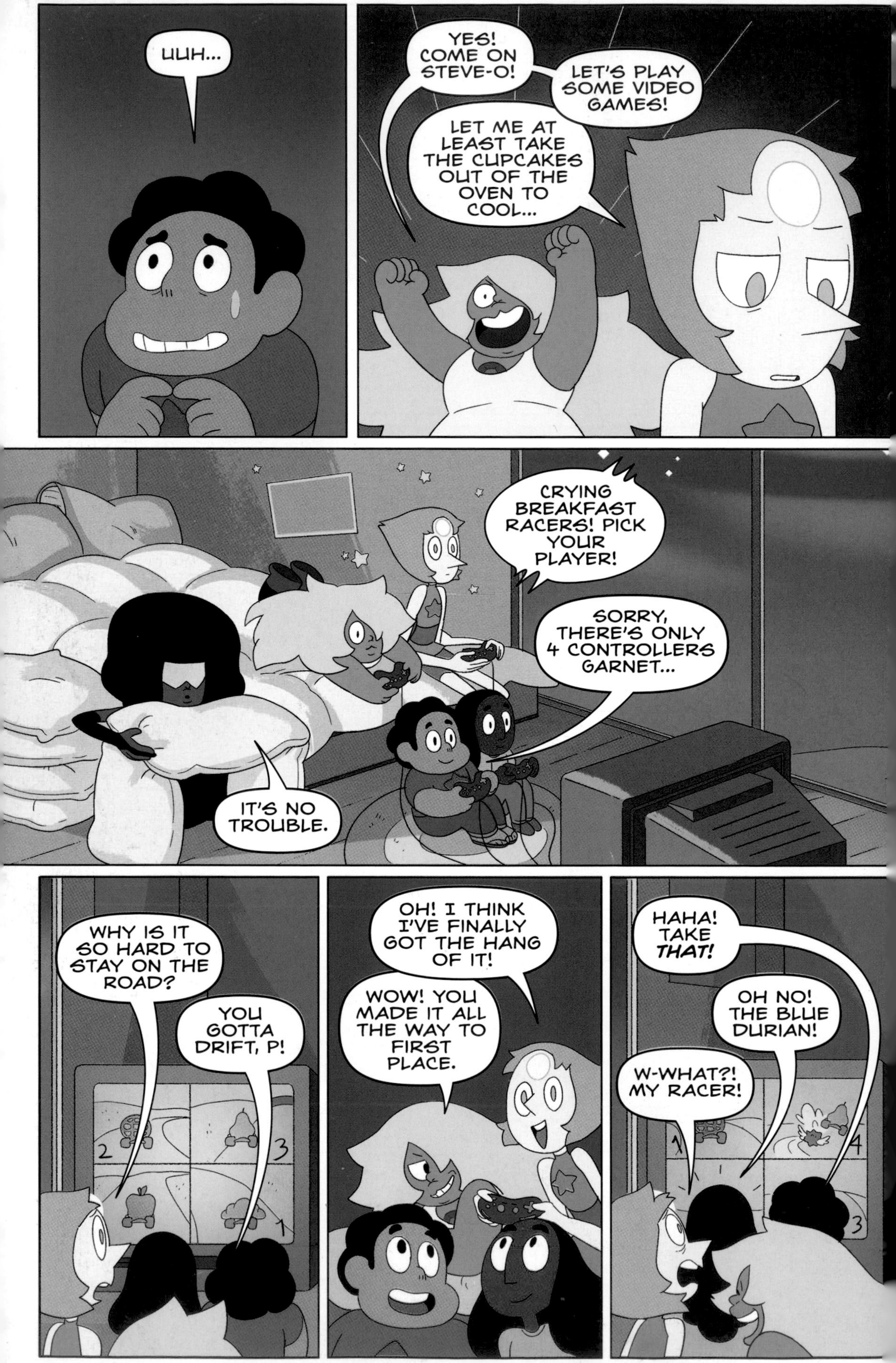
UUH...
YES! COME ON STEVE-O!
LET'S PLAY SOME VIDEO GAMES!
LET ME AT LEAST TAKE THE CUPCAKES OUT OF THE OVEN TO COOL...
CRYING BREAKFAST RACERS! PICK YOUR PLAYER!
SORRY, THERE'S ONLY 4 CONTROLLERS GARNET...
IT'S NO TROUBLE.
WHY IS IT SO HARD TO STAY ON THE ROAD?
YOU GOTTA DRIFT, P!
OH! I THINK I'VE FINALLY GOT THE HANG OF IT!
WOW! YOU MADE IT ALL THE WAY TO FIRST PLACE.
HAHA! TAKE *THAT!*
OH NO! THE BLUE DURIAN!
W-WHAT?! MY RACER!

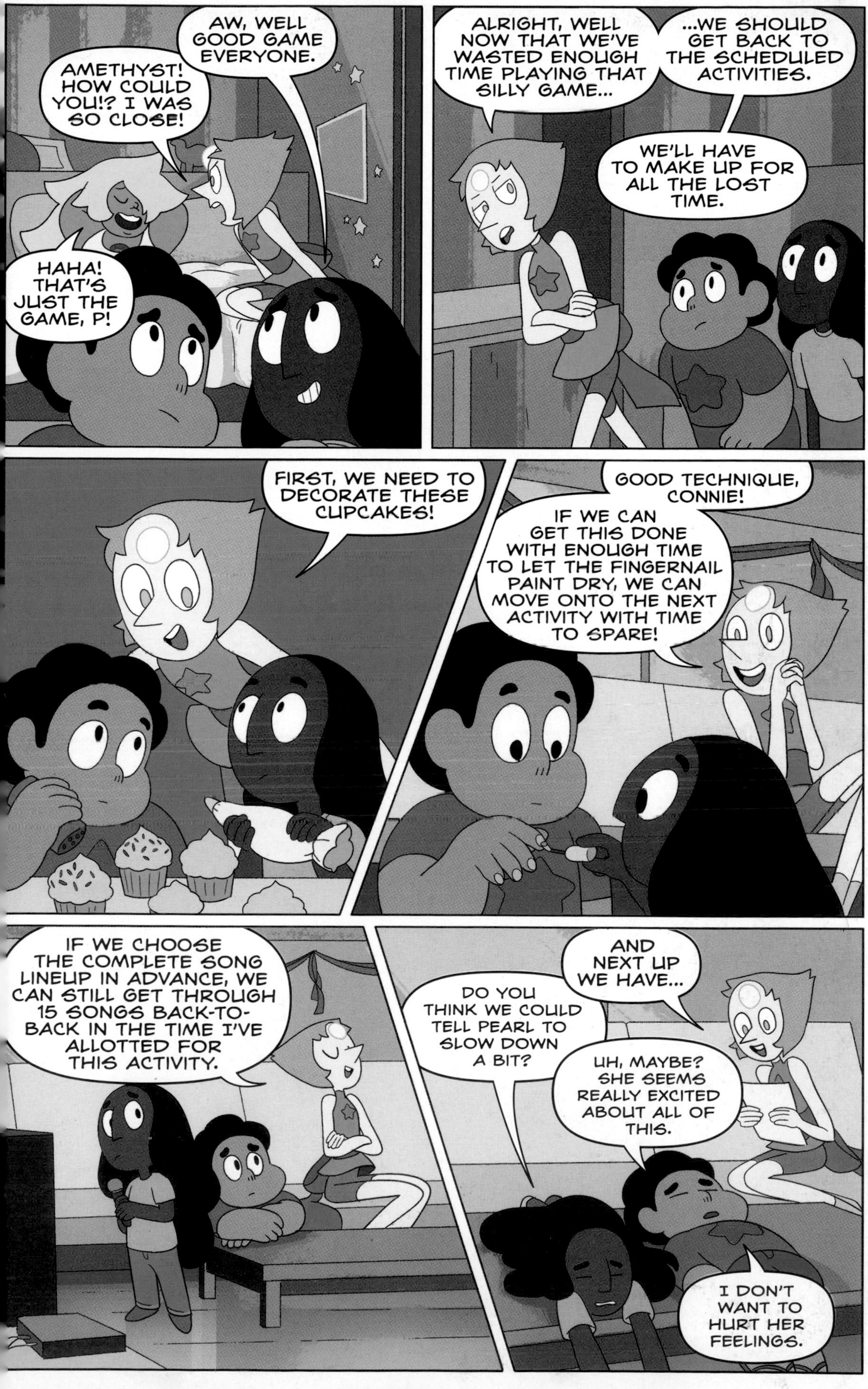
AW, WELL GOOD GAME EVERYONE.
AMETHYST! HOW COULD YOU!? I WAS SO CLOSE!
HAHA! THAT'S JUST THE GAME, P!
ALRIGHT, WELL NOW THAT WE'VE WASTED ENOUGH TIME PLAYING THAT SILLY GAME...
...WE SHOULD GET BACK TO THE SCHEDULED ACTIVITIES.
WE'LL HAVE TO MAKE UP FOR ALL THE LOST TIME.
FIRST, WE NEED TO DECORATE THESE CUPCAKES!
GOOD TECHNIQUE, CONNIE!
IF WE CAN GET THIS DONE WITH ENOUGH TIME TO LET THE FINGERNAIL PAINT DRY, WE CAN MOVE ONTO THE NEXT ACTIVITY WITH TIME TO SPARE!
IF WE CHOOSE THE COMPLETE SONG LINEUP IN ADVANCE, WE CAN STILL GET THROUGH 15 SONGS BACK-TO-BACK IN THE TIME I'VE ALLOTTED FOR THIS ACTIVITY.
AND NEXT UP WE HAVE...
DO YOU THINK WE COULD TELL PEARL TO SLOW DOWN A BIT?
UH, MAYBE? SHE SEEMS REALLY EXCITED ABOUT ALL OF THIS.
I DON'T WANT TO HURT HER FEELINGS.

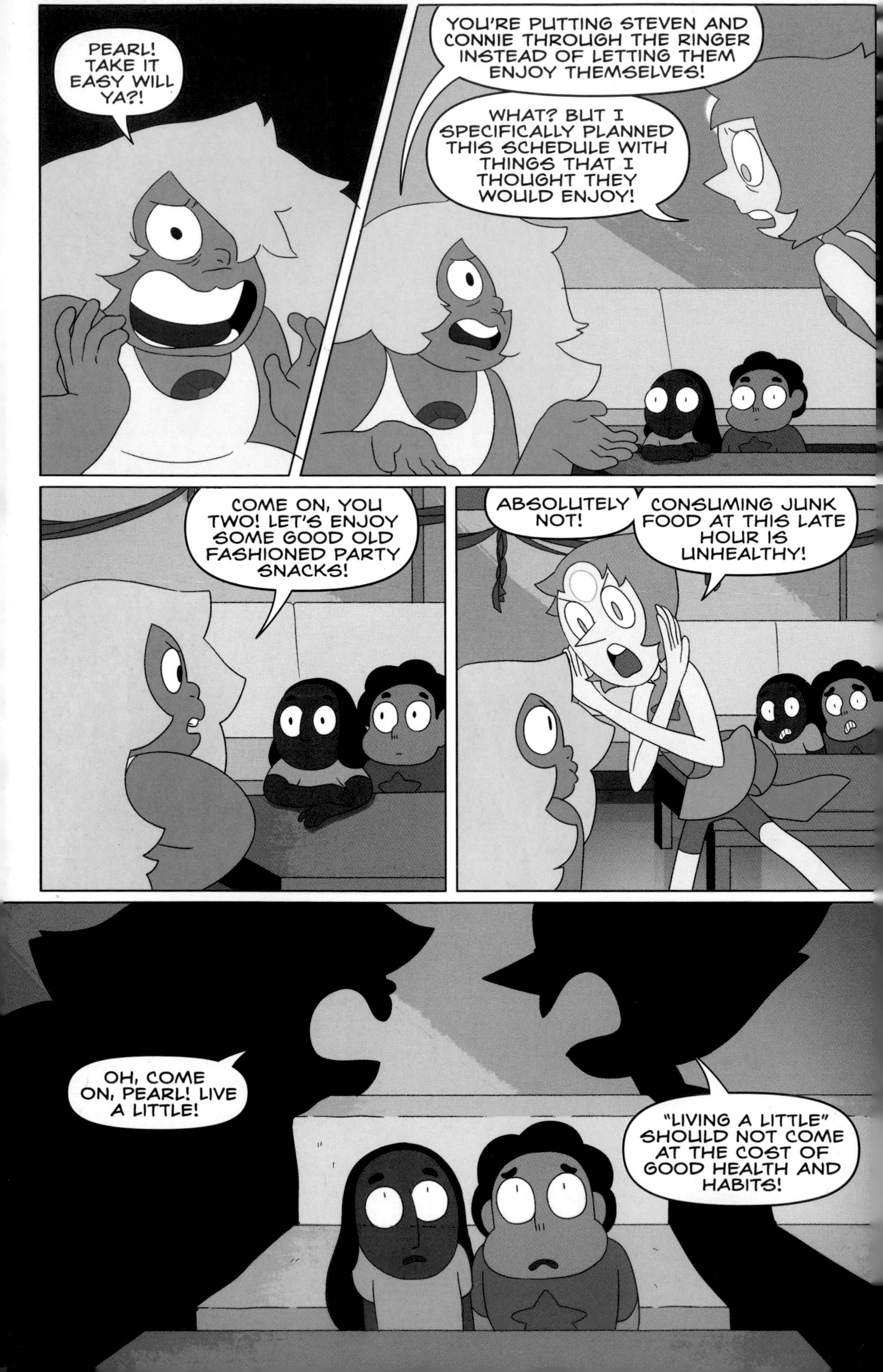
PEARL! TAKE IT EASY WILL YA?!
YOU'RE PUTTING STEVEN AND CONNIE THROUGH THE RINGER INSTEAD OF LETTING THEM ENJOY THEMSELVES!
WHAT? BUT I SPECIFICALLY PLANNED THIS SCHEDULE WITH THINGS THAT I THOUGHT THEY WOULD ENJOY!
COME ON, YOU TWO! LET'S ENJOY SOME GOOD OLD FASHIONED PARTY SNACKS!
ABSOLUTELY NOT!
CONSUMING JUNK FOOD AT THIS LATE HOUR IS UNHEALTHY!
OH, COME ON, PEARL! LIVE A LITTLE!
"LIVING A LITTLE" SHOULD NOT COME AT THE COST OF GOOD HEALTH AND HABITS!

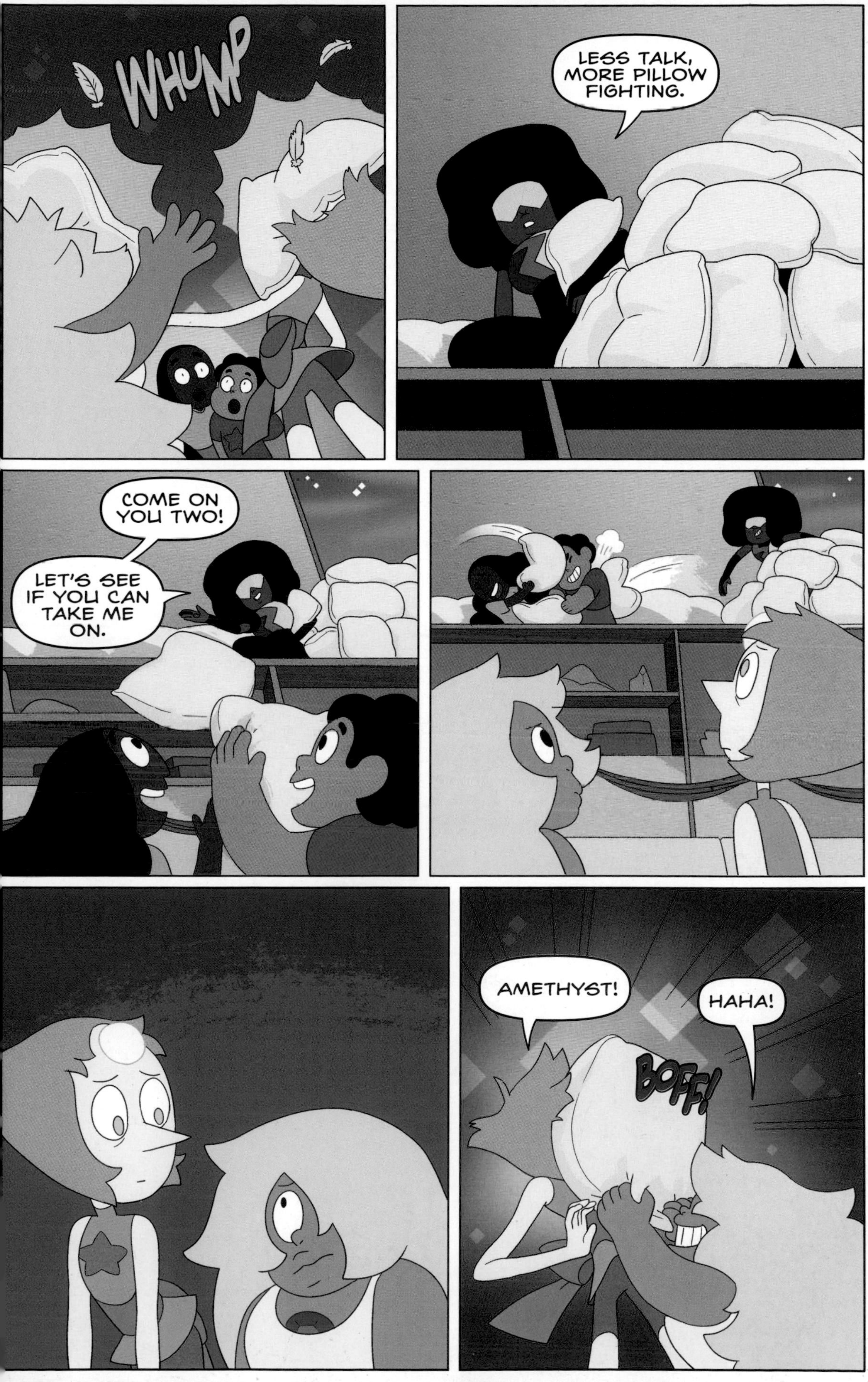
WHUMP
LESS TALK, MORE PILLOW FIGHTING.
COME ON YOU TWO!
LET'S SEE IF YOU CAN TAKE ME ON.
AMETHYST!
HAHA!
BOFF!

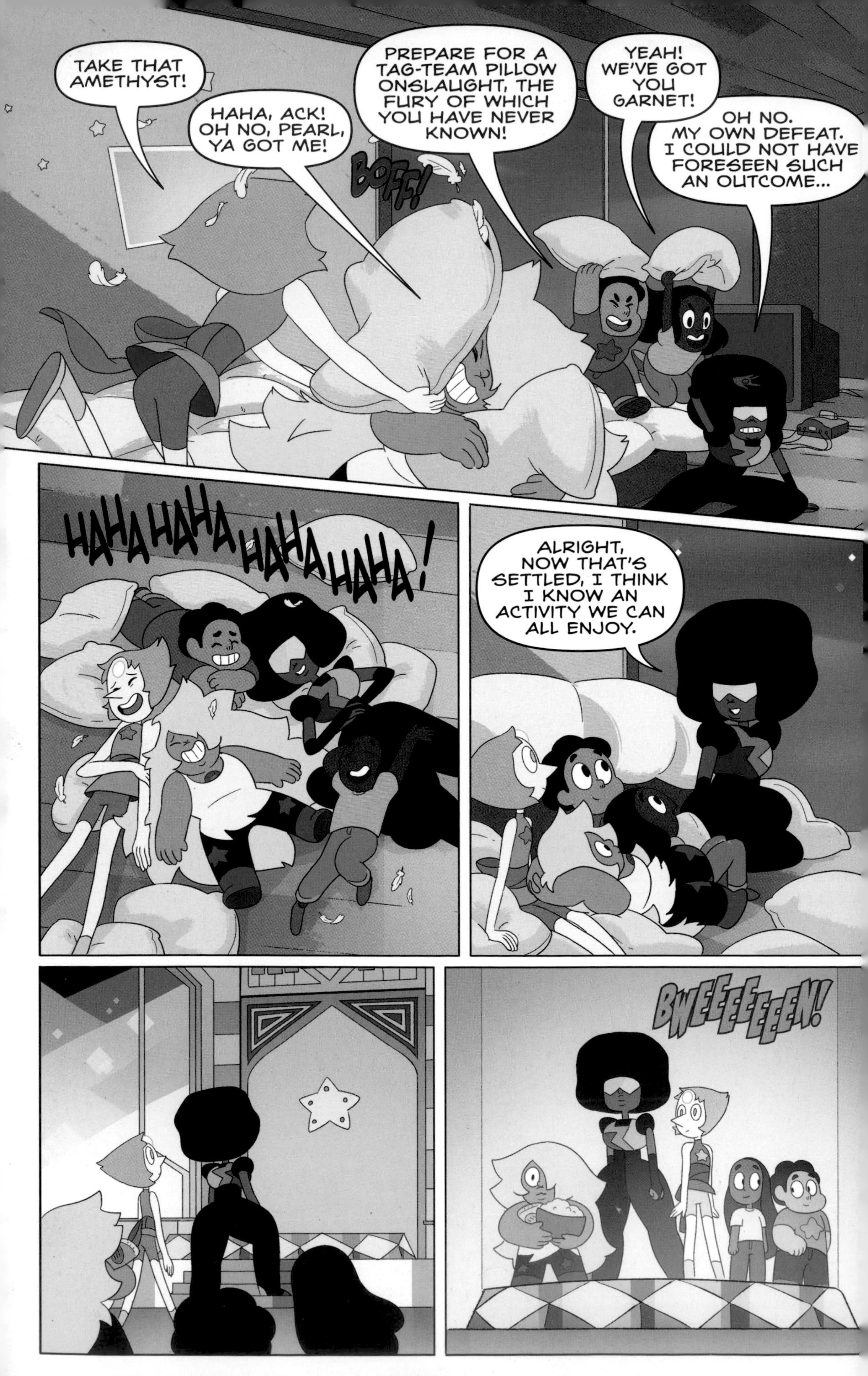
TAKE THAT AMETHYST!
HAHA, ACK! OH NO, PEARL, YA GOT ME!
BOFF!
PREPARE FOR A TAG-TEAM PILLOW ONSLAUGHT, THE FURY OF WHICH YOU HAVE NEVER KNOWN!
YEAH! WE'VE GOT YOU GARNET!
OH NO. MY OWN DEFEAT. I COULD NOT HAVE FORESEEN SUCH AN OUTCOME...
HAHAHAHAHAHAHAHA!
ALRIGHT, NOW THAT'S SETTLED, I THINK I KNOW AN ACTIVITY WE CAN ALL ENJOY.
BWEEEEEEEN!

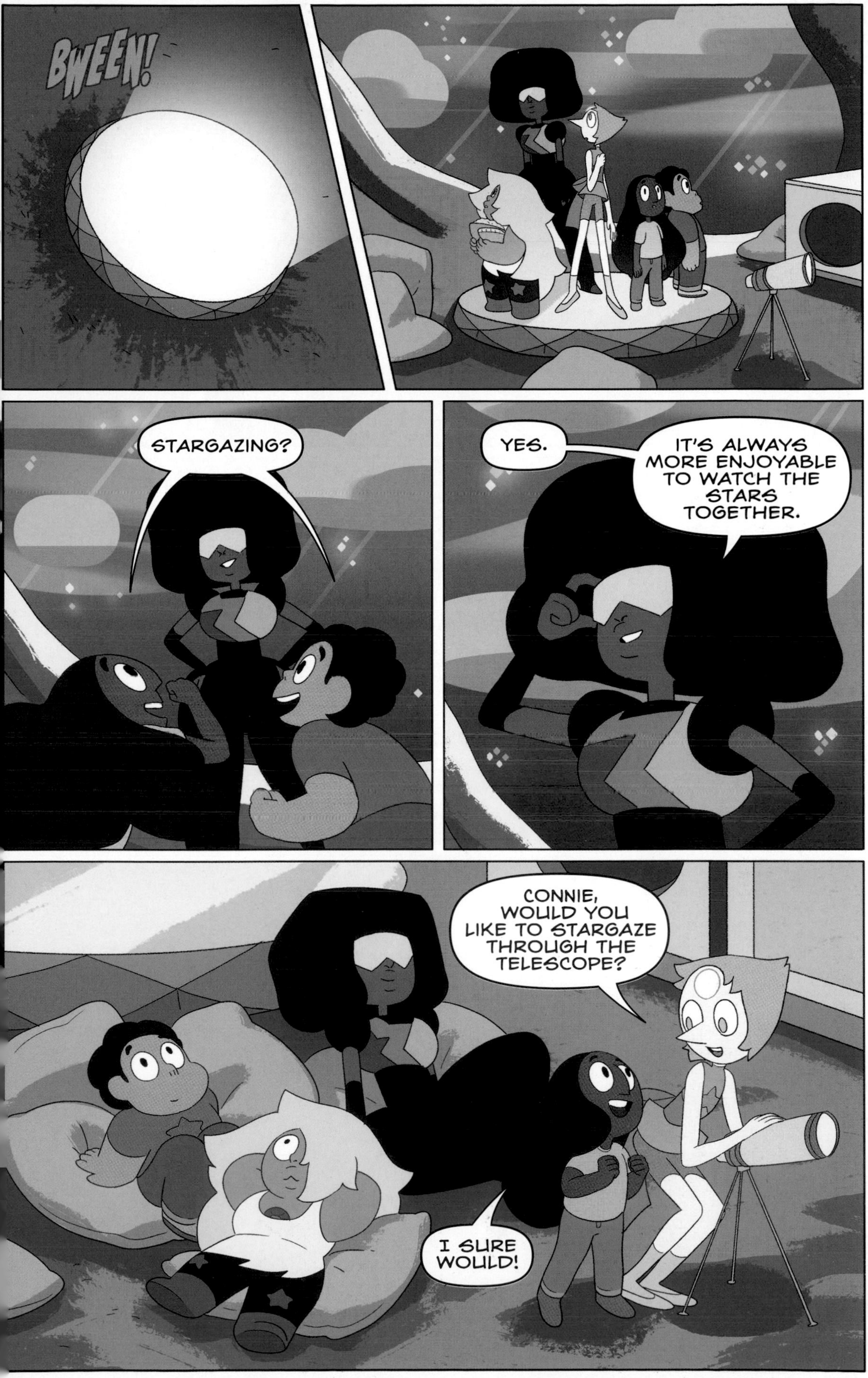
BWEEN!
STARGAZING?
YES.
IT'S ALWAYS MORE ENJOYABLE TO WATCH THE STARS TOGETHER.
CONNIE, WOULD YOU LIKE TO STARGAZE THROUGH THE TELESCOPE?
I SURE WOULD!

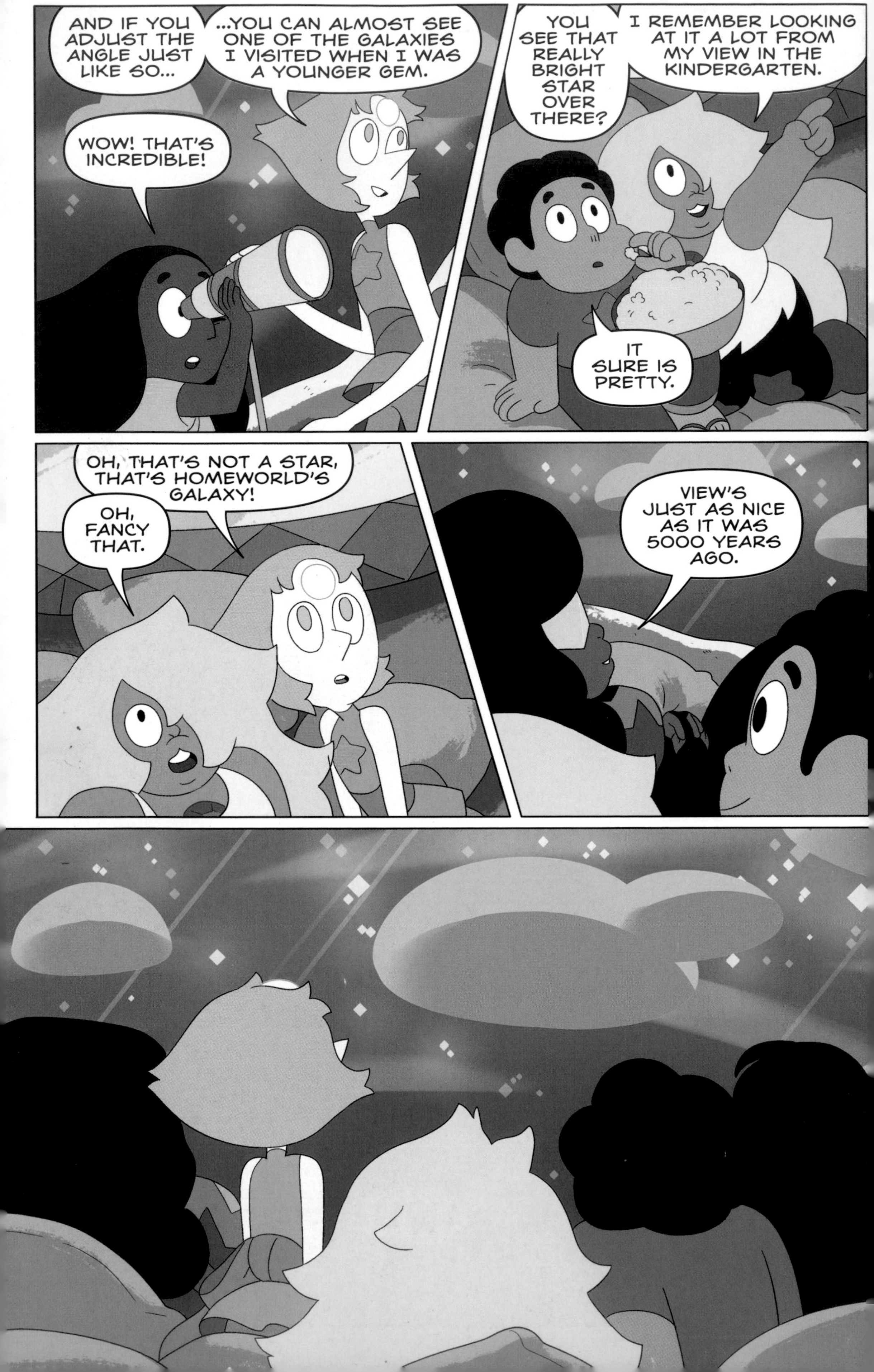
AND IF YOU ADJUST THE ANGLE JUST LIKE SO...
...YOU CAN ALMOST SEE ONE OF THE GALAXIES I VISITED WHEN I WAS A YOUNGER GEM.
WOW! THAT'S INCREDIBLE!
YOU SEE THAT REALLY BRIGHT STAR OVER THERE?
I REMEMBER LOOKING AT IT A LOT FROM MY VIEW IN THE KINDERGARTEN.
IT SURE IS PRETTY.
OH, THAT'S NOT A STAR, THAT'S HOMEWORLD'S GALAXY!
OH, FANCY THAT.
VIEW'S JUST AS NICE AS IT WAS 5000 YEARS AGO.

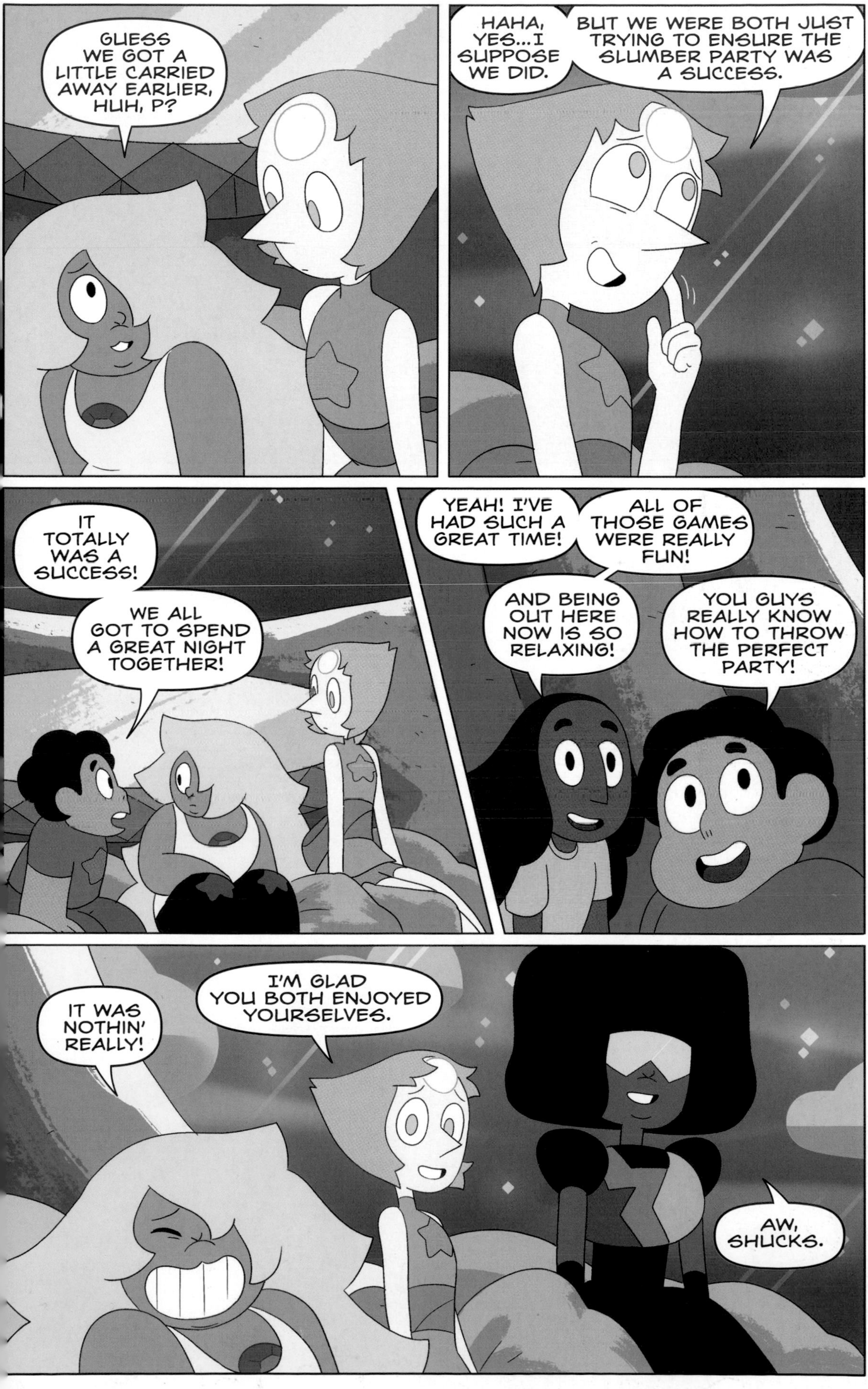
GUESS WE GOT A LITTLE CARRIED AWAY EARLIER, HUH, P?
HAHA, YES...I SUPPOSE WE DID.
BUT WE WERE BOTH JUST TRYING TO ENSURE THE SLUMBER PARTY WAS A SUCCESS.
IT TOTALLY WAS A SUCCESS!
WE ALL GOT TO SPEND A GREAT NIGHT TOGETHER!
YEAH! I'VE HAD SUCH A GREAT TIME!
ALL OF THOSE GAMES WERE REALLY FUN!
AND BEING OUT HERE NOW IS SO RELAXING!
YOU GUYS REALLY KNOW HOW TO THROW THE PERFECT PARTY!
IT WAS NOTHIN' REALLY!
I'M GLAD YOU BOTH ENJOYED YOURSELVES.
AW, SHUCKS.

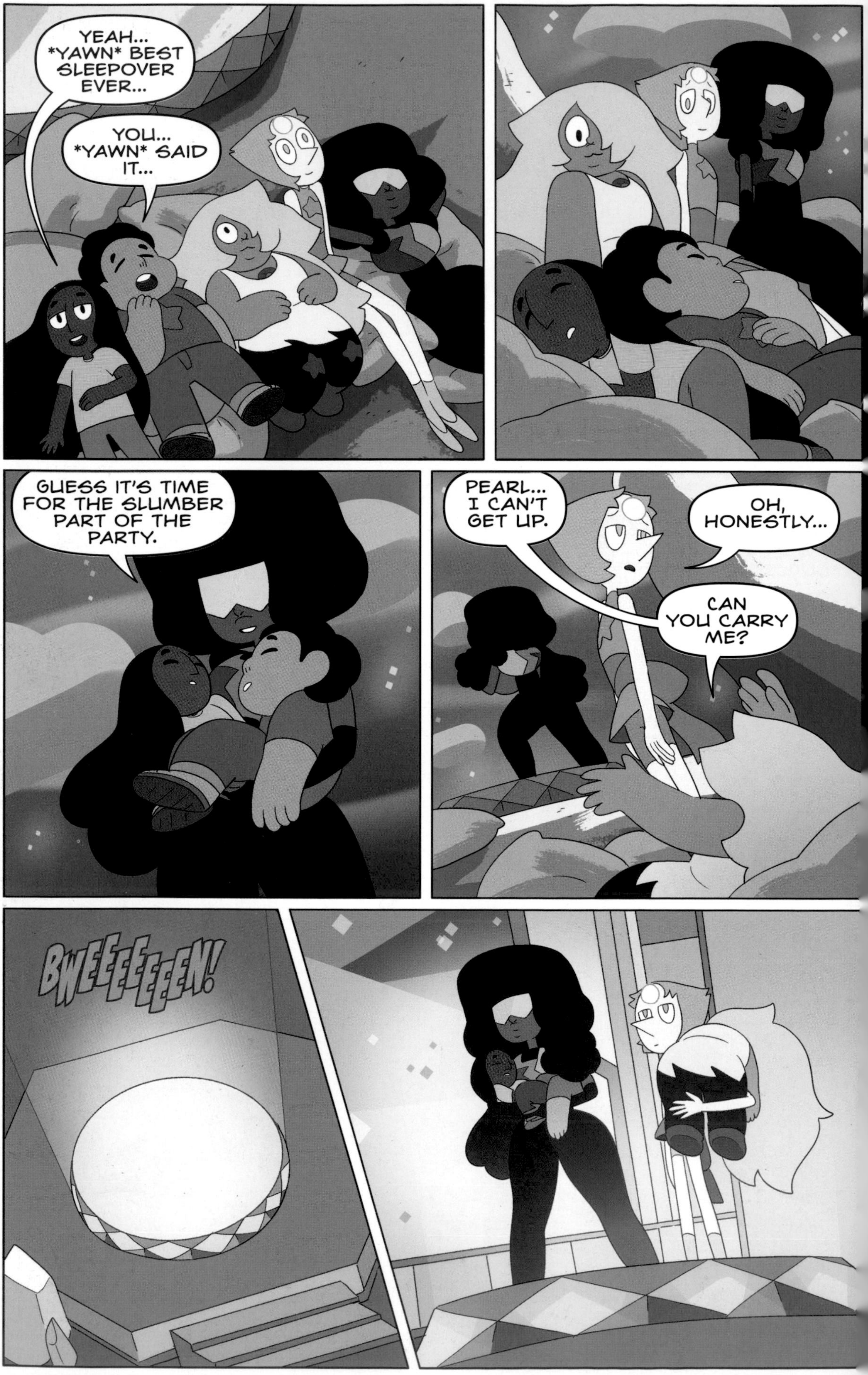
YEAH... *YAWN* BEST SLEEPOVER EVER...
YOU... *YAWN* SAID IT...
GUESS IT'S TIME FOR THE SLUMBER PART OF THE PARTY.
PEARL... I CAN'T GET UP.
CAN YOU CARRY ME?
OH, HONESTLY...
BWEEEEEEEN!

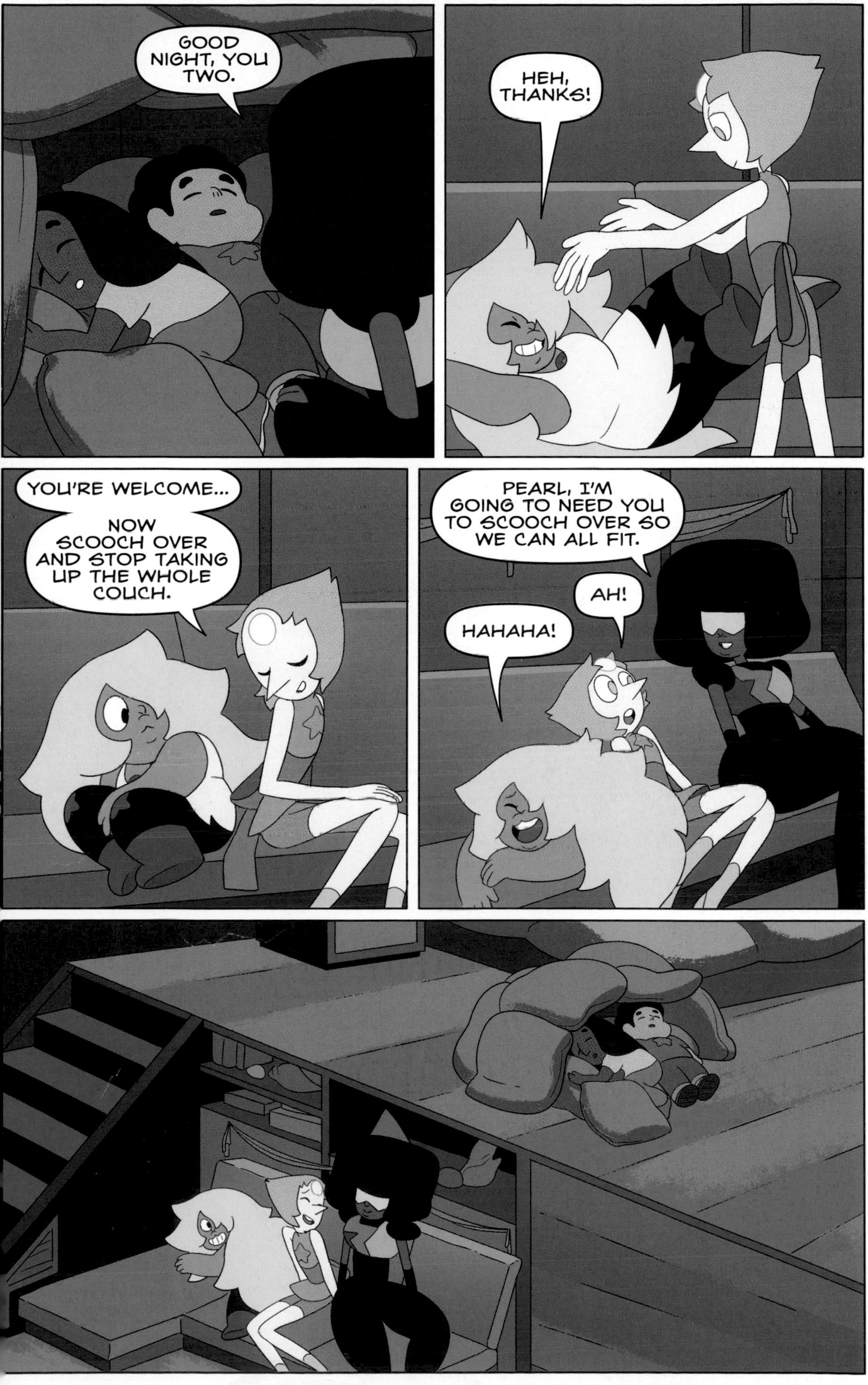
GOOD NIGHT, YOU TWO.
HEH, THANKS!
YOU'RE WELCOME...
NOW SCOOCH OVER AND STOP TAKING UP THE WHOLE COUCH.
PEARL, I'M GOING TO NEED YOU TO SCOOCH OVER SO WE CAN ALL FIT.
AH!
HAHAHA!

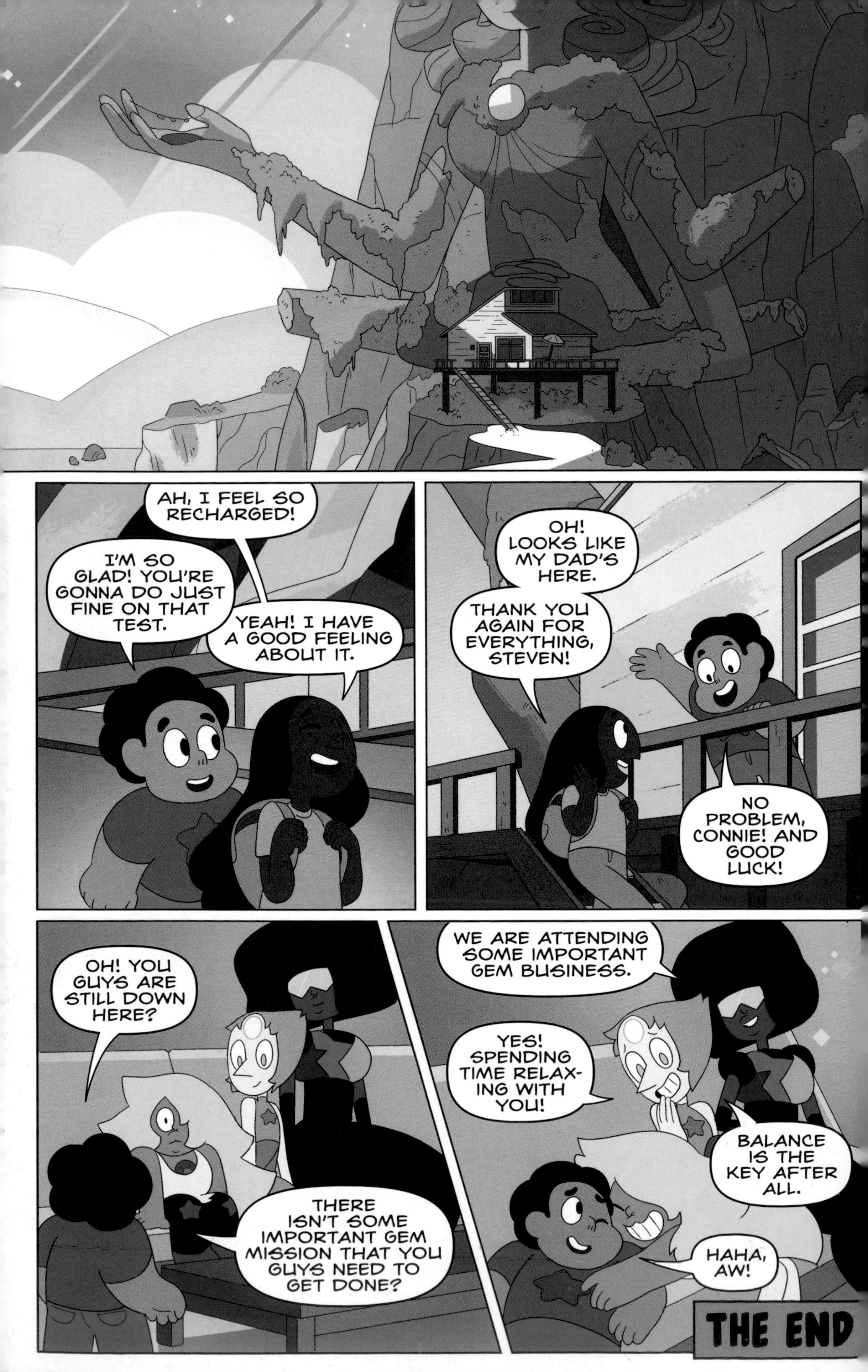
AH, I FEEL SO RECHARGED!
I'M SO GLAD! YOU'RE GONNA DO JUST FINE ON THAT TEST.
YEAH! I HAVE A GOOD FEELING ABOUT IT.
OH! LOOKS LIKE MY DAD'S HERE.
THANK YOU AGAIN FOR EVERYTHING, STEVEN!
NO PROBLEM, CONNIE! AND GOOD LUCK!
OH! YOU GUYS ARE STILL DOWN HERE?
THERE ISN'T SOME IMPORTANT GEM MISSION THAT YOU GUYS NEED TO GET DONE?
WE ARE ATTENDING SOME IMPORTANT GEM BUSINESS.
YES! SPENDING TIME RELAXING WITH YOU!
BALANCE IS THE KEY AFTER ALL.
HAHA, AW!
THE END

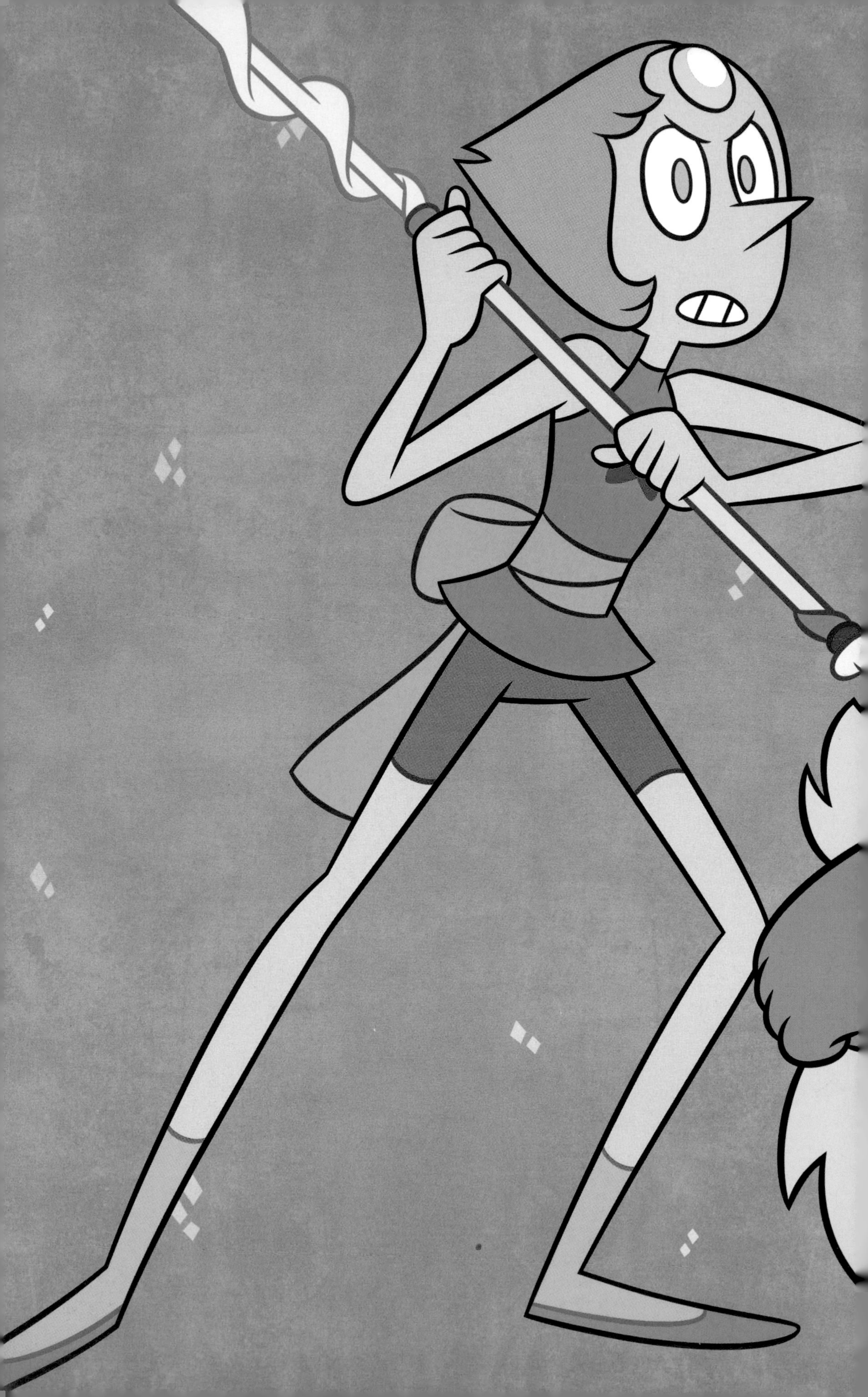

COVER GALLERY

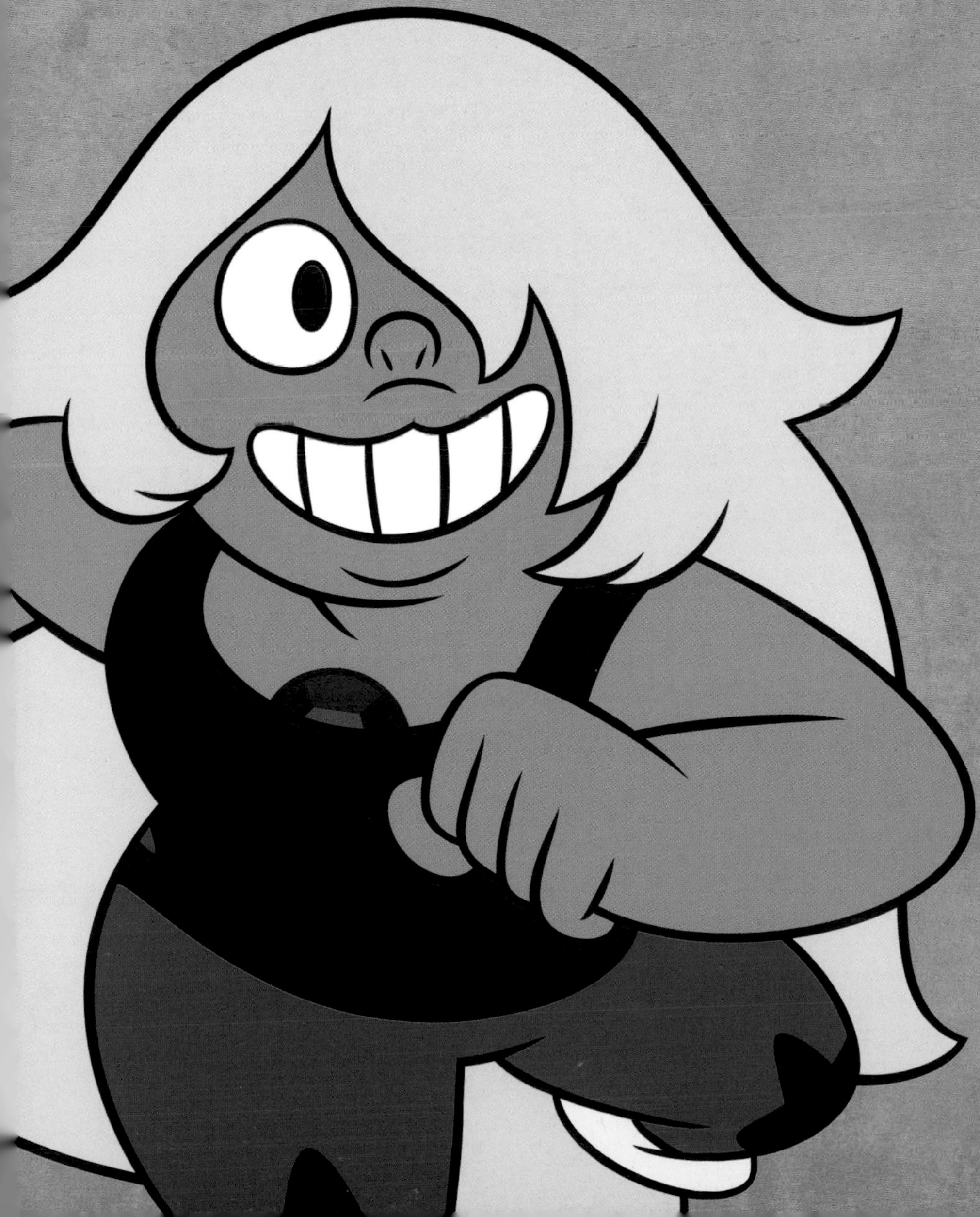

issue nine main cover

MISSY PEÑA

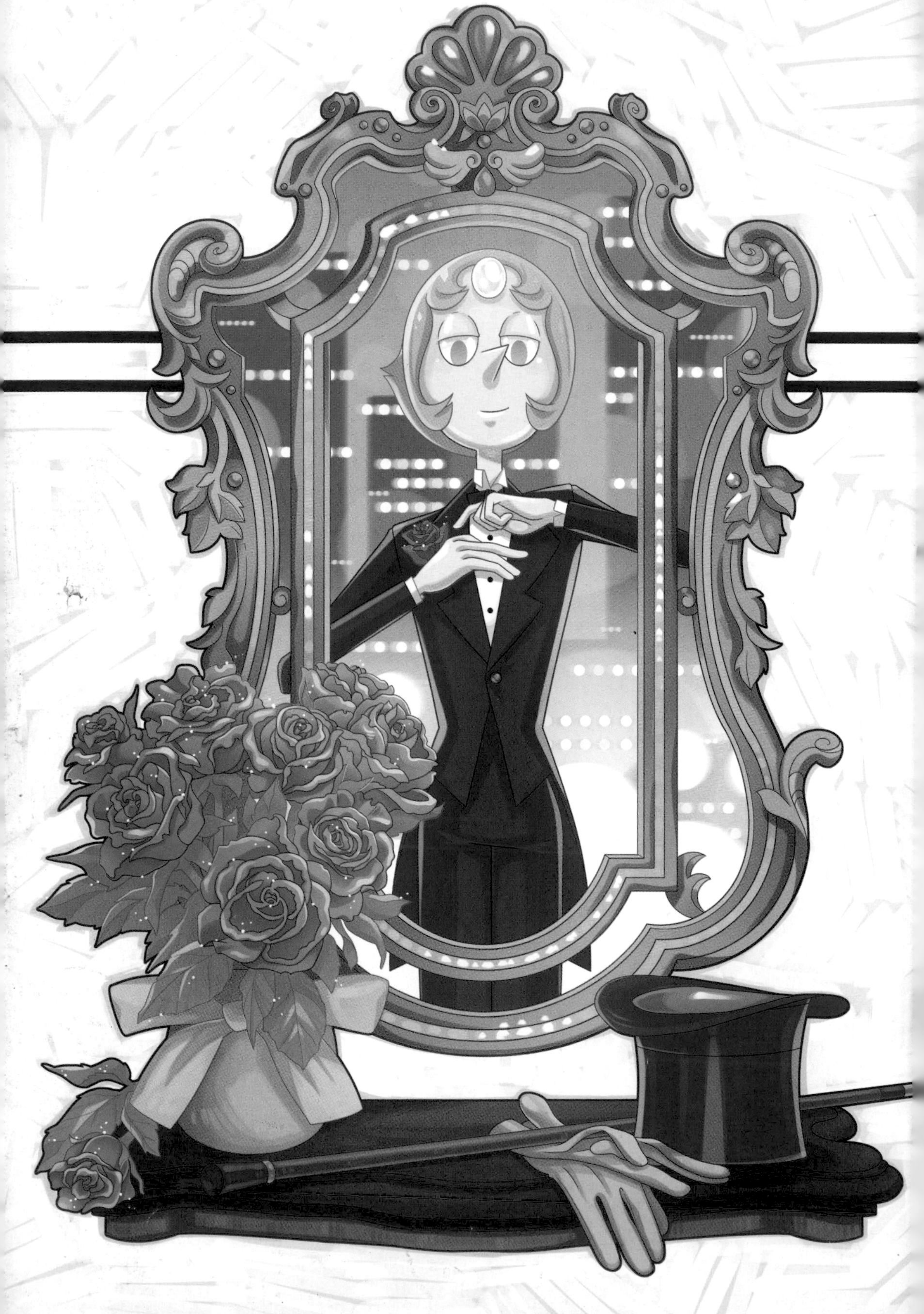

issue nine subscription cover
SIBYLLINE MEYNET

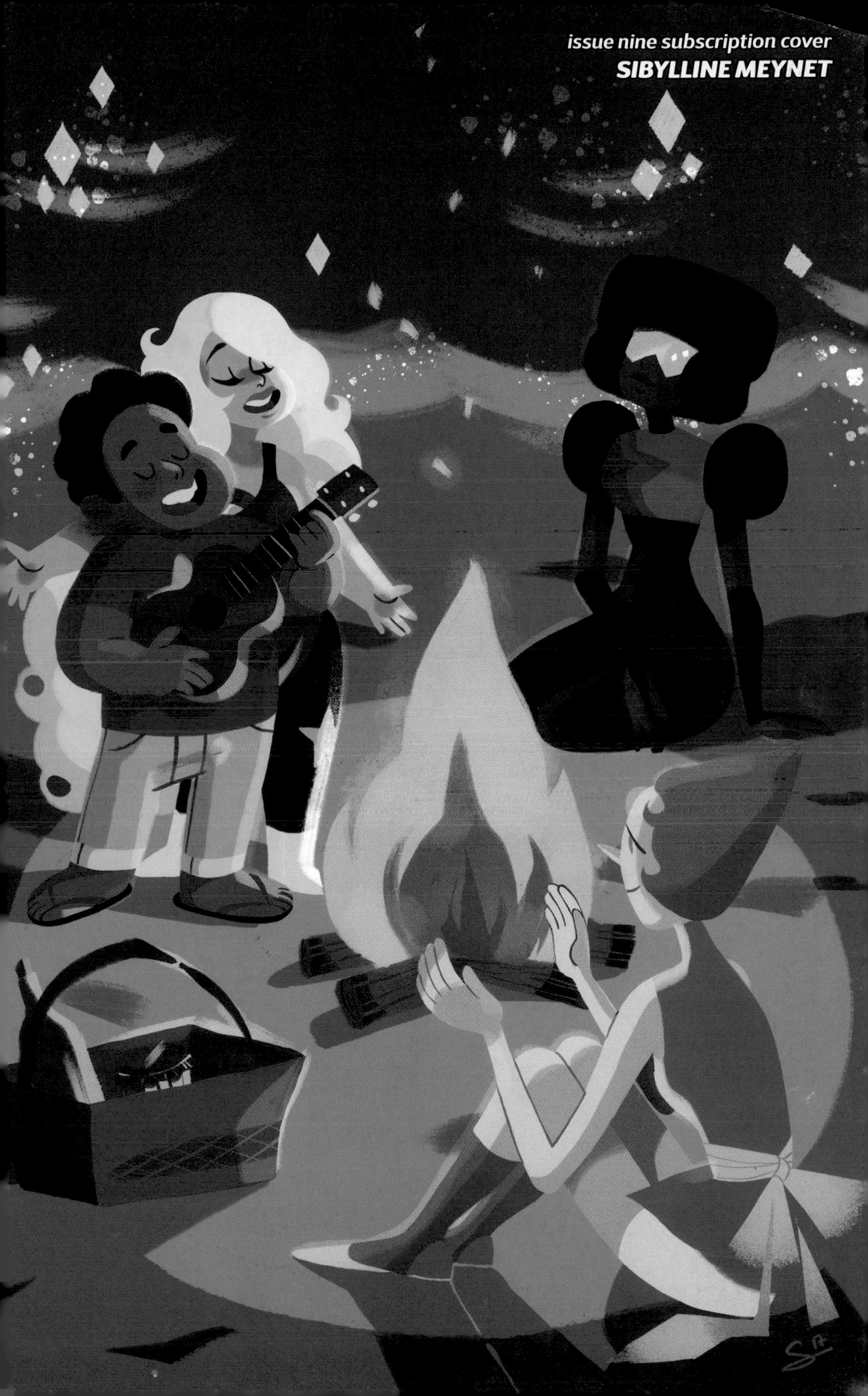

issue ten main cover
MISSY PEÑA

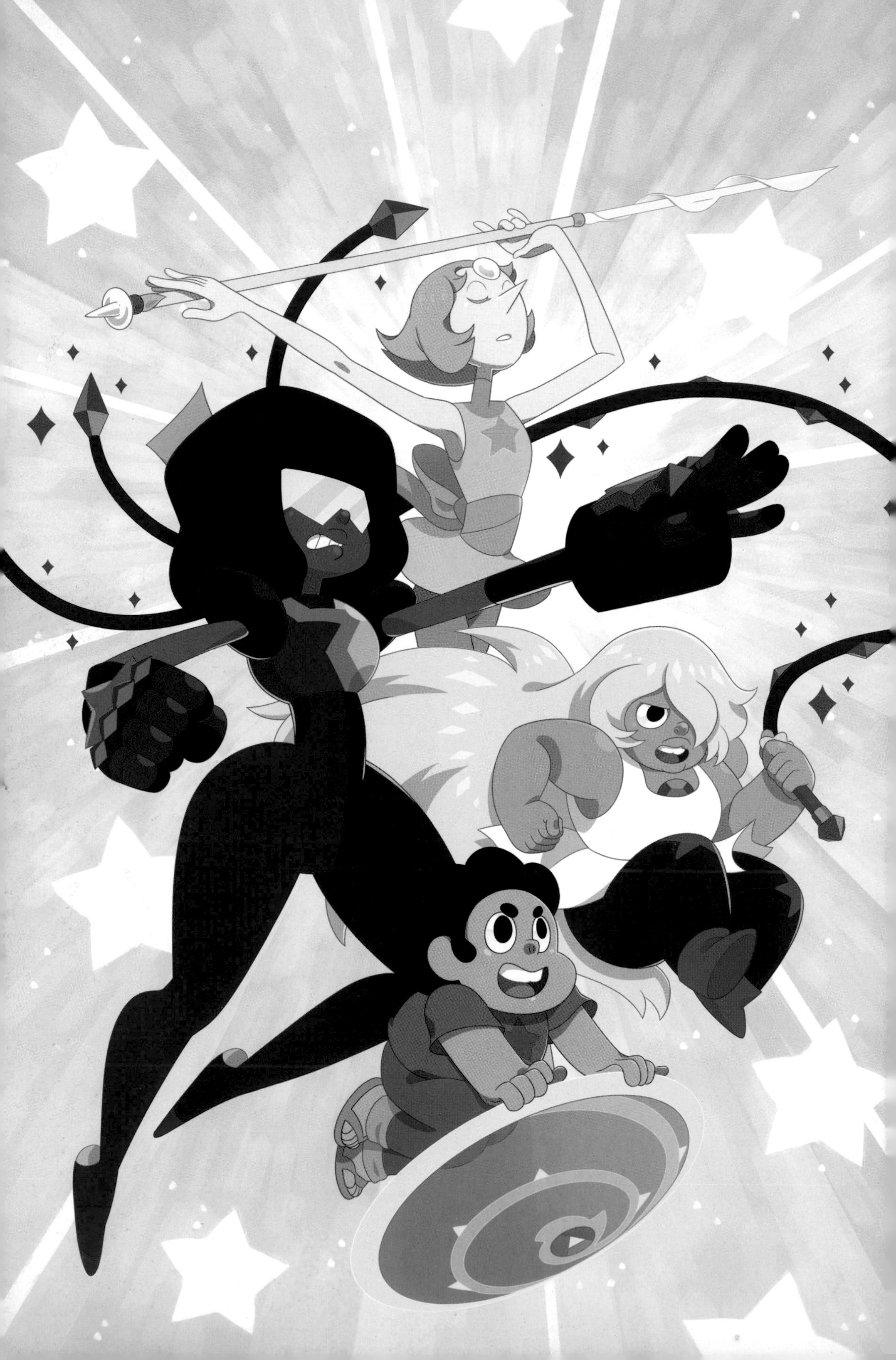

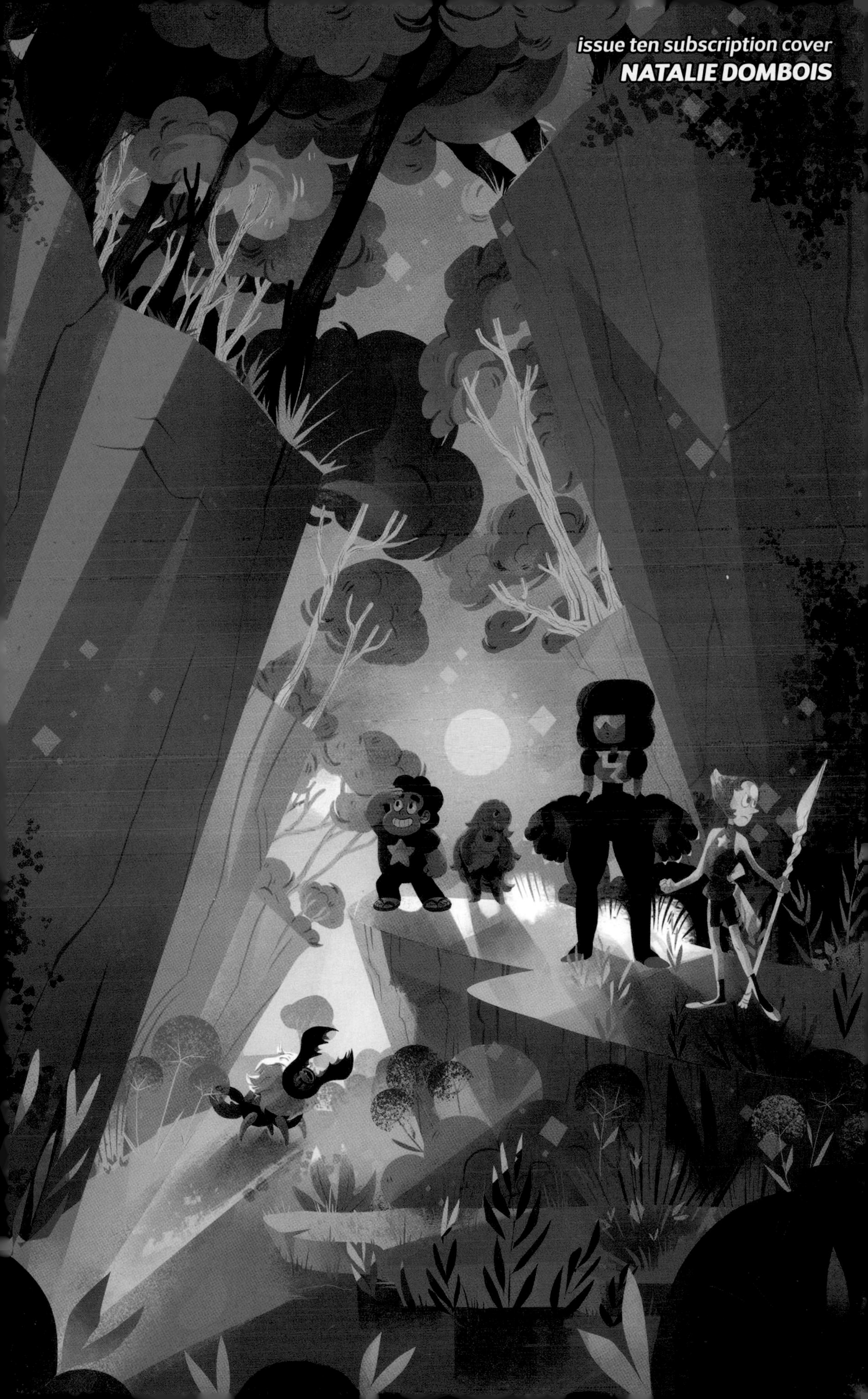

issue ten subscription cover
NATALIE DOMBOIS

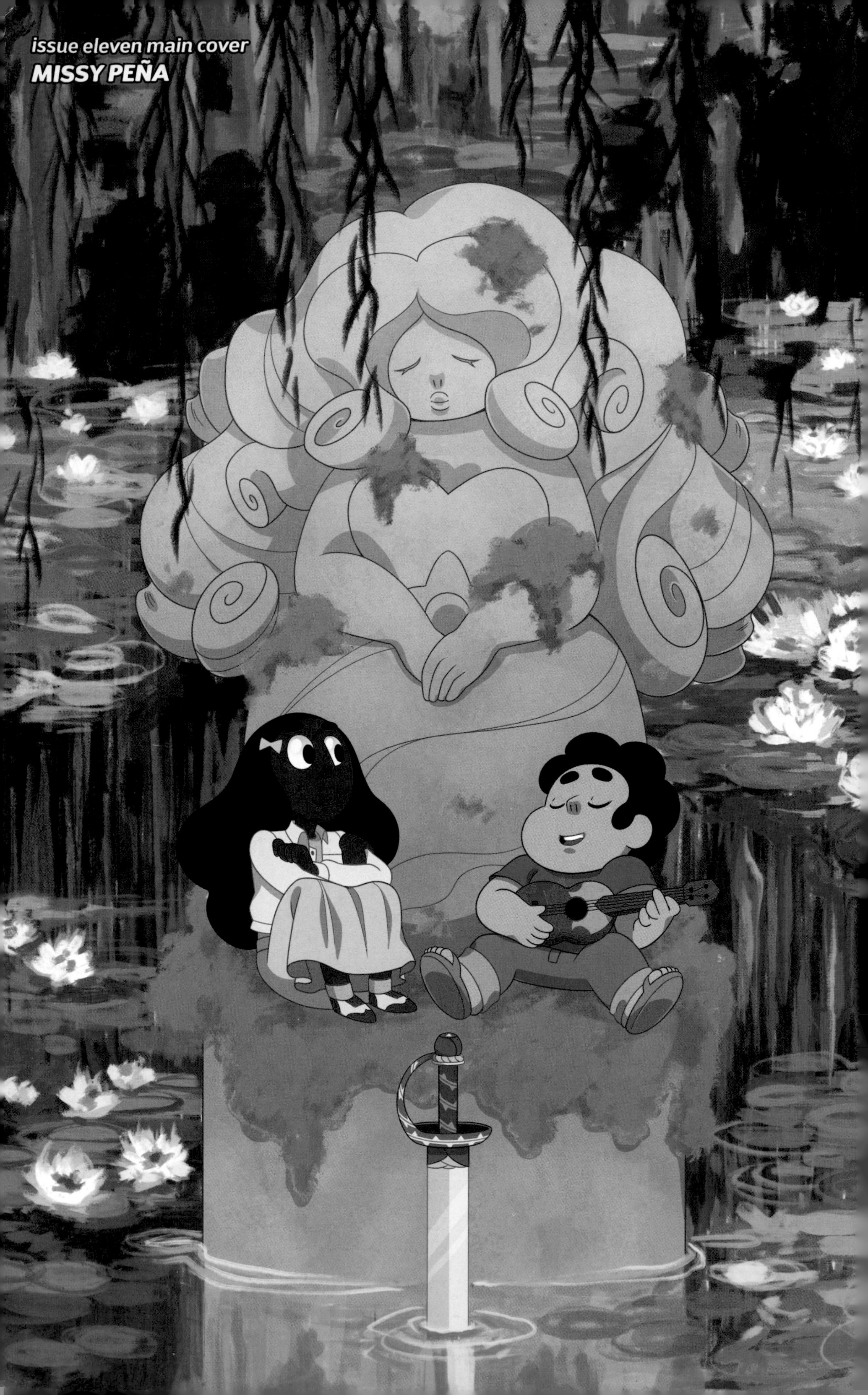

issue eleven main cover
MISSY PEÑA

issue eleven subscription cover
KAT TSAI

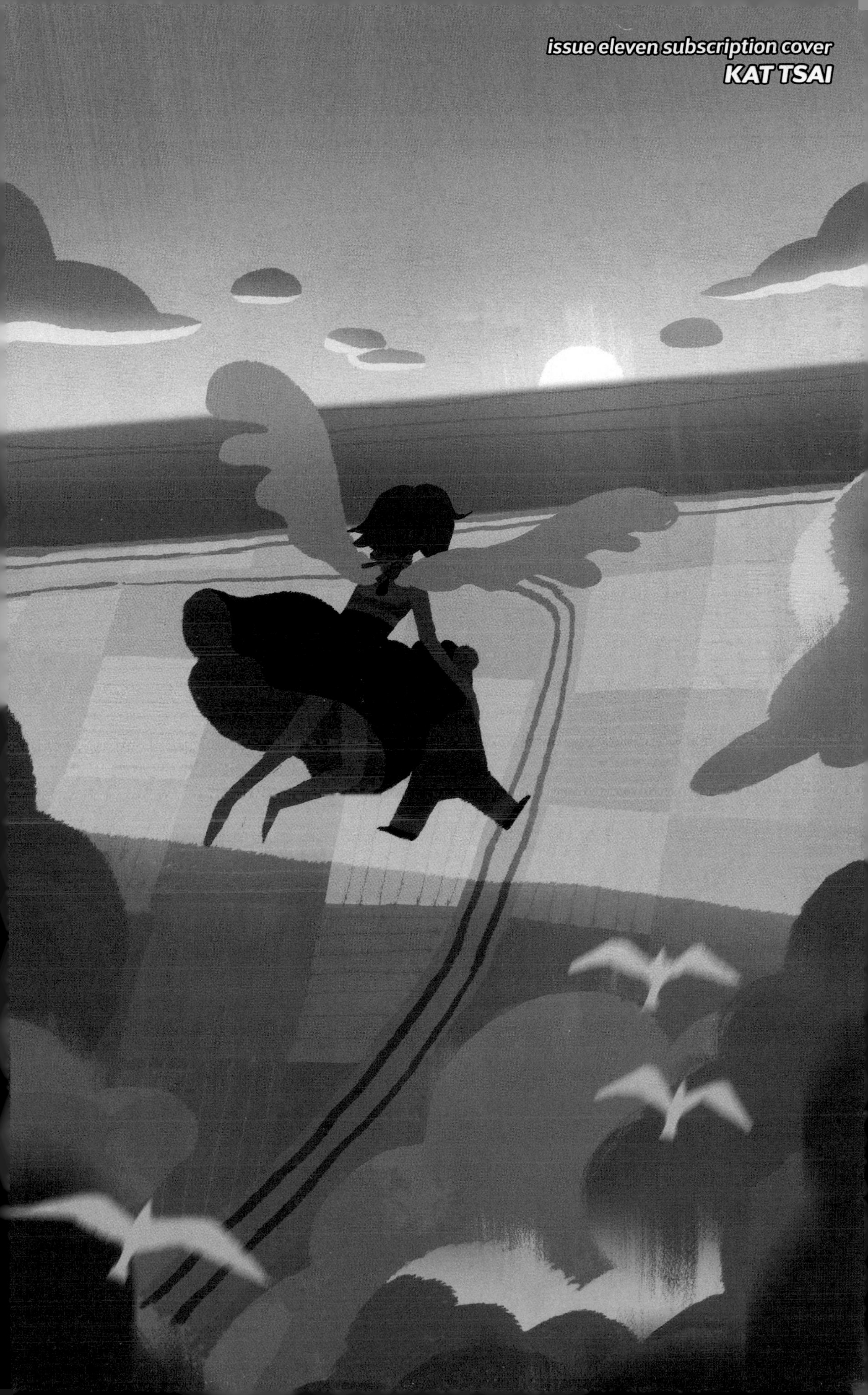

issue twelve main cover
MISSY PEÑA

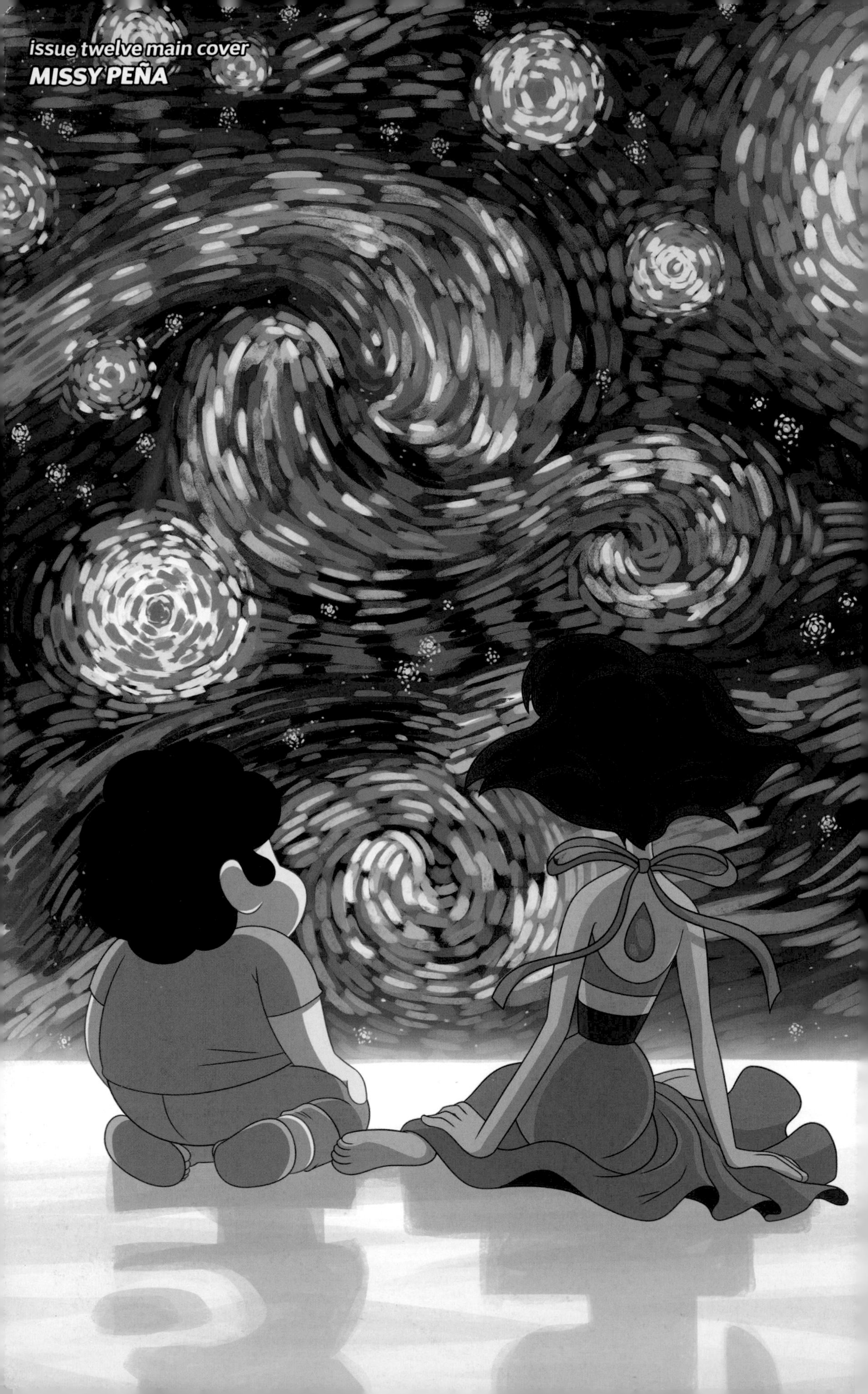

issue twelve subscription cover
NATALIE DOMBOIS

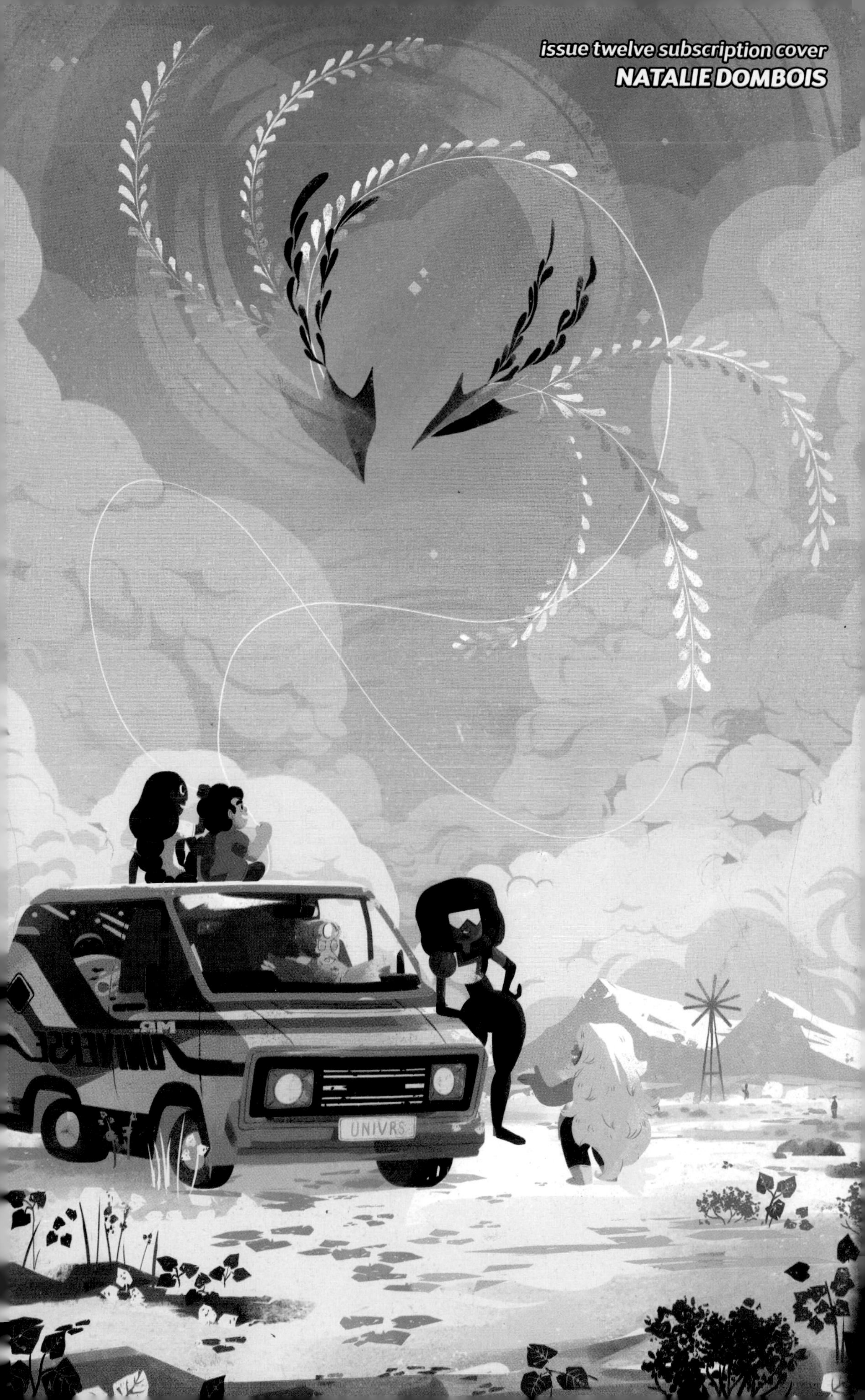
UNIVRS

DISCOVER
EXPLOSIVE NEW WORLDS

ADVENTURE TIME

Sam Sykes · Selina Espiritu · Sarah Stern
Brave Chef Brianna

KELLY THOMPSON BRIANNE DROUHARD M. VICTORIA ROBADO
MEGA PRINCESS

THE NOT-SO SECRET SOCIETY
DALEY · CRAFTS · CLARK · BRUNI

OVER THE GARDEN WALL

STEVEN UNIVERSE
VOLUME ONE

Adventure Time
Pendleton Ward and Others
Volume 1
ISBN: 978-1-60886-280-1 | $14.99 US
Volume 2
ISBN: 978-1-60886-323-5 | $14.99 US
Adventure Time: Islands
ISBN: 978-1-60886-972-5 | $9.99 US

The Amazing World of Gumball
Ben Bocquelet and Others
Volume 1
ISBN: 978-1-60886-488-1 | $14.99 US
Volume 2
ISBN: 978-1-60886-793-6 | $14.99 US

Brave Chef Brianna
Sam Sykes, Selina Espiritu
ISBN: 978-1-68415-050-2 | $14.99 US

Mega Princess
Kelly Thompson, Brianne Drouhard
ISBN: 978-1-68415-007-6 | $14.99 US

The Not-So Secret Society
Matthew Daley, Arlene Daley, Wook Jin Clark
ISBN: 978-1-60886-997-8 | $9.99 US

Over the Garden Wall
Patrick McHale, Jim Campbell and Others
Volume 1
ISBN: 978-1-60886-940-4 | $14.99 US
Volume 2
ISBN: 978-1-68415-006-9 | $14.99 US

Steven Universe
Rebecca Sugar and Others
Volume 1
ISBN: 978-1-60886-706-6 | $14.99 US
Volume 2
ISBN: 978-1-60886-796-7 | $14.99 US

Steven Universe & The Crystal Gems
ISBN: 978-1-60886-921-3 | $14.99 US

Steven Universe: Too Cool for School
ISBN: 978-1-60886-771-4 | $14.99 US

kaboom!™

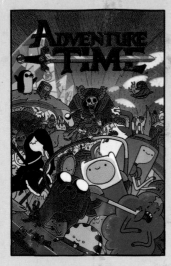

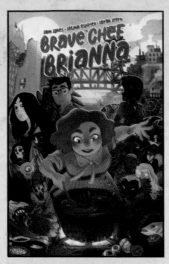

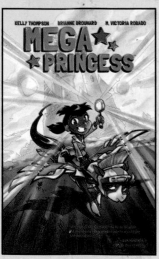

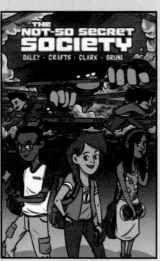

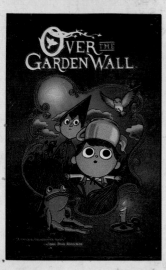

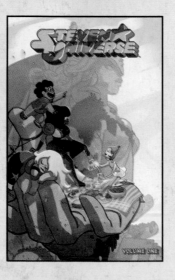

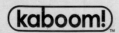

AVAILABLE AT YOUR LOCAL COMICS SHOP AND BOOKSTORE
WWW.**BOOM-STUDIOS**.COM